RAW JUSTICE

A FRANK LUCE THRILLER

RICK BOSWORTH

Whoever fights monsters should see to it that in the process he does not become a monster. And if you gaze long enough into an abyss, the abyss will gaze back into you.
   —Friedrich Nietzsche

PART I

That which does not kill us makes us stronger.
—Friedrich Nietzsche

CHAPTER ONE

JANUARY 17, 2017
DC JAIL GYM
WASHINGTON, DC

I STOOD OVER MY CELLIE JAMAL AS HE STRUGGLED TO push the fourth rep off his chest. A fog of sweat hung in the air and gave the windowless gym a fetid, rainforest feel. As Jamal dropped the bar to his chest to bounce up his fifth rep, I noticed them. To my right. Movement in my peripheral vision. Head still down, I glanced up through my eyebrows and saw four men, close together and moving as one. A pack of hyenas. Men don't move like this in a gym. Especially the DC Jail gym. Not good.

I looked away and back to Jamal. He was squirming under the bar as he fought to raise his sixth and final rep, big-framed oval glasses askew on his contorted face. He was losing the battle, his spaghetti arms unable to raise the 135 pounds to me. I leaned in and spotted him, gave him just enough help to rack the bar with a clang that shook the rickety bench.

"Six—motherfucker!" Jamal shouted.

He sprang from the bench and stood facing me. Adjusted his glasses back into place. He searched my face for approval. I had just started showing Jamal a few moves in the gym, and he was anxious to make an impression. He was tall and lanky, all skin and bones, and wanted to put on a few pounds for the ladies. He was getting out in seven months.

This was the first time Jamal had got six reps at 135. His bench-press form was for shit, but I didn't have the heart to correct him. His big smile was infectious.

I returned that big smile and said, "Good set."

We each added a forty-five-pound plate to the bar and traded places. I took a seat at the end of the bench and sized up the hyena pack, holding my stare until the pack looked my way. But instead of the usual mad dog stare I was hoping for, I got a matching set of arrogant smirks, barely visible, before they all looked away again. This, too, was not good.

There were four of them, all different shapes and sizes. Inked-up Hispanic guys. All of them had a handprint tattoo or the number 13 prominently displayed in black ink, large enough to be visible from across the gym.

The pack sauntered over to two other prisoners at the pull-up bar and spoke with them in hushed voices. The two men glanced my way, then back to the pack, and then nodded and left the gym without a word. They did not look back at me.

"C'mon, man. Do your set," Jamal said with exasperation. He was still standing at the rear of the bench, waiting for me to start my third set of bench presses. Jamal was a high-strung, jumpy sort of guy. A fast talker. Always in motion.

I leaned back towards him, my eyes still fixed on the pack, and whispered, "Look at those four guys at the pull-up bar. They're up to something."

"What're you talking about?" Jamal retorted in a voice louder that I would have preferred.

I shushed him and lay down flat on the bench, looking up at him. I grabbed the bar and took my grip.

"Those guys. By the pull-up. They're watching us," I said quietly. "You know those guys?"

Jamal looked over and then back down at me. "Those dudes are La Eme. Mexican Mafia." Jamal was whispering now too. "I've seen them around. Their head is a dude named Swoll. He's a real badass. Duckie don't even fuck with him."

"What do you think they want?" I asked.

"Don't know," Jamal said. "Let's finish our sets and get the fuck outta here."

The Mexican Mafia began in the California prison system in the 1950s and now controlled thousands of Hispanic inmates and street gang members. They are particularly, and oftentimes creatively, violent. La Eme specialized in murder-for-hire, extortion, drug dealing, and assaults. Most wore a black handprint tattoo or the number 13, signifying the letter M, the thirteenth letter in the alphabet.

I hoisted the 225 pounds and did six smooth reps, four short of my usual. The cancer had weakened me, and I fatigued more easily now. I had been denied treatment in the month or so I'd been incarcerated in this place. This had come as no surprise to me but had infuriated my girlfriend Sarah and my friend and mentor, mob boss Quinn Doyle.

Both were currently hiding out in Boston from the woman who had put me here: Prisha Baari.

I spoke to Quinn regularly on the jail telephone; all our conversations were recorded and reviewed by DC Jail Intel investigators. They need not have bothered. Quinn and I spoke in riddles, using coded language we had honed since I was a child and he was my hero. Quinn had survived many FBI wiretaps and thousands of overhears. We were Navajo Code Talkers on that jailhouse phone, Quinn and I, discussing operational plans right under the noses of the guards. They had as much chance of breaking our code as the Japanese had had during World War II.

Let them listen all they wanted. They would hear nothing.

I racked the bar and sat up. The pack had gathered around another prisoner now. Two more guys left the gym, both stealing looks at me and Jamal as they left. One of the hyenas looked my way now and flashed his teeth.

I had thought going to the gym during off-hours would be safer, but now realized my mistake. It only meant fewer witnesses.

I knew Prisha Baari would make a move on me in jail but had not expected it quite so soon. Jamal had earned his $100 and made contact with Duckie on my behalf. That had been over a week ago, and Duckie had yet to respond to my overture. Duckie was the toughest, meanest man in DC Jail—hell, in all of DC—and I intended to secure his protection while I was inside. But I had no such benefactor now. It was just me and spindly Jamal with his big oval glasses and 135-pound bench press.

I had been harassed and roughed up a bit by the guards in here. No doubt for the benefit of Victor Reyes, the asshole

DC cop whom my girlfriend Sarah was currently divorcing. In all fairness to me, I had not broken up their marriage. It was already broken when I reappeared in Sarah's life. We had dated all through high school, and Sarah was the only woman I had ever loved. Victor had caught Sarah on the rebound years after we broke up, and I'd impulsively married her younger sister, the equally impulsive Nicole Phillips. Nicole and I, predictably, didn't last long. We divorced just before my now-mortal enemy (and then boss) Prisha Baari fired me from the CIA for spurning her romantic advances.

Five years of vagabond homelessness followed, which ended with me back in DC, clinging to life in the ICU after having been beaten almost to death by a group of my fellow down-and-outers who had seen fit to rob me of the few valuables I had. I awoke to Sarah, cancer, and the news that Nicole and I had a five-year-old son named Teddy.

Putting it mildly, 2016 was quite a year.

The gym was nearly empty now. Just me, Jamal, and the pack.

I tried to appear nonchalant—hyenas will pounce on weakness—but my breathing felt shallow and I could hear my heart thumping in my ears. I wiped my moist hands on my shorts. It wouldn't be long now. Jamal pretended to ignore the pack while he did his last set. I stood at the rear of the bench spotting him as the last man left the gym.

The door closed, like the toll of a bell, and the pack turned on us, making no further effort to hide their true intention. They fanned out, shoulder to shoulder, in front of the gym door. Our only exit. In unison they took one step closer to me and Jamal. Then another. The biggest guy grimaced. I suspected this man hadn't smiled since the third grade and had lost the ability or inclination to do so ever again. He had two gold teeth—a front tooth and an incisor, both on the left side of his mouth. I took this man for the pack leader and began to take his measure, looking for an opening.

The gym door flew open again. The pack parted in the middle, and a large man stepped in and moved towards us. The hair on my arms stood on end as I took him in. He had a good four inches and forty pounds on me. On my best day. His face was scarred, and a black-inked hand, bearing a skin-toned capital M, covered one side of his bull neck. He stared at me with dark shark eyes that never blinked.

"Shit." Jamal leaned into me. "That's Swoll."

Swoll was the leader of the pack, and the head of the Mexican Mafia in the DC Jail. His reach and reputation went far beyond the jail. He was equally feared and respected by inmates and street gang members on the outside.

Swoll came by his name for his love of swoll, a prison delicacy made from disparate foodstuffs obtained from the commissary. Basically a ramen noodle–based casserole. His favorite iteration included Jack Mack (canned mackerel), canned chili, and squeeze cheese, seasoned with hot sauce and crushed Doritos. Nothing made Swoll happier than a big plate of his favorite food, and his crew and other supplicants made sure he was well fed. Everyone wanted a happy Swoll. It made life a lot easier.

Swoll stopped a few steps in front of me and Jamal. He took a wide stance, thick arms crossed over his chest. His merciless black eyes looked me and Jamal up and down. Slowly and casually, like a customer at a butcher shop. Still unblinking. A calm man on the verge of extreme violence was extremely unnerving. I'd seen his type before. No preening or posing. This was not his first rodeo.

"You Frank Luce?" Swoll asked. I did not like the sound of my name in his mouth.

"Yeah," I replied, my words light and tinny in my ear. I cleared my throat.

"You've got some enemies out there, my friend," Swoll said. "Enemies with money that'll pay big for your ass."

Swoll smiled, but it left his face as quickly as it came. No flicker of it reached his dark eyes.

"What enemies?" I asked, already knowing it was Prisha Baari and that she had come early for me.

"Your enemies ain't my problem," Swoll said. He looked to his pack, flanking him on either side. They chuckled.

"I can pay you," I said. A stall for time while my mind raced for a solution, a way out of this. "How much is she paying you? I'll beat it."

Swoll looked me over again and laughed out loud. An explosive, violent laugh that made his head snap back and those shark eyes roll up in their sockets.

"You don't have that kind of money, my friend," Swoll said. He looked at Jamal. "And I doubt your friend here does either."

"I know Duckie!" Jamal shouted. "You'd best leave us alone, or he'll beat down all you motherfuckers."

"I'm not afraid of Duckie," Swoll said. "Let him come." He waved his hand dismissively. "All I know is," he said, taking a step closer to us, "Duckie's not here now. Is he, Jamal?"

Swoll reached his right hand behind him and pulled something from the back of his waistband. It came back around with something in it, palmed from view. I didn't have to see it to know it was a shank. The pack closed rank, sticking tight to Swoll as they advanced. Jamal and I took a step back, and then another. I bumped up against the forty-five-pound plate, leaning against the side of the bench rack. I hit it with my heel, with enough force to send a vibration up my leg and spine. It rang my brain like that old-time carnival game where the strapping man smashes down the heavy mallet to ring the bell and win the stuffed bear for his girl-friend. I looked down at the weight, a little bigger than a toy spare tire.

It was a bad plan, but our best hope. I had been a decent discus thrower in high school track and hoped the muscle memory was still there. Swoll was our biggest threat. Partly because he had a knife and partly because he was Swoll and the others weren't. The timing was crucial. And I would only get one shot at this.

Swoll was now within a couple steps of me, his pack a step behind at his shoulders. I muttered to Jamal to wait for my move and blew out a deep breath. I had only seconds to act. I tried to visualize it. High school me in the discus pit, loose and fluid, taking warm-up throws before a meet. No thinking, just move. I'd thrown that three-pound metal disk thousands of times, enough to own the habit for life. Or so I hoped.

Swoll took one more step, putting him at arm's length in front of me. He now turned his right hand over to display his prison shank, a four-inch blade taped to a piece of wood. His grimace and those shark eyes were the last thing I saw.

I bent over and grabbed the forty-five-pound plate with both hands. I closed my eyes. Tried to summon the ghost of all those past discus throws. I planted my feet and started my thrower's spin. I let my mind take my body and opened my eyes as I came out of my final spin. I judged the distance between me and Swoll, extended both my arms, and slammed the plate into the side of his head.

I felt the crash of the weight against Swoll's face. Heard the melon thump. Swoll buckled and fell to the floor. His shank fell from his hand and skittered across the concrete.

There was an eerie pause after Swoll hit the ground, like the delay between a lightning strike and crashing thunder. Everything was still. And then it wasn't. The pack rushed me and Jamal in unison, screaming. My next memory was of me and Jamal at the bottom of a pile, being kicked and punched. We were both throwing punches but getting the worst of it. Things slowed down. My vision became more acute. I could sense the impact of the blows inflicted upon me but felt no pain.

I rolled to my side and saw one of the hyenas had Jamal around the neck. Jamal's eyes bulged with fear; his face was ashen. I noticed the shank on the concrete floor a few feet away. I threw a man off me and lunged for the knife. I got to it and wrapped my hand around the wooden handle, covered in duct tape. It felt substantial in my hand.

I spun and slid the blade into the ribs of the man choking Jamal. He howled, then turned to face me. I stabbed him a second time. The guy let go of Jamal and dropped to his knees, choking and gasping. Another hyena came at me, and I stabbed him too. I don't remember stabbing him, but I do remember all the blood.

The guards rushed in and jerked me and Jamal to our feet. I looked down at my hands and didn't see the knife. I never saw it again. I was covered in blood. Jamal was too.

Swoll was still on the floor, unconscious. I had landed that forty-five-pound weight perfectly. He was out before he hit the floor. It was a lucky shot. Probably couldn't do it again in a hundred tries. Luckily, I had thrown discus and not shot put, like my high school coaches had wanted me to. If I'd been a shot putter, I would be dead right now. Life's funny that way.

The guy who'd been choking Jamal was still bleeding out on the floor. The other two—one of whom I'd stabbed, plus the other guy I hadn't gotten to yet—were on their feet and being restrained by the guards. I looked at Jamal. The color had returned to his face, but his breathing was labored. It was alarming to see Jamal without the big glasses he always wore. Like Santa Claus without his big white beard.

The guards had a tight grip on me, one on each side and both digging their fingernails into the insides of my biceps. Suddenly, heavy fatigue and blunt pain racked my whole body to the marrow of my bones. My adrenaline had dried up, and the cancer returned to its place of primacy. My knees buckled. The guards held me up as I sagged.

As they started to drag me away, one of the standing guys, the one I'd stabbed, yelled something at me that I didn't catch. I turned to face him, and he yelled again.

"Hey, Luce—you gonna get what's coming to you! You hear me, *pendejo?*"

I turned away and let the guards drag me out of the gym. I didn't respond to the guy.

I knew he was right.

CHAPTER TWO

JANUARY 19, 2017
PRISHA BAARI'S TOWNHOUSE
GEORGETOWN, WASHINGTON, DC

HENRIK KARLSSON CHECKED HIS FAITHFUL TAG HEUER watch, the one he'd worn since his days in the Swedish Armed Forces Special Operations Group. 9:05 p.m. He cocked his head back and exhaled a cloud of condensation into the chilled night air. It was a clear night, with a faint half-moon.

Karlsson stood on the covered front porch of the swank Georgetown townhouse belonging to his boss, Prisha Baari. Their relationship was... complicated. Atypical, at least. Karlsson was neither subordinate employee nor independent contractor. Either way, Prisha was the boss and both of them knew it. Prisha paid Karlsson a deep six-figure tax-free salary. In exchange, he had a short memory and tight lips. It helped that he excelled at his job, which, as head of security, was to keep Prisha alive and out of trouble. Karlsson had worked for Prisha for over six years. It had been better at first, even fun at times. Now, mostly Prisha just rubbed him raw. He stayed for the money.

Karlsson looked up and down the bucolic, tree-lined street. All appeared normal. He opened the front door with his key and went inside. He heard the faint sound of a television emanating from the lower floor and shuffled to the door leading down to the two-car garage. Karlsson put his hand on the doorknob. He paused, closed his eyes, and drew a few deep breaths. He turned the knob and headed downstairs to the small exercise room off the garage.

Prisha was running on her treadmill in the center of the room, a concrete-block bunker no larger than a parking stall. Karlsson approached her from the rear and noted the view. He had to give Prisha her due; she was in her early forties but worked hard to avoid the touch of Father Time. She wore only black yoga pants and a purple-and-black sports bra. Karlsson stepped forward now and stood beside the treadmill, once again enjoying the view. Prisha's augmented breasts gently rolled with each stride. Karlsson held his gaze a moment too long.

"Eyes up, perv," Prisha said with a cackle. She liked to flirt with Karlsson, and she relished catching him looking. Her smile lingered; her lips were adorned with lush red lipstick.

Karlsson didn't take the bait. He silently chastised himself for allowing Prisha her satisfaction.

"You wanted to talk?" Karlsson asked in his business voice.

The smile drained from Prisha's face. She jerked her

thumb at the fifty-five-inch television monitor mounted to the concrete wall at eye level in front of the treadmill, which was playing the *Rachel Maddow Show* on MSNBC. Tonight's guest was the Speaker of the House, a shrill and vocal critic of President Mo Udell.

"Can you believe this guy?" Prisha asked. She stabbed her finger at the control panel of the treadmill to increase her speed. Her breathing soon became more labored.

Karlsson remained silent.

"I mean, he's trying to repeal the Twenty-Second Amendment," Prisha said. "The balls on this guy to think America wants him for a third term." She grabbed a fluffy white towel that hung over the front of the machine and wiped the sweat from her face. "He thinks he can get seventy-five percent of the states to agree to repeal. How the hell does he think he can get thirty-eight states to agree to anything right now?"

Her feet thumped rhythmically on the belt as she awaited her answer.

"I wouldn't know," was all Karlsson said.

"I'll tell you how," Prisha continued. She looked away from the television and over to Karlsson. He stood to her left side, five feet away from the treadmill and with his back braced against the concrete block wall. "I'll bet you that bastard is using ODYSSEUS."

ODYSSEUS was the top-secret government project to input false memories into the brains of the American people by grafting suggestive messages onto innocuous sound waves delivered into hundreds of millions of American homes via music streaming apps like Spotify and Apple Music. The FBI and law enforcement saw ODYSSEUS as an investigative tool, an advanced form of wiretapping. The CIA viewed it as a propaganda and disinformation technology. Only Prisha saw it as a way to brainwash and manipulate the American public to her ends. But now she wasn't so sure. She had briefed ODYSSEUS to President Udell, but at the time she'd thought him too obtuse to realize its true potential. But maybe he wasn't the dullard she thought he was. Maybe he had accessed ODYSSEUS behind her back and was using it now to ensure his third term. This was something Prisha would not abide, as she had her own thoughts on the 2020 presidential election.

Karlsson started to speak. Prisha cut him off.

"Yeah, I bet that bastard got his hands on ODY somehow," she said, striding furiously, arms swinging faster. "That's just another problem you and I have to address, Henrik."

Karlsson sighed and rested the back of his head against the concrete wall.

Prisha turned from Karlsson and back towards the television. She went silent, enjoying the spectacle of Rachel Maddow skewering President Udell. Karlsson, familiar with all Prisha's little power plays and mind games, endured the silence. He would wait her out as always. He knew why he had been summoned here and awaited her wrath.

He didn't have to wait long.

"Henrik, what the hell happened with Luce at the DC Jail?" Prisha asked in a clipped tone, her eyes still glued to the television.

Karlsson pushed off the concrete wall and took a half-step towards her.

"I just got the full story myself today. From one of our guards," Karlsson replied. He briefed his boss on the failed assassination attempt on Frank Luce at the DC Jail two days ago. It had been all set up and scheduled to go as planned. Luce's cellmate had unexpectedly been with him at the gym, but the Mexican Mafia had been okay with killing them both. The corrupt guard had told him afterwards that Luce had just got lucky, and that he'd cracked Swoll in the head with a forty-five-pound weight. Stabbed a few of the others. Everyone, including Luce, had ended up in the infirmary. There were no fatalities. Swoll and one of his guys had gotten the worst of it, but they were both expected to recover.

"How did this get so screwed up, Henrik?" Prisha shouted. "Luce got the best of you at the bodega, and now again. Even while he's in jail." Prisha grabbed the handrails of the treadmill hard and turned to face Karlsson. "He's my bad penny. Why can't you fix this problem and make him go away—once and for all?"

"May I remind you I was the one he shot that night in the bodega. Not you," Karlsson said. He took another step forward. "I want this guy as bad as you do, Prisha. Sometimes ops just don't work out."

"We've got to be better than that, Henrik," Prisha snapped, still running and breathing hard. "We've gotta wrap this up now—right now! I can't move forward with Luce still around." Prisha turned back to the television and shook her head in disgust, her raven ponytail bobbing to and fro. "This guy's been one big pain in my ass," she panted.

She increased her treadmill speed again and sprinted for five minutes. Karlsson took his place back against the wall. He watched Prisha's taut body going through its exertions and promised himself he would get to the gym tomorrow. He tried to watch the television, but Rachel had nothing to say that was of any interest to him. Karlsson studied his boots and thought maybe it was time for a new pair. He checked his watch. He had been there for almost twenty minutes. That was enough.

"Hey. Prisha, if that's all, maybe I'll just get going. I—"

Prisha grunted and slapped at the control panel to slow the treadmill down to a fast walk. She wiped her face with the towel and draped it around her neck. She was sweating freely now.

"Do you think the cancer will get him?" she asked, taking a long pull from the tube sticking out of her water bottle. She paused to catch her breath. "I mean, we denied him treatment in jail, right? How much time can he have left?"

"I don't know, Prisha," Karlsson replied. "But I don't think that's our best option."

"Well," Prisha said with a tinge of sarcasm, "what *is* our best option?"

Karlsson did not hesitate to answer. "I think we should hire another inmate to take him out."

Prisha snorted, which caused her to choke on her water. "Another inmate?" she rasped when she was done coughing. "You've got to be kidding me! What makes you think the same failed plan will work the second time?"

"Prisha..." Karlsson paused to swallow his rising anger. "I told you. It was a good plan. The Mexican Mafia picked the location. How was I to know Luce would pick up a forty-five-pound plate and crack the guy's head open? Shit happens in my business. This is no time for overreaction."

"Overreaction?" Prisha asked incredulously. She placed both her hands on the handrails and squeezed tight. "Do you think I'm overreacting?"

Karlsson again pushed off the wall. He jammed his clenched fists into the front pockets of his jeans.

"I'll find another inmate. Maybe Aryan Brotherhood. Luce got lucky the first time. Maybe not so much next time."

"What about a guard?" Prisha asked. "Or Luce's girlfriend's ex—the cop? Maybe they could do it? I'll bet that cop might want a piece of Luce right about now."

Prisha smiled her big, open smile.

"No," Karlsson said, jerking his head from side to side in a quick, violent motion. "Too much scrutiny. Inmate-on-inmate violence draws much less attention. It's our best play inside the jail."

Prisha dabbed her face with the towel and took slow sips of her water, looking straight ahead and deep in thought. Karlsson kept silent and stewed.

Prisha stood fully erect, back straight, as she strolled through the machine's cool-down cycle. She released her grip on the handrails and let her arms hang at her sides. Her breathing had slowed to conversational level. She turned towards Karlsson, her face now relaxed. A grin began to form at the corners of her mouth. Her dark mahogany eyes twinkled.

"Maybe we should be looking for a solution outside the jail," Prisha said.

"What do you mean?"

"I know a man," Prisha continued. "I learned of him from one of my European colleagues at the CIA."

"So you've never met this man?" Karlsson interrupted.

"He has impeccable credentials and comes highly recommended. Besides, you don't meet this guy. That's not how it works."

"You don't know anything about him? He's a ghost?"

"All I know is that he's an Israeli, or purports to be. Or maybe my colleague made that up. Doesn't really matter.

The man is uniquely qualified for this job. I'm told he is an older man. Nondescript and nonthreatening in appearance. Able to blend into the background wherever he goes. An expert knife fighter and skilled in Krav Maga. A real pro. Never failed a contract. They call this guy in when others have failed. He's expensive, but he delivers."

Prisha pressed the stop button and stepped off the treadmill. She took a step towards Karlsson, who backed up against the wall. Karlsson took Prisha's words for what they were: a rebuke.

"What do you think?" Prisha asked.

Karlsson sighed, pulled his hands out of his pockets and folded his arms tightly across his chest.

"I don't work with ghosts," Karlsson said. "You don't know this guy any more than I do. I've come across all kinds of guys with big reputations. And inevitably, the bigger the reputation, the bigger the disappointment. Most of these guys turn out to be full of shit. What do your Texans say— big hat, no cattle."

"But my colleague—"

"So this guy's roaming around Europe somewhere, and Luce is sitting in DC Jail. How the hell would this even work?" Karlsson's voice had a sharp tone to it now. Prisha's face registered this and she mirrored him. Her eyes went flat; her posture stiffened.

"We get ACA Calderon and his corrupt cop on board," Prisha replied. She gestured emphatically to make her point. "They'll arrest the guy on some bullshit charge and stick him in DC Jail." Prisha smacked her fist down against the palm of her other hand like a gavel. "Bang! That puts the guy in with Luce, and we just sit back and let him fix our problem."

"So now we've got three outside people involved in this?

The ghost assassin, the corrupt ACA, and his little cop minion?" Karlsson huffed an indignant breath out his nose. "And I don't like corrupt cops. Can't trust them worth a shit."

"That cop did what we asked of him with Luce's girlfriend," Prisha retorted. "Her arrest went down as planned. No problems."

They glared at each other for a long moment. The silence grew heavy. Karlsson spoke first.

"Too risky. I don't like it. Three outsiders. Three points of failure. We need a plan with the fewest possible assumptions. Keep it simple and—"

"You're giving me Occam's Razor?"

"I'm saying we can handle this ourselves, Prisha. Our guard can hook me up with the Aryans. They'll get the job done. Nice and simple."

Prisha remained impassive long enough to give Karlsson the impression she was considering his argument. Then came the big open smile. The one that displayed Prisha's prominent ivory-white teeth. She had already made up her mind.

"I want you to know I heard you, that I value your opinion and loyalty," Prisha said. "However—I think it's time we go with the ghost."

"But, Prisha—"

"I've made up my mind, Henrik. It's our best option. I'll contact my colleague tomorrow and get this thing going. Trust me. It'll work."

Karlsson did not trust this decision, and said so. He was also beginning to doubt Prisha as well. At least his standing with her. This he kept to himself.

Prisha took another step towards Karlsson, smile still in

place. She reached out and affectionately touched his arm. Told him everything she thought he wanted to hear: how important he was to her; how much she respected him and relied on his counsel; how she considered him a dear friend; how much she cared for him.

Karlsson fought his emotions. This performance had worked in years past, but not tonight. He had broken Prisha's spell over him. This he decided to keep to himself as well.

Karlsson put on his own best fake smile.

"Sure, Prisha. We'll do it your way. Whatever you want."

CHAPTER THREE

I WALKED TWO STEPS BEHIND A BEHEMOTH OF A MAN, my eyes fixed on the thick, ebony neck rolls below his glossy bald head. The sounds of general population assaulted my senses; I had been released from thirty days in solitary just yesterday. I'd mostly recovered from the beating I'd taken at the hands of the Mexican Mafia, but still felt the grinding fatigue and bone pain of my leukemia on a daily basis. My orange prison scrubs hung off me now, such that I had to roll the waist to keep my pants up. I guessed I'd lost about ten pounds in the hole.

My weight loss and aches and pains were not the worst part of my thirty-day retreat, however. Jamal, who had gone from the infirmary to solitary just like me, had been reassigned to a new cell. Which meant I had a new cellie, a fat Hispanic guy named Carlos whom I took an immediate dislike to. I didn't know if he was Mexican Mafia, and I had slept with one eye open last night. Carlos was my reminder that the DC Jail was still out to screw me. This was going to get worse before it got better. If it ever got better, that is. At least Jamal was okay. He had not said a word under questioning. Good man.

My big bald escort stopped abruptly mid-block in front of an open cell. He waved me inside without a word, a scowl etched on his face. He had come by my cell early this morning, and the mere sight of him had caused Carlos to scurry away. He'd told me to follow him, that someone wanted to see me. He didn't say who and I knew better than to ask.

What I saw stopped me in my tracks just outside the cell door.

It was a single cell, unheard of given the epic overcrowding at the DC Jail. Mid-morning sun filtered through the window at the back of the cell, projecting a bar-and-window shadow onto the floor. The bedding was real cotton, not the standard sandpaper sheet and blanket. Artwork adorned the walls. Some were reproductions of famous paintings, like *The Scream*, by Edvard Munch. Others were painted with a more amateur hand. There was plenty of contraband in plain sight: meats and cheeses not sold in the commissary; a painting easel and assorted brushes and paints; an older model iPhone; and a few porn magazines. Normally, any of this contraband would draw immediate confiscation and thirty days' solitary confinement. What shocked me was how brazenly all this stuff was displayed, easily seen by any guard who cared to look.

The man occupying this cell sat at a table facing the wall

opposite his bunk. He had a pen in his hand and had been writing on a yellow legal pad. He remained seated and turned to face me when I stepped to his cell door. He was the largest man I had ever seen, even sitting down. He didn't introduce himself. He didn't have to. I knew in an instant that this must be Duckie.

He was a dark-skinned African American, closer to four hundred than three hundred pounds, with a shaved head and a thick, black beard, graying slightly at the chin. His eyes were almond shaped and wide-set, the color of toffee, the kind of eyes that made one feel like prey. The eyes of an apex predator.

He motioned me into his cell. I shuffled in on leaden legs and stopped two steps in. I wasn't going to sit on this man's bed with its real cotton blanket. He motioned me to a second chair next to his bed and across from him. I took my seat and waited.

"You all good in there, Duck?" my bald escort asked from out in the hall.

Duckie nodded and waved the man off, not breaking his focus on me.

"All right, then," the man said, then took his post outside Duckie's door.

Duckie nodded for me to begin. So I cleared my throat and did.

"My name's Frank Luce, and I—"

"I know who you are, Frank Luce," Duckie said. His voice was melodic and higher-pitched than I expected from such a colossus of a man. "Medal of Honor winner. Murderer."

"I'm no murderer. I'm innocent," I said.

"Too bad," Duckie replied with a grin. "Being a killer

comes in handy in here." He leaned forward in his chair. It groaned under his bulk. "C'mon, Frank. You must have killed your share of men in the army. They don't give those Medals of Honor out to no Boy Scouts now."

I was nervous, not knowing where this was going. He sat back and awaited my answer.

"That was different," I finally mumbled. "That was war. Combat. I was a soldier following orders."

"Is that right?" Duckie roared. "I've been a mother-fucking soldier all my life. Fighting the war on poverty." He smirked. "I guess that makes us both soldiers, then, don't it?"

I held my silence.

"So why did you want to see me?" Duckie cut me with his stare. "You're no murderer, but you be looking for one. Is that it?"

I nodded. "Something like that."

Duckie snorted. He held his arms wide and tilted his head back.

"Look around you, man. There's killers everywhere around here." He pointed outside the cell to my bald escort. "Homeboy's killed three dudes. One just for the fuck of it. Just about everybody I mess with has killed a dude or watched a dude be killed. It ain't no thing around here."

"I'm not looking for any murderer. I'm looking for you."

"Is that right?"

"Yeah. Jamal said you were the guy in here."

"Jamal," Duckie said, shaking his head and smiling. A friendly, honest smile that lit up his face. "Scrawny lil' Jamal. He can be a pain in my ass, but he's a solid dude."

I nodded.

"That's why I sent for you. I heard you handled yourself against Swoll and his crew when they came at you in the gym. Jamal says you saved his life. Stabbed the shit out of a guy that was choking him out. That true?"

I nodded again.

Duckie said I had five minutes to say what I had to say. I glanced at the cell door, and Duckie dismissed my bald escort so we could talk in private. I inched my chair as close to Duckie as I dared, and ended up in the patch of sun that was streaming through the window. The warmth eased the aching pain in my bones. Duckie looked even bigger at this distance. I was close enough now to be within his grasp, should he choose to reach out and grab me. I swallowed my fear, leaned forward in my seat, and made my case.

"I'd like to hire you. For protection, while I'm in here."

"Protection from who? Mexican Mafia? You double-cross them?"

I told Duckie that I had no beef with the Mexican Mafia. He found this funny and informed me that I had a beef with them now, after taking out Swoll and stabbing a couple of his men. Duckie asked me who had hired Swoll to kill me, and why anyone would want me dead that bad. I told him I couldn't say, for his own good.

That was the wrong thing to say to this man.

"You mean to say you're asking me for help, but you can't tell me the truth? For my own protection?" Duckie said in a mocking tone. "Does it look like I need protection?"

Duckie slid his chair closer to me. He leaned forward so that we were now less than three feet apart. My heart raced. My body tingled in its fight-or-flight neurochemical dump.

"Are you calling me a bitch, Frank?"

I emphatically explained to Duckie that I had not just called him a bitch.

"You want my protection, you come at me straight,"

Duckie said. "I gotta have the truth... gotta know what I'm stepping into here. You feel me?" Duckie fixed me with a hard stare. "I pick my own enemies... know what I'm saying?"

I told Duckie that made sense.

"Damn right," he responded, then made it clear I had to tell him what was going on, or else I was on my own in here.

My mind raced. I knew Prisha would reload and come back for me a second time, and I was pretty sure I wouldn't get lucky again. So I decided to tell him everything. Well, mostly. I told Duckie about Prisha, and how our one-night tryst had turned into my nightmare. My five years of home-lessness. My cancer, and my vow to get my government money to Nicole and Teddy before the cancer got me. How all of this had led to my discovery of ODYSSEUS, which marked me for death. How Prisha had used Sarah to get to me, and how she'd framed me for Hewitt's murder just so she could kill me in jail. I filled him in on Quinn Doyle and Gerry Gonzalez, our ethics-challenged attorney. Finally, I told Duckie that Prisha was up to something, I didn't know what as yet, but that she was anxious to have me dead—and probably Sarah and Quinn as well.

I went well over my allotted five minutes. The only rele-vant thing I left out were the details of ODYSSEUS, which I figured he really didn't need to know. Duckie was spell-bound, like he was watching a good murder mystery on television.

"So, you got the damn CIA, the ACA, and some killer Viking all after you?" Duckie asked, counting each one of my tormentors off on his fingers.

"Yeah, that's about right."

"What did you do to piss all these people off?"

"I wonder that sometimes myself."

"And what makes you think I want all these people up my ass too?"

"I'll pay you."

"How much?"

"Whatever you want."

Duckie sat back in his chair and laughed. "You ain't got that kind of money, Frank."

"Try me."

Quinn had already agreed to pay to keep me alive in jail; he'd trusted me to look after the details.

Duckie stroked his beard as he thought. "Five grand down. Five grand a month. Cash," he said at last.

"Done."

Duckie's face went cold. He drew closer.

"I want you to understand what this is gonna mean, going into business with me. Unlike you, I am a killer. Killed my first when I was eleven years old. Too many since then to count. Shot 'em, stabbed 'em, choked 'em, beat 'em to death—with pipes and my bare hands. I've got no qualms about killing a man that needs killing. You partner with me, some of that might get on you. You know what I'm saying?"

I did know what Duckie was saying. This was a decision that, once made, I could not walk back from. It would cause me to see and do things I would not have considered a few short years ago, before I'd stumbled back into Prisha Baari's life. But I was sure I would die in custody if I didn't throw in with Duckie. I was prepared to get a little dirty if I had to.

I rose to my feet and stuck out my hand. "Five down, five a month. And you keep me alive?"

Duckie stood slowly. He kept rising and rising. I looked up at him. All six foot nine inches of him. A full head and shoulders taller than me. Jamal was right. I could see why they called him Duckie. This man was terrifying.

He reached out and grabbed my hand. Swallowed it whole. He tightened his grip and pulled me to him like I was a rag doll. We were now chest to chest. He leaned down close to my face, his eyes fierce.

"I'm gonna check your shit out. I've got eyes and ears everywhere. On the streets and inside. You lie to me—you cross me—and I'm gonna kill you, Frank. And not easy, but hard. You understand?"

My mouth went dry, my throat tight. I just nodded. I knew he was serious. Knew if I betrayed him, he wouldn't stop at just me. Sarah and Quinn would be next. There is no negotiation with apex predators. You kill the lion or let him be.

"Good!" Duckie exclaimed, releasing his death grip on my hand.

I stepped back from him.

"Me and you are gonna be fine, Frank. You got nothing to worry about. As long as you keep your word, I'll always deal you straight. All I ask is you do me the same."

I nodded, dry-mouthed, and Duckie motioned me out of his cell. Our meeting was over.

CHAPTER FOUR

GERRY GONZALEZ SAT ALONE IN THE ATTORNEY visiting room at the DC Jail. It was a small, sparse room, containing not much more than a small table and two chairs. He had been here many times before in his two decades as a misdemeanor and minor-felony criminal defense lawyer. DUIs, simple assaults, domestic cases. The good old days. His client list now included a retired Irish mob boss, a disgraced ex-CIA analyst everyone seemed to want dead, and his newest client, who was about to walk through the door. This guy frightened him most of all.

Gonzalez longed to return to the legal work he had done before Frank Luce strolled into his life. Staged car accidents and slip-and-fall cases that were good money and low risk.

Not exactly honest work, but who really cared if a multi-million-dollar insurance company got squeezed out of a little money? Not Gerry Gonzalez, that's for damn sure.

Gonzalez had grown fond of Frank and Quinn, and of course Sarah. He didn't mind handling their legal work. But this new client was different. Gonzalez didn't want any part of him, but Quinn and Sarah had convinced him this was the only way. Their pleas, and a generous up-front fee paid in full, had gotten him here. He fidgeted in his chair. Gonzalez wanted out, even if that meant refunding his fee—a sacrilege to him.

Just as Gonzalez rose to leave, the door opened and a guard delivered his new client. He filled the room. The guard was jocular, almost deferential to this man, who called the guard by his first name. A chill ran down Gonzalez's spine. He stood mid-chest to the man and had to crane his head back to see his face. This man was much bigger than he looked in all the mug shots. Gonzalez waited for the guard to leave and shut the door.

"Gerry Gonzalez," he said, offering his hand. Duckie shook it. Gonzalez immediately tried to wriggle free. Duckie's massive paw reached past Gonzalez's wrist. He wasn't shaking his hand, but his entire arm.

One look at Duckie told Gonzalez the man's extensive criminal history was true, that he had done everything they said he'd done. And much more. Gonzalez had built up quite a network of street snitches, and he had done his homework on Duckie. He learned that Duckie had a reputation for keeping his word and punishing those who didn't keep theirs. People were terrified of him, thought of him as some type of larger-than-life bogeyman. As they took their seats across from each other, Gonzalez now understood all of this.

Frank must have let his thirst for vengeance against Prisha Baari cloud his judgment, he thought, inwardly shaking his head. Why else would he go into business with such a man? To Gonzalez's way of thinking, Duckie was a monster. A monster he wanted no part of. But he was in too deep now. It frightened him to be in such a confined space with Duckie. He would make this visit quick and get the hell out of there.

They got right down to business.

"I now represent you as your attorney," Gonzalez said, fighting to control the tremor in his voice. "As your attorney, I will meet with you in private, just like today. Anything you say to me from now on will be protected by attorney–client privilege. Do you understand?"

Duckie chuckled. "I know what attorney–client means."

Gonzalez slid Duckie some papers to sign: a client agreement and conflict of interest waiver, as he also represented Frank, Sarah, and Quinn. Duckie signed all the forms without reading them, then slid them back across the table.

They discussed their new arrangement. Gonzalez would make payments to Duckie, five thousand dollars a month, on the first of every month, for as long as Frank was incarcerated at the DC Jail. For his part, Duckie would provide his protection, meaning no one raised a hand to Frank while he was inside. Gonzalez said the first payment of ten thousand dollars would be made today: five thousand down and the first month's payment in advance. Duckie nodded.

With their business concluded, Gonzalez started to gather his papers. "How's Frank doing?" he asked. "His health, I mean."

"Well, I don't take his temperature every day, so I wouldn't know, would I?"

"You need to know Frank's got leukemia," Gonzalez said. "It gives him persistent fatigue, weakness. Makes him bruise and bleed easily. I'm sure you can appreciate how this makes your job more difficult." Gonzalez looked up from his neatly stacked papers. "And important."

"How long's he got?"

"Five years, if he's lucky," Gonzalez responded. "I'm working on getting DC Corrections to give him the treatment he needs. But you know how these people are."

Duckie nodded and blew out a heavy sigh across the table. "That man's got a dark cloud over him. ACA put a murder case on him, and now death cancer. Damn."

Gonzalez finished stuffing his papers into his briefcase and started to stand. Duckie gave him a look that said their meeting was not over yet. Gonzalez melted back into his chair.

"Did Frank really kill that CIA guy?"

"I currently represent Frank, and as his lawyer I can't disclose—"

"We're all friends here now," Duckie said with a smile, displaying straight, white teeth any dentist would applaud. "You're my lawyer too, right? Just said so. So you're gonna tell me, right, Gerry?"

Gerry heard the threat behind the smile. "No," he said. "Frank didn't murder Charles Hewitt. He was framed by the people who are trying to kill him."

"Is Frank CIA?"

"He used to be. He was a desk analyst, not a spook. He only worked for the CIA for three years before he crossed the wrong person. And that's when the wheels came off his wagon."

Duckie appeared satisfied with the answers Gonzalez provided.

"One more thing, Duckie. Do you know who Quinn Doyle is?"

"Frank said he's some kind of gangster from Boston or some shit."

"Quinn led the Irish mob in Boston for decades. He's a very powerful, dangerous man. Retired now, but still holds the loyalty of his crew. This is Quinn's money I'm giving you. His personal funds. And Quinn thinks of Frank as a son. Do you understand what I'm saying here?"

"As long as the money's right, you got no problem with me."

"Good," Gonzalez said. He did not want to get in between Quinn Doyle and Duckie. Ever.

Gonzalez and Duckie wrapped up their first attorney–client meeting by discussing the logistics for the monthly payments. Duckie instructed Gonzalez to deliver the money, hundreds and small bills, no fifties, to his girl Nia Green. He gave him Nia's cell number and code word.

"Nia'll tell you where to meet for the money drop. And she'll count every bill, 'cause Nia don't play, neither. She handles all my business while I'm inside. Keeps fools in line too." Duckie smiled, cocked his head at Gonzalez. "Nia's meaner than me. Don't mess with her."

Gonzalez nodded and said he didn't want any trouble.

Duckie stood to leave. He turned and signaled for the guard through the small slot window in the door, and Gonzalez heard the jingle of keys. Duckie spun back around to face Gonzalez and leaned his bulk over the table, so that he was face-to-face with him. His piercing eyes bore into Gonzalez, freezing him in his chair. Gonzalez swallowed hard. Duckie held his stare for an extended moment as the guard entered the room behind him, then leaned in even closer.

"I'm gonna be your best friend or your worst enemy, Gerry," he whispered. "You decide."

CHAPTER FIVE

"Ever been shot, Frank?" Duckie asked.

"Been shot at plenty of times. In the 'Stan."

"I mean been shot."

"As yet, I have not had the pleasure," I replied. "You?"

"Three times," Duckie said. He lifted his orange scrubs to reveal a discolored divot on the left side of his abdomen. "Once in the gut." He fingered the wound and dropped his shirt. "Once in the elbow." He raised his huge right arm, bent it at the elbow, and pointed it at me. "That one hurt like a motherfucker." Duckie shook his head and let out a low whistle.

"And I got this one right here." Duckie leaned in and turned his big bald head at a slight angle. "Damn bullet just bounced off my head. Feel it." He grabbed my hand and traced my finger over a spot a half-inch above his right temple. The dent in his head was the size of a dime. I'd never noticed it before. It blended right in with all the other scars and knots on Duckie's shaved head.

"Some fools be thinking that's why they call me Duckie. That my dumb ass forgot to duck." A mischievous smile spread wide over his face. "Did Jamal tell you for real why they call me Duckie?"

I nodded and started to answer when Duckie dropped his shoulder back and fired a straight jab my way. I turtled and bobbed my head to my left. Duckie pulled his punch inches from my head.

"Jesus, Duck!" I gasped.

The big man's laughter boomed, filling every corner of his cell. It was an honest laugh that softened his face and gave him a childlike expression. If only for a moment.

"Motherfuckers always duck," he said, still chuckling.

"Do you blame 'em?" I gathered myself. "You gotta stop doing that, man."

"I love seeing your face," Duckie said, bugging out his eyes and bobbing his big bucket head from side to side in pantomime.

It had been almost a month since I came under Duckie's protective wing. Gonzalez had made the first payments on time, and Duckie was good to his word. He worked a few favors with some of the guards and got my cell moved to his tier, about halfway down the block from his. He wasn't able to get Jamal moved, so I still had Carlos as my cellmate. I still didn't trust him, but Duckie put the word out that I was not to be touched and everyone knew what that meant. Especially Carlos, who suddenly discovered his civility and stayed out of my way.

I still had a serious problem with the Mexican Mafia, though. Swoll had lost face in our encounter and wanted to even the score. This meant that Duckie was my shadow for now, and we spent a lot of time together. We swapped life stories. He told me of his street life, how he had come up and become the most feared gangster in Southeast DC. I told him of my youth, my father Arthur's murder and how Quinn had stepped in and raised me. Duckie had never met his father, a failure he'd rectified with his own two daughters. We talked about my son Teddy, and how I had some rectifying of my own to do. He asked me about my Medal of Honor. I told him the whole story, including why I'd left the military. He told me some hair-raising stories of his exploits on the streets, which had given rise to his reputation and myth. It turned out we had a lot in common.

We were both soldiers, like he said. His war was the war on poverty. Mine, I wasn't so sure. I burned with a vengeful rage against Prisha Baari. I had made her the root of all my problems and vowed to kill her. So I guess my war was Prisha Baari. I knew I would have to fight hard to keep from falling into the darkness of my rage, but I was willing to lose a few of these battles to win my war.

It was getting late. I told Duckie I was heading back to my cell to read a bit. We bro-hugged and I left him at his table. He started to take out his brushes and paints.

I walked the hundred feet down the narrow catwalk hallway back to my cell, my white Velcro strap shoes slapping against the cracked concrete floor. Duckie and I were on the third tier. A black steel safety railing, four feet high, ran the length of the hallway at its edge. Many an inmate had gone over this railing and taken the thirty-foot plunge to the concrete floor below. Some made it. Some didn't.

I turned into my cell. Carlos lay in the bottom bunk, still as a corpse and eyes shut. Upon my arrival he jerked up and took a sitting position at the side of his bed. His jail scrubs stretched against his fat stomach, which caused his gut to spread into the one-inch gap between his scrub shirt and pants.

Carlos greeted me with niceties that I ignored. He seemed even more jittery than usual. I grabbed my book and jumped into my top bunk, but I felt his attention lingering on me. After a moment or two, he asked me if I was going to be around for a while, a question that struck me as odd. I leaned over my bunk, close to his blotchy, pock-marked face, and stared daggers into his dull, yellowed eyes. He harrumphed, then got to his feet and left the cell. I watched him waddle off and returned to my book.

"Hey, man."

I disengaged from the story world of my book and looked up. Jamal was standing at my cell door.

"What's up?" I bent the page to mark my place and put the book down. I sat up at the end of the bed, feet dangling.

"Ah, you know, homey," Jamal sang as he sat on my only chair by the door. "How's Duck?"

"We're good."

"That's cool, man," Jamal said. "I told you, man. No one fucks with Duckie." Jamal beat his fist into his palm for emphasis.

A loud crash rose from the bottom floor, followed by rapid footfalls and screamed commands from the guards. Jamal and I exchanged looks. He broke for the hallway. I leapt off my bunk and followed him out. We looked down over the railing to the bottom floor. Two Hispanic inmates were rolling around on the ground, fighting. Two guards jumped in, then two more, and they separated the two combatants. One was much larger than the other, but neither one appeared to have any real injuries.

The guards barked questions at them. They held their silence at first, but then grew insolent and began sassing the guards, their voices heavy with sarcasm. The guards threatened them with solitary time, and they just laughed. Giggled, really. I thought I saw one of them, the smaller one, flash a glance up at me.

This all felt odd. I got the kind of creepy feeling that puts goosebumps on your arms. The feeling they say you're supposed to pay attention to. But I didn't. Instead, Jamal and I lingered at the railing, clowning a bit and joking about the fight for a minute or two.

For the remainder of my life, I wished I could have those two minutes back.

I turned away from the railing and faced my cell. I saw movement to my left and turned to see Swoll approaching at a fast walk. He smiled when our eyes met. I hissed "Shit!" under my breath and grabbed Jamal. He saw what I saw. We both spun to our right. Another man approached. He was white, early fifties, with thinning dark-gray hair. He was of small stature; his orange jail scrubs were ill-fitting. He walked slowly but with purpose, his face expressionless. His right hand hung limply by his side. He was cupping something in that hand. I had a pretty good idea what it was.

I raced back into my cell, Jamal at my heels.

"Fuck! You got anything on you?" I asked.

Jamal shook his head no. I scurried to my hidey-hole and pulled out the shank Duckie had given me. Jamal looked around wildly for a weapon and settled for the chair he had been sitting on. We backed into the rear of my cell and stood shoulder to shoulder.

The white guy stepped into the doorway. He was calm and contained, with perfect posture. He was also too clean and had an expensive haircut. One thing was clear to me: despite the orange jail scrubs, this man was no inmate.

"Hello, Frank," the man said, in a slight Israeli accent.

"What do you want?" I asked. "Who sent you?"

"I'm afraid we do not have time for all of that. Be a good boy and I'll spare the life of your friend here."

I turned to Jamal and nodded towards the door.

"Listen to your friend," the Israeli told him, not taking his eyes from me. "I've got no interest in you tonight. This is the one and only opportunity I will afford to you." He stepped inside, away from the doorway, offering Jamal safe passage.

"Fuck you," Jamal said without pause.

The man sighed. "Very well. As you wish." He slowly turned his right hand around, and I saw what he had hidden. I shuddered in recognition. It was a gleaming karambit combat knife.

It had a three-inch curved blade shaped like a tiger's claw. The man had a finger looped through the safety ring at the end of the four-inch handle, which made it impossible to disarm him. The knife was designed to make lightning-quick slashes in close combat. It could slice through vital arteries like butter. In the proper hands, it killed or incapacitated in seconds.

I took a hard look at the Israeli now, noticing how he held the karambit. He was clearly a skilled knife fighter and had used this weapon before. Jamal and I were in deep trouble.

The man took one step towards us, and I instinctively moved backward. My heel bumped against the wall. Trapped. He took another step. Now only three feet separated us. Fight or flight. There was nowhere to go. That left only one option.

I lunged forward, my prison shank extended, and thrust my blade at his heart. The Israeli gracefully sidestepped my bull rush and grabbed my knife hand at the wrist. His grip was shockingly strong. He applied a wrist lock and cranked hard. I saw a white flash as he snapped my right wrist. It flopped down at a grotesque angle, completely useless now.

Jamal screamed as he charged. He held the chair over his head; his face was filled with rage. The Israeli spun to parry the blow of the chair, which caused him to release my broken wrist. He brought the karambit up in one fluid, arcing motion and raked it hard against the inside of Jamal's thigh, at the crotch. Jamal's eyes filled with fear. The orange fabric of his scrub pants sliced open and bloomed bright red with arterial blood from his severed femoral artery. Jamal never said a word, just silently slumped to the floor. He bled to death in less than a minute.

Enraged, I turned and ripped Carlos's blanket off his bed with my one good hand and charged the Israeli. He sliced through the blanket but failed to strike me a fatal blow. My momentum carried me into him, and we both tumbled out into the hallway. Our bodies bounced as one mass off the railing, and we fell to the concrete floor. We wrestled. I got on top of him, wrapping him in the blanket as best I could. He bucked and slashed. I punched with my left hand.

Swoll, who had been waiting outside the door, joined the fight now and struck a heavy blow to the middle of my back. It took my breath away. The Israeli pushed me off him and swept the blanket aside. Still on his back, he reached up and sliced me deep across the chest. I felt the karambit bite and rip through my flesh. My left arm fell limp now. I was out of the fight. I staggered up and off the Israeli, away from his deadly karambit—and right into Swoll.

Swoll hit me again, this time on the back of my head. I dropped to my knees. Everything went silent. I turned my head and looked up. Everything was moving in slow motion. I felt dizzy and nauseous. My vision narrowed. Another blow from Swoll. Dimly, I saw the Israeli regain his feet.

Suddenly, the catwalk shook like an earthquake tremor. I squinted over Swoll's shoulder and saw Duckie barreling down the hall towards me.

Swoll landed another blow and it all went dark.

CHAPTER SIX

March 25, 2017
Quinn Doyle's Beacon Hill condo
Boston, Massachusetts

Sarah sobbed into the shoulder of Quinn Doyle as they sat together at the four-top circular table in the small kitchen nook of their rented two-bedroom condo in downtown Boston. Quinn held her tight, pressing his cheek against the top of Sarah's head and gently stroking her mane of long blonde hair. He comforted her in a low, soothing voice while alternatively looking past her to Gerry Gonzalez. It was a look that froze men's souls.

Gonzalez quickly looked away and out the window as the midday sun shone over the cobblestone and brick of Beacon Hill. He hated the sound of women crying. Hated worse being the cause of it, even as the messenger.

Gonzalez had got the call from Duckie's girlfriend Nia

late the previous night, saying they had to meet immediately. He had been alarmed by the emotion in her voice, a cross between anger and dismay. He'd jumped out of bed, got dressed and met Nia at the designated spot, where he'd listened, sickened, as Nia repeated what Duckie had told her. He'd raced to the hospital to gather further information, then jumped in his Mercedes and drove I-95 North for nine hours until he'd arrived in Boston. Only then had he called Quinn to tell him he was in town and needed to talk to him and Sarah. Gonzalez knew Quinn well enough to harbor a legitimate fear of how he might respond to this news. He could do better damage control face-to-face.

All Sarah had heard was that there had been a second, more serious attempt on Frank's life. That he was unconscious and in serious condition at GWU Hospital. The men's voices had faded into the background as she lost it. Sarah had been on edge since the first attempt at the hands of Swoll and his minions. She was not accustomed to this life, as Quinn was, and her anxiety had steadily escalated, even after the hiring of Duckie. She had insisted that something else was going to happen, that she could just sense it. Now she was right.

Sarah pulled herself off Quinn's shoulder and wiped her eyes. Then they both turned to Gonzalez and demanded answers.

Frank's vital signs were unstable, Gonzalez began. He had suffered significant head trauma and loss of blood. A deep cut to the outer side of his pectoral muscle had partially severed the cephalic vein, which had bled profusely. Surgeons had thankfully been able to repair the vein and close the wound, but it had taken over two hundred sutures.

They had then put Frank's right wrist back together with pins and screws.

"Just tell us—is Frankie gonna make it?" Quinn asked, his voice taut with anger.

"I spoke to both the floor nurse at the hospital and his surgeon on the phone this morning," Gonzalez said. "They both said the same thing—that Frank's lucky to be alive. And although it's too early to tell, they think he is going to pull through."

Sarah exhaled deeply and grabbed Quinn's hand tightly. "Oh, thank God." She turned to face him. "I've got to see him, Quinn. I've got to go down to DC and see Frank."

Quinn shook his head. "It's too dangerous, Sarah. We don't know enough about this yet. There may be people monitoring the hospital." He paused a moment. "No."

"I know a nurse at GWU. Jill Everett!" Sarah exclaimed.

"That's not who I spoke with," Gonzalez said.

"Then go back to GWU, find Jill, and ask her to call me," Sarah pleaded.

Gonzalez was about to respond, but he looked uneasily at Quinn.

Quinn sat quietly, deep in thought; eyes narrow, face flushed. He started to speak, then stopped himself, putting a hand to his face. Seeing Quinn this angry frightened Gonzalez to the marrow of his bones. Would Quinn hold him accountable for this? He suspected the Irishman had sent many men to the bottom of the Charles River for less.

A moment later Quinn began to speak again, his voice dangerously low and tense. "Do you mind telling me what the fuck happened down there, Gerry? I thought we were paying this guy Duckie to stop this shit."

Gonzalez told them what Nia had told him.

Duckie had heard the diversionary fight by the Mexican Mafia just as he had put brush to canvas. He had gone to the railing to look, and not knowing it had been staged by Swoll, had sighed and gone back to his cell and his paints. A few moments later Duckie had heard a faint scream from down the hall, near Frank's cell, and this time he got up to investigate. As he stepped into the corridor, he'd seen Swoll, his back to him, and started running. Duckie was fast, but before he could get to him, Swoll had attacked a man from behind and started to beat him. Hard. As he drew up, Duckie saw it was Frank, on his knees, one arm hanging limp and crooked, and bleeding from a chest wound.

Swoll never saw the punch that knocked him cold. Duckie landed it without slowing down, with almost four hundred pounds of momentum. Swoll crumpled to the floor, and in one smooth movement Duckie picked him up, held him over his head and launched him headfirst over the railing. With force. Swoll's head made first impact with the concrete thirty feet below. He never regained consciousness and died later that night.

Duckie had then whirled around to see a middle-aged man he didn't recognize standing over an unconscious Frank, karambit in hand. Duckie had jumped him, getting slashed on the arm in the process. He'd pinned the man to the concrete floor with his knees and forced the knife from his hand with brute strength. That done, Duckie had wrapped his huge hands around the man's neck and squeezed with all he had. The man had stopped flailing after twenty seconds and had gone limp. Duckie got off him, stepped over to retrieve the karambit, then turned and raked it hard over both sides of the man's neck. He'd bled out rapidly.

A knot of guards arrived and cleaned up the mess. Frank,

still unconscious, went to GWU trauma center. Duckie was escorted to the infirmary and got stitched up. The bodies of Swoll, the Israeli, and Jamal were carried off.

"What Nia told me jibes with what I learned at the hospital and from Frank's surgeon," Gonzalez concluded. "As I see it, we're not paying this guy enough. Frank would be one hundred percent dead if it weren't for Duckie."

Quinn and Sarah sat mute, absorbing Gonzalez's accounting of last night's events.

"Who was the guy with the knife?" Quinn asked at last.

"No idea," Gonzalez responded.

"Prisha Baari." Sarah spat the name out. "This is her doing."

They all conceded the point.

Quinn's eyes went cold. He leaned back in his chair and placed his hands on the table, lacing his fingers together with enough force to turn them crimson. Gonzalez stared at Quinn's hands, dreading what was going to come next.

"I'm going to make some calls," Quinn said. "Get the crew together. Time to get rid of this bitch. Her Viking too. I'm going to finish this right now. Once and for all."

Both Gonzalez and Sarah stared at him, realizing he was dead serious. Quinn was prepared to kill the deputy director of the CIA and, in consequence, ignite a war with the United States government.

Gonzalez pressed his lips together. Picking this fight, at this time, he knew, was futile and would get them all killed. This was why he had driven all night up to Boston: he had known Quinn would want to seek immediate vengeance. And now he knew he had to talk him out of it.

Gonzalez started gingerly, first acknowledging Quinn's point and mirroring his anger. "But killing Prisha and

Karlsson will not get Frank out of jail," he said. "He's still facing a lengthy prison term for Hewitt's murder."

Quinn dodged this logic. "We have to kill them both. Now. It's the only way to eliminate the threat. Frank's already survived two attempts on his life, and I don't want to give this bitch a third shot."

"Prisha's a senior federal government official," Gonzalez said. "Killing her is a capital offense. We'll all get the death penalty for it."

Quinn gave a shrug of indifference. He was dug in.

Gonzalez looked furtively to Sarah for help, but she sat silently opposite him, her face ashen. Gonzalez wiped the moisture from his forehead with the back of his hand. His only hope was for Sarah to see things his way.

At last, she cleared her throat and turned to Quinn. "Quinn, I know how you feel... and I want this woman dead as much as you do," she said. "But I agree with Gonzalez. I don't think killing her is the answer right now." She turned fully in her seat to face Quinn straight on and grasped his hands in hers. "Frank's vulnerable in jail, and you're right: they're gonna try again. So we have to focus on getting Frank out. Somehow."

"Break him out of jail?" Quinn asked dubiously.

"I don't know," Sarah responded, blowing out a sigh. "It's better than going to war with the CIA right now. And even if we did kill Prisha, and none of us were caught, Frank would still stay in prison for Hewitt's murder for a long, long time. He'd die in there, one way or another." Sarah frowned. "If we kill her, even if we get away with it, her supporters aren't going to stop coming after us. We don't know who Prisha knows, or what her people are capable of. The bottom line is, if Frank stays inside, it's a death sentence for him. We've got to get him out somehow. Then we worry about taking care of Prisha."

Gonzalez sat back and studied Quinn as Sarah spoke. She was a formidable woman. Quinn respected her. And more importantly, he listened to her.

After a few moments, the storm clouds passed from Quinn's face. "You don't just walk someone out of jail," Quinn finally said. "It's not that easy."

Gonzalez saw his opening and pounced. "Maybe it is," he said. "I have an idea."

He knew a guy, he said, a crooked attorney, who had direct access to Aaron Geller, a corrupt Fairfax commonwealth's attorney. Geller was a five-term republican who had run afoul of the governor. Subsequently, Geller had lost his taste for politics and had already declared he would not stand for reelection in 2019. The word had been passed that Geller was looking to cash out. One last big score.

This crooked attorney had previously paid Geller to fix criminal cases for a couple of high-profile clients of his. Gonzalez thought that, with enough money, they could bribe Geller to drop the case on Frank. But it wouldn't be cheap. Mid-six figures, Gonzalez thought. Maybe more. But it would get Frank out of jail for good, and he would legally be a free man. Frank and Sarah could get new identities— Quinn could help with that—and then start over. A nice quiet life somewhere. Together. It could work. After all, he finished, Whitey Bulger and his girlfriend had been fugitives for seventeen years, most of that time on top of the FBI's Most Wanted List.

"I know all about Whitey Bulger—that fucking rat," Quinn said with disgust. He turned to Sarah. "You want to be a fugitive for the rest of your life?"

"No. Of course not," Sarah said. "But what other choice do I have? What I want is for me and Frank to have a life together. If we have to be fugitives, so be it. But we've got to get him out of there, Quinn."

"You think you can beat this case, Gerry?" Quinn asked. "Maybe we bribe the jury."

"No," Gonzalez said. It was too risky to roll the dice with a jury. Frank would be convicted at trial, at which time Geller would no longer be in a position to help them.

"You said this thing might cost six figures?" Quinn protested. "That's a lot of money."

"I'll pay it," Sarah interjected. "I've got that much put away. Money Victor and his sleaze attorney didn't get their hands on."

"How are you two gonna live, if this does work?" Quinn asked. "You're gonna need money when you're underground."

"We'll get by," she said stubbornly.

Quinn grimaced. "I don't know." He looked directly at Gonzalez. "What if Geller screws us? Takes the bribe but doesn't do what he's supposed to do?"

Gonzalez assured him they would own Geller once he went for the bribe: blackmail (his job) and intimidation (Quinn's job) would keep Geller in line.

Quinn still didn't like this, and wore the face of a child about to be force-fed a tablespoon of cough syrup.

It was Sarah who closed the deal.

"Quinn," she said, placing her hand on his. "I know this won't ensure that Prisha is held accountable now, but we'll make her pay once Frank is out and we are all safely underground." Sarah's eyes misted over. "Both Frank and I love you... and we really need your help now." Her voice broke with emotion.

Quinn's face softened. It was love that got the cough syrup down. "Okay," he said, and sighed. And that was it. Sarah embraced him. Kissed his cheek and thanked him over and over.

Gonzalez relaxed for the first time since he'd arrived in Boston. His repose was short lived.

"I want your word, Gerry, that you will do what you say and that this will work," Quinn said.

Gonzalez squirmed in his chair. "I'll get on this as soon as I get back to DC, Quinn. I'll talk to the lawyer and see what I can work out." Gonzalez tried to give himself an out. He was an attorney, after all. "But of course there's no guarantee that Geller will go for it. I know this lawyer well, and he'll have to get paid too, and I think he'll—"

Quinn cut him off, his voice hard. "Your word, Gerry."

Gonzalez stiffened. Swallowed hard. Cleared his throat. "I... I give you my word... that I'll do my best."

A tight-lipped smile slowly crossed Quinn's face. Gonzalez withdrew into his chair.

Both men knew what it meant to give your word to Quinn Doyle.

CHAPTER SEVEN

April 28, 2017
DC Jail
Washington, DC

I murdered a man tonight.

Carlos was not the first man I had killed. But he was my first homicide. I lay on my top bunk, hands clasped behind my head, staring at the cracked ceiling less than three feet from the tip of my nose. Enveloped in darkness, I felt the absence of the dead man in the lower bunk. I searched for all the feelings murder was said to conjure—remorse, anguish, self-loathing—but found nothing. Felt nothing. I was glad Carlos was dead. Glad I had been the one to do it.

I had been in the hospital for ten days. I saw Jill Everett a few times at the end of my stay. She was very emotional about the current state of my health. I was told I would have no permanent injuries, but I had a new scar running from one side of my chest to the other. And my right wrist still hurt like hell. It would heal but never be the same.

I promised Jill I had no cancer symptoms and that my attorney was close to getting me access to treatment. White lies all, but I couldn't stand to see her cry. Jill told me she had been in touch with Sarah and had given her a complete update on my condition. I asked her how Sarah was, how she was taking all this. Jill said Sarah sounded strong, and said she had a plan to fix all this. I pressed Jill for more details, but she had none to give. On her last visit, before they shipped me back to jail, I told Jill I would see her again. I hoped that was true.

They put me right back in my same cell, with now-dead Carlos. It was clear to me that Prisha was behind this latest attack, as she had been with the first one. Which meant the jail administration was complicit as well. This was confirmed by how quickly the incident was covered up. Swoll's death had been ruled accidental, his swan dive to the concrete merely a tragic mishap. I confessed to killing the Israeli in self-defense, in an effort to keep Duckie out of this. The authorities readily accepted this fiction, despite the fact that the crime scene said otherwise. That was when I knew they wanted me right back in my cell. Like nothing had ever happened. They had other plans for me yet.

I never learned who the Israeli was or how he'd got admitted to DC Jail. The prison authorities said he and I had had some beef, and that was why he came at me with a knife. They quickly cremated him, and his true identity was never revealed. At least as far as I know. All I did know was that he was Prisha's guy and that he would have killed me if Duckie hadn't come along when he did. Duckie also had no charges brought against him.

They held the Israeli accountable for Jamal's death, which was the only truth in the whole investigation. Jamal's family buried him in a nice cemetery, close to the neighborhood where he grew up. It saddened me greatly that Duckie and I couldn't be there. We held our own ceremony for our dear friend in his cell.

Everyone knew Carlos had snitched me out to Swoll and the Israeli. And if there's one thing that everyone agrees on in jail, inmates and guards alike, it's that snitches get stitches. The Mexican Mafia would come after me and Duckie for Swoll's death, but they would not intervene on Carlos's behalf. The guards would not protect him, either. Carlos would pay for Jamal's death. It was just a matter of time. Everyone knew this. Carlos most of all.

This made for a rather awkward three weeks bunking with him. He tried to explain himself to me. I ignored him. He tried to find safe harbor with anyone who would have him, but got no takers. Duckie put a hands-off order out on him. So Carlos was an island for those three weeks. He lost twenty pounds, and his jet-black hair became streaked with gray.

Finally, Duckie and I decided to make our move. A month had passed since my attack, and I was feeling strong enough to do this. We picked a Friday night. Carlos worked in the kitchen, and Duckie arranged for a guard to hold him there post-shift. We strolled into the back area of the kitchen where the guard had Carlos detained. Duckie thanked the guard and he left.

Carlos knew immediately what this was. He tried to bolt for the door. Duckie swatted him with an open hand, like a grizzly bear does a salmon, and he crashed to the ground. Carlos whined and howled at Duckie's feet. He protested his innocence. Duckie grabbed Carlos under the chin with both hands. Lifted him right off the ground. Feet dangling, arms flopping, face going purple. It didn't take Carlos long to come clean. Duckie put him back down. Asked who got him to snitch, and who the Israeli was. Carlos made the mistake of saying "I don't know" one too many times, then compounded it by swearing on his mother's life. Duckie was very close to his own mother and took umbrage at this affront to motherhood. He smiled and said fine, we'd do this the bitch way.

As it turned out, the bitch way involved a cheese grater and a salt shaker, and it didn't take long for Carlos to find his truth.

Carlos said the Israeli had approached him, saying he had a score to settle with me. A beef we supposedly had from the outside. Carlos said he was to get a hundred bucks on his books every month for a year, plus a little something for his girl and her two babies. Duckie asked Carlos if that was how much Jamal's life was worth—twelve hundred bucks? My life too? Especially after Duckie had put the word out that I was not to be touched. Carlos had no satisfactory response to this. More grating commenced, followed by the salt shaker.

But no matter how much salt Duckie seasoned him with, Carlos insisted he didn't know anything else about the Israeli. On this point I believed him.

In between all the screaming and begging, Carlos kept repeating that Jamal wasn't supposed to die. That he shouldn't even have been there. That he'd liked Jamal. The more I heard Carlos say the name of my dead friend, the more rage I felt. I thought of the daughter Jamal had left behind. I heard the joy in his voice as he read aloud passages from her letters to me at night from his lower bunk. Jamal had died because of me. He deserved better.

I'd heard enough. I grabbed a big iron skillet lying on the counter and swung it with my left hand. The blow impacted Carlos's shoulder and glanced off the side of his head. He wailed, covered up. Folded his arms over his head. I swung again, which knocked him to the ground. I threw the skillet to the floor with a crash and stood over him, breathing heavily.

Duckie pulled Carlos to his feet. He slapped him and told him to put his hands down. Carlos did so with a hesitant jerking motion, wondering what was coming next.

I stared at Carlos. All I saw was my friend Jamal. All I thought of was Prisha Baari. I felt the rage build within me. The eye of a hurricane gathering strength. My hands began to shake. An energy, like none I'd ever felt before, flowed through me.

What happened next, I only recall as an out-of-body experience. Looking down at myself from above as I moved in slow motion. Sound muted and far away.

I heard myself calling for Duckie's knife and watched him place it in my left hand. I saw myself thrust the blade deep into Carlos's chest, planting it like a flag. I took a back-ward step, and time stopped. In this snapshot I saw Duckie watch me impassively, and I saw myself staring at the knife protruding from Carlos's chest. And I saw Carlos sway and begin to lean like a felled tree.

Time resumed with me standing over Carlos, now dead. Blood was everywhere. Duckie pulled the knife from Carlos's heart and led me away. I followed Duckie's lead as we wiped the blood off us and changed into our spare pairs of scrubs. I sleepwalked with Duckie back to our cell block, where we embraced and went our separate ways.

I lay in my bunk for over an hour, eyes closed.

I recalled something else about this night, a memory snippet. A YouTube video in my mind. Carlos stood before me. I held Duckie's knife down by my side in a tight overhand grip. Carlos's dying words to me, right before I plunged the knife into his chest, were, "You don't have to do this."

It was just one more thing Carlos had been wrong about. I did have to do it.

CHAPTER EIGHT

I DIDN'T TELL MY ATTORNEY ABOUT MY FIRST HOMICIDE. He'd already betrayed my trust: against my wishes, he had told Sarah about the first attempt on my life, at the hands of the now-dead Swoll. I liked Gerry Gonzalez, but sometimes he didn't know when to shut up. He apologized. Told me it had been a mistake, that he hadn't meant to tell Sarah. I was trying my best to shield Sarah from the darker side of my incarceration. Things that, in my estimation, she was better off not knowing.

Carlos's death went unsolved. Not much effort was expended to find his killers. Of course, I was a logical suspect. But I was also a Pandora's Box for my jailers. Prisha wanted me dealt with in her way, and in the jail's avoidance of me I saw her invisible hand. She would try again. Soon, I thought.

I had seen a lot of Gonzalez in the two months since the Israeli's attack. First at the hospital, then almost weekly in the attorney visiting room at the jail. I looked forward to these visits, not so much for Gonzalez, although I mostly enjoyed his company, but for what news he brought of Sarah and Quinn in Boston. It was too dangerous for them to visit me here, and I ached to see them both. Gonzalez brokered personal messages back and forth between us. It was what kept me from drifting into my darkness.

For every visit, Sarah would send me a selfie of her standing at famous landmarks around Boston—Faneuil Hall/Quincy Market, Fenway Park, Old North Church—always holding a small piece of paper to her chest with a loving message scribed in her own looping cursive. I lived to see those pictures every week. Looking at them made me feel whole again, made me feel that someday I was going to get out of here alive and Sarah and I would have our life together. Looking at Sarah's photos gave me that most precious of commodities: hope. Of course, I couldn't risk keeping any of the selfies. They always went back into Gonzalez's briefcase with the rest of his legal papers at the end of each visit.

Other than Sarah's photos, the main purpose of these visits was to discuss the plan to get me out of jail before Prisha took another go at me. I shared Quinn's concerns, as well as his objections about Gonzalez's bribery plan. Too expensive, too risky, too benign. Like Quinn, I wanted Prisha dead now. In the end, what won me over was what had worked on Quinn: Sarah. Gonzalez convinced me that Sarah needed it this way. That it would break her if I spent the rest of my days away from her in prison. He said that Sarah had picked me over Prisha, and that I had to do the same. Gonzalez was a good lawyer. I was his jury of one. He got my vote.

This didn't mean I liked it. Not all of it, anyway. The plan, if successful, would reunite Sarah and me to live out our days in fugitive bliss. At least I hoped it would. I was confident in our ability to live an anonymous life below the radar. I was less confident that the bribes would actually work. I didn't trust politicians, bribe seekers least of all. I worried about a double-cross. And I really hated the idea of Sarah spending a good chunk of her savings to fund this risky plan. What if this shitty guy, Aaron Geller, took the money and did nothing? Quinn would go ballistic. Me too. More violence would follow. More bodies. You can't kill a sitting commonwealth's attorney and just walk away. We'd all likely go down for it.

My biggest objection to the bribery plan was that Prisha would not be my second homicide victim. I did not voice this objection in those terms. My vow to kill her by my own hand was made in silence and became a promise I carried inside me. I feasted on it in times when I needed strength to endure another day. It slaked my thirst for vengeance. It would cleanse my soul, or so I told myself. My personal baptism. I would lose my religion, and Prisha would live, because my love for Sarah was stronger that my hatred for Prisha. The simplest choices are often the most difficult. My god of vengeance could not be so easily ignored. He would relentlessly call me back to the flock to worship at his altar. Good and evil are both absolute and abstract. I would struggle with this in the months and years ahead.

And so I submitted to the bribery plan—with one caveat.

I insisted that Duckie be included and that his case be dropped as well as mine. I didn't tell Duckie this. I didn't want to get his hopes up, as I still harbored serious doubts as to our prospects of success.

Gonzalez vehemently opposed this, on the grounds that Duckie's case was not with Fairfax County, but the United States Attorney's Office for the District of Columbia. It would be much more difficult to deal with the USAO. Gonzalez said it couldn't be done. I pointed out that I was charged with first degree murder, while Duckie was incarcerated only for a drug possession case. Gonzalez said that didn't matter. Duckie had an extensive criminal history, including convictions for violent felonies, and the USAO would not stomach being responsible for putting such a man back on the street. I countered that Gonzalez was a skilled lawyer, at home in the shadowy world of slippery jurisprudence, and that he would find a way. It would be both of us or neither of us. I would not leave DC Jail without Duckie. To their credit, both Sarah and Quinn supported me on this point, and Gonzalez reluctantly moved forward with his directive.

———

They came for me early one morning. Two guards rattled my cell door open and told me to pack up my shit. Now. I shook myself awake and jumped down from my bunk. The bottom bunk had remained empty, but for the ghost of the departed Carlos. I had enjoyed my time in my solo cell.

I asked what was going on. The smaller guard, a skinny guy with big jug ears we called Goober, told me to shut my mouth or he'd do it for me. I inwardly smiled at the thought of Goober trying such a thing on the outside. But I was on the inside, so I silently gathered my things as Goober barked commands and cursed at me to hurry up.

I got my small kit together and followed the guards out of my cell and into the hallway. I was handcuffed in the front. Some inmates awoke and wanted in on the drama. They greeted me with catcalls that were silenced by the guards' sharp threats. I followed the guards down the hallway. One in the front, one in the back. They walked briskly. I adjusted my stride to keep my proper distance.

I wondered what this was all about. I thought I was being moved to another cell, that I had lost my solo and was getting another roommate. I wondered how far away from Duckie my new cell would be. The Mexican Mafia were lurking, awaiting their opportunity to avenge the death of Swoll. The further away my new cell was, the worse it would be for me. We walked past Duckie's cell. It was empty. My stomach clenched in a knot. I stopped dead in my tracks. All of Duckie's stuff—his paintings, cotton bedding, everything—was gone. His cell was stripped bare. This was bad. My heart rate soared. Goober shoved me from behind, cursed at me to keep moving.

We kept walking. Off the third tier and down the stairs to the first floor. Shit. The tier one cells were the worst. The most dangerous cells in the jail. We kept walking. We left the inmate section and continued to the front part of the jail, where all the jail administration was housed. Walked past dark, empty offices. The threadbare carpet was a novelty underfoot. I'd touched nothing but concrete since I'd been in this place. We took a hard right by a vending machine that glowed in the half-light of the hall. We walked to the end and stopped at a door with a small slit window. The front guard motioned for me to enter. I stepped up to the door and squinted into the room through the scratched windowpane. Inside, Duckie sat in a chair against the wall at the back of the room. He was front handcuffed as well.

Our eyes met. Duckie's face was etched in a scowl. Goober stepped up, shoved past me and opened the door, and then pushed me forward. I swallowed my anger and entered the room.

It resembled the attorney room but was not as spartan. It was larger, four chairs instead of two. Upholstered instead of hard plastic. There was even a lonely fake ficus tree in the corner, sitting crooked in a faded wicker basket. The thing that really got my attention was the round clock on the wall. It was an ordinary wall clock: white face, black hands, ticking second hand. We were in civilian, not inmate, space now. For us inmates, time was the elephant in the room, something that must not be acknowledged or dwelled upon. Inmates had no need or use for clocks. We marked our time by season or calendar. Goober and the other guard left without a word, closing the door behind them, and I stood with my back to it. The clock read 5:45 a.m.

I went over and grabbed a chair, slid it next to Duckie and sat down. We compared notes. His morning had been similar to mine. We both had no idea what was happening or why we were in this room. We discussed various theories, careful to speak in whispers. One of our theories was that the jail had put us together in a bugged room to see if we would slip up and incriminate ourselves for the murders of the Israeli or Carlos. This had already gone beyond a simple cell reassignment. Maybe they were going to feed us to the Mexican Mafia? We decided probably not. They wouldn't have paraded us out here like this, with all our belongings, to do such a thing. They would have just taken us to the showers in the middle of the night to meet our fate.

We concluded it was most likely that they were about to put a case on us. Probably take us to court and charge us with Carlos's murder. I apologized to Duckie; told him I was sorry I'd got him involved in all my shit. He waved me off, said he'd beat murder raps before. We just had to keep our mouths shut and be cool. See how this thing played out.

Duckie slid the back of his chair against the wall. He put his head back and was asleep in two minutes. It amazed me how this man could fall asleep anywhere. I guess that's what a clean conscience can do. I envied him.

It was 6:50 a.m. I let Duckie sleep. I listened to the cadence of his breathing as I paced the room. I studied the ficus tree, its green silk leaves dulled with a dusty film. A feeble and ludicrous attempt to soften this hard place. It saddened me, like a caged bird or a beast of burden pulling its load.

I turned my back to the tree. The clock now read 7:22 a.m. Duckie had been fast asleep while I'd been wrestling the thoughts in my head. I couldn't help but think that somehow Sarah and Quinn were in trouble too.

I was busy trying to talk myself out of this notion when the door burst open. Duckie instantly pulled out of his slumber and shot to his feet. I stared, wide-eyed, as Gerry Gonzalez entered the room. He was smiling.

Two guards followed. They walked right up to both me and Duckie and removed our handcuffs. We rubbed at our wrists and exchanged confused looks. Gonzalez waited for the guards to leave. The smile never left his face.

"Good morning, Frank!" he said when the guards were

gone, stepping deeper into the room. "And good morning, Duckie."

"Gerry—what is this all about?" I asked.

"We're going to court this morning! At nine o'clock, ACA Calderon will advise the judge that he is dropping all charges, and the judge will dismiss your case!" Gerry said with the flair of a circus ringmaster.

I eyed Gonzalez sharply. "Whose case, Gerry?"

Gonzalez paused a beat. "Yours and Duckie's." He looked over at Duckie and then back to me, beaming. "You're both going to walk out of that courtroom free men! We did it, Frank—we did it!"

My mouth hung open. He and Sarah and Quinn had pulled it off. For an extra two hundred and fifty thousand, Geller had somehow wrangled control of Duckie's dope case from the USAO. We were both getting out.

Duckie's face was twisted into a mask of confusion. He looked between me and Gonzalez until he found his voice.

"What? What the hell's going on here?" Duckie studied the smile inching across my face.

"I've been working behind the scenes for two months to get charges dropped on old Frank here," Gonzalez told him. "And thanks to him, the Fairfax commonwealth's attorney agreed to drop your case too."

"My case is in the District," Duckie said, still confused.

"Don't worry about that," Gonzalez said. "It's all been taken care of."

"Why didn't you tell me any of this last week?" I asked. "That you were this close."

"Things were delicate there at the end." Gonzalez stole a quick look at Duckie. "I didn't want to get your hopes up... or for you two to do anything stupid to screw this up." He chuckled as he said that last part.

"Same price?" I asked.

"Uhm, no," Gonzalez said. "The cost went up a bit."

"What do you mean, cost?" Duckie asked, his voice deepening.

"As I said, I've been negotiating (air quotes) to get justice for Frank in his case. It turned out that some new evidence (more air quotes) had come to light. Compelling evidence that made the commonwealth change its mind about the viability of its case against Frank. So in the interests of justice (more air quotes still), it got dropped."

"But you said I'm getting out too?" Duckie asked.

"This guy here," Gonzalez said, jerking his thumb at me, "insisted I look at your case too. And Frank can be very persuasive when he wants to be. So I did some more work, talked to a few people I know, and bingo-bango, they dropped your drug case too."

Gonzalez studied Duckie, who stood stunned and silent. The smile fled from Gonzalez's face. He backpedaled half a step. "I, uhm, I hope you don't mind, Duckie. I know I told you I wouldn't get involved in your case, but Frank insisted, as I said." Gonzalez held his hands out in front of him. "I was only trying to help."

"And you say I'm getting out today? For real?"

Gonzalez nodded.

Without warning, Duckie rushed in and wrapped Gonzalez in his arms. He raised him off the floor in a full bear hug and swung him around, whooping for joy. He planted Gonzalez back down on the ground, then patted and brushed his suit jacket back into place. Gonzalez's face was crimson. He bent at the waist a moment to catch his breath, then straightened and finger-combed his hair back into place.

"Okay, well... you're welcome, Duckie," Gonzalez said, relief washing over him. "But it's Frank here you really have to thank. He's the one who insisted. Said he wouldn't leave here without you."

The big man turned to me, his eyes wide. His face went slack. He tried to speak, but his voice broke. He put a hand to his lips and fell silent, blinking back a tear.

I stepped to Duckie and we embraced. He leaned down so that his mouth was at my ear.

"Thanks, man," Duckie whispered. "I owe you one."

"We're even."

"If you ever need anything—"

"I know," was all I said.

And that was that. Duckie and I walked out of the courtroom free men that beautiful spring day in May 2017.

I would no longer live my life behind bars. But I was not exactly free. Not yet.

CHAPTER NINE

KARLSSON WALKED OUT OF THE GYM. A BAG CONTAINING his sweaty workout clothes was slung over his sculpted shoulder. He raised his hand to shield his eyes from the sun directly overhead. It was leg day at the gym: thirty minutes of cardio on the treadmill, followed by squats, hamstrings and calves. He took his usual cold-water shower and was enjoying a nice post-workout high when his phone vibrated in his pocket. Karlsson looked at the screen and frowned. Prisha Baari. He let it go to voicemail.

Prisha had been particularly difficult these past two months, since the failure of her invincible assassin at the hands of Frank Luce. She had become short tempered and distracted, and had begun spending many more late nights at the office. Karlsson inwardly celebrated her failure but dared not say "I told you so." He still believed his idea—same plan, different prison gang—was best. He had secretly been working with his corrupt jail guards and the Aryan Brotherhood for the past two months to develop a foolproof plan. He was almost ready, and would spring this on Prisha only when the plan was airtight. Everything had to be perfect this time.

Karlsson hit the voicemail button and immediately pulled the phone from his ear.

"Henrik!" Prisha screamed. "Fucking Frank Luce got released from jail this morning! And I had to learn about this on fucking Twitter? Shit! Now listen to me. Go see that bastard and find out how this happened. I want meet with him tonight. Not tomorrow, not the next day—tonight! Got it?"

Karlsson knew what bastard Prisha was referring to: Assistant Commonwealth's Attorney Andrew Calderon, the corrupt Fairfax County prosecutor she had paid handsomely to falsely convict Frank Luce for the murder of her CIA colleague and onetime lover Charles Hewitt and lock him in the DC Jail. Karlsson knew Luce was innocent because he himself had killed Hewitt. But now it seemed Luce was out again, although God only knew how. From the sheer decibels of Prisha's voicemail, it sounded like this latest setback might just push her right over the edge. He felt bad for Calderon. Tonight was going to get ugly.

Karlsson didn't want to talk to Prisha right now, especially in the mood she was in. He texted her instead: *copy. driving to Calderon now. will set up meet at staging at 830p. 30m SDRs, at the spot by 900P. copy?*

Prisha responded instantly: *get him there. tell him he better have some good answers for me.*

Karlsson: *I'll pick you up at 8oop. usual spot.*

Prisha: *how the hell did this happen? tell him this is unacceptable.*

Karlsson: *k. 8oop.*

———

The sky had darkened by the time Prisha Baari stepped out of the front passenger seat of Karlsson's black-over-black 2017 Mercedes Benz GLS 550 SUV. The sun had set behind the clouds and last light was waning. Karlsson heard a thunderous rumble. The Mercedes shook. He leaned over the dashboard and looked up through the windshield. A huge commercial jet passed directly overhead at a ridiculously low height. The airplane looked cartoonishly big. It landed seconds later across a small inlet of the Potomac River on runway 1/19 at the north end of Ronald Reagan Washington National Airport.

The meeting spot this evening was the parking lot at Gravelly Point, a thirty-eight-acre park in Arlington County, along the George Washington Parkway and across the Potomac River from Washington, DC. Gravelly Point was one of the premier plane-spotting locations in the U.S. As the plane, about the size of a large dinosaur, flew overhead, Karlsson thought how easy it would be to take any one of these airliners down with a shoulder-launched surface-to-air missile, readily available to any self-respecting terrorist organization. He cleared his head of such musings. He and Prisha had bigger problems tonight.

Karlsson had picked Prisha up at her Georgetown townhouse at 8:00 p.m., sharp. Punctuality was paramount to him. They drove to a Walmart parking lot in Fairfax,

Virginia, where they met ACA Calderon. Calderon left his vehicle there and jumped into the back passenger seat of Henrik's Mercedes for a routine thirty minutes of surveillance detection routes, or SDRs, designed to flush out anyone who might have followed Calderon—or worse, anyone he had brought along himself. Satisfied that they were clean, Karlsson pulled into the Gravelly Point parking lot a little after 9:00 p.m.

Prisha opened the door, stepped out of the front seat, and got into the back behind Karlsson and next to Calderon. She slammed the door hard enough that Calderon jumped. Karlsson adjusted his rear-view mirror and watched Prisha go to work.

Calderon squirmed in his seat; he wore a Washington Senators baseball cap pulled low over his face. Prisha told him to take his stupid hat off. He reluctantly did, revealing eyes that were red rimmed and tired. He needed a haircut. His face was puffy, and he had gained a good thirty pounds. He was in over his head and going down.

Normally Prisha liked to take an indirect approach with her targets, but not tonight. She went right at Calderon. Asked him to explain how it was possible that Frank Luce was a free man. Calderon stammered his response in fits and starts. He said he didn't know. He had gotten called in to see the commonwealth's attorney, Aaron Geller, last week. Geller had told him to drop the Luce murder case, he said, but nothing more than that. Prisha pressed him, but Calderon stuck to his story. He said he'd tried to argue, that his case against Luce was strong, but Geller had cut him off. He'd already had his mind made up. Calderon said Geller's deputy was also at this meeting but had just sat there and said nothing. Without meeting Prisha's eyes,

Calderon said he was sorry, but there was nothing more he could do.

"You knew about this last week, and you didn't call me?" Prisha asked, her voice rising. "I had to learn about this today, on fucking Twitter? After he got out and was already on the street?"

Calderon mumbled an apology, then something about losing Prisha's number and not wanting to call her at CIA.

"Luce could've tried to kill me today, you dumb shit!"

Calderon looked down at his lap and repeated his apology.

"Did you say anything—do anything—to make Geller dismiss the case?"

"No!" Calderon exclaimed. "I didn't do anything. I swear."

"Then why did he do it?"

"I don't know. I don't know anything."

"Where's Luce now?" Karlsson asked Calderon in a low voice through the rear-view mirror.

"I told you. I don't know."

"We pay you to know, Andrew," Prisha responded. She moved closer to Calderon now. He leaned away from her and pushed up against the door. He put his head in his hands, then rubbed his eyes. He looked at Prisha for some compassion and came up empty.

Calderon then tried to talk his way out. He said he had learned that there was another case being dropped at the same time as Luce's case, and that both cases were being handled by the same attorney. On a hunch he'd checked into this, called some sources he had at the DC Jail, and learned that the other case involved a guy by the name of Duckie.

Some big-time local gangster and thug who had provided Luce with protection in the joint.

Calderon mentioned there had been two failed attempts on Luce's life. "Did you guys know anything about this?" he asked.

"Why would you think that?" Karlsson asked through the mirror.

"No, I'm just saying... that... you know..." Calderon trailed off and broke eye contact with Karlsson in the mirror.

"You promised to take care of this, Andrew," Prisha said. "And I ask you: does this look like it's taken care of?"

Calderon blew out a long breath. "I did everything I could do. I fixed the case against Luce. I coached Webb as a witness—and she's a huge pain in my ass." Calderon was referring to Linda Webb, an ODYSSEUS project manager supplicant of Prisha Baari. "I called in a big favor with the judge to get Luce's shit arrest warrant signed. And don't forget, I also got Luce sent to DC Jail when he should have gone to County. You think all this was easy?"

"That's what we paid you to do," Karlsson said flatly. "And yet—here we are."

"And I got Luce's case dismissed without prejudice," Calderon pleaded. "It can be refiled someday. Geller wanted to dismiss it outright, but I got him to come around. That's gotta be worth something, right?"

"Are you asking us for a bonus, Andrew?" Prisha said.

"No... no." Calderon paused. "I mean, not unless you think—"

Karlsson tapped the rear-view mirror to get Calderon's attention. He looked up.

"Get the fuck out of my car," Karlsson said.

"Wait... I didn't mean that. I wasn't asking for any more

money." Calderon waited long enough to see Karlsson was serious. "Oh, c'mon, man. My car's miles from here. You're not gonna make me—"

Karlsson, for the first time all night, turned fully around in his seat to address Calderon. The weaker man gulped and pushed back into his seat.

"Are you going to make me ask you again?" Karlsson asked, without a hint of emotion in his voice.

Calderon looked to Prisha for assistance. All he got back was an empty smile.

Calderon fumbled with the door handle. He finally opened the door and stumbled hastily out of the SUV. Prisha threw his ball cap at him. He struggled to his feet, put the cap on his head, and started to fast-walk across the parking lot towards the open fields of Gravelly Point. With a deafening roar, another large jet flew directly overhead. Calderon started to run.

Prisha got out of the back seat and slammed the rear door shut. She walked around the SUV, got back into the front passenger seat, and slammed that door shut. Karlsson punched the accelerator, and the tires on the big Mercedes chirped against the asphalt. He pulled out of the parking lot and headed north on the George Washington Parkway. They drove in silence for many miles before either of them spoke.

"This Frank Luce," Karlsson said. "He is—how you say—a bad penny."

CHAPTER TEN

MAY 24, 2017
DUCKIE'S ROW HOUSE; EAST CAPITOL HILL
WASHINGTON, DC

I WAS AT THE WHEEL OF A LATE-MODEL, DULL GRAY Chevy sedan provided to me by Duckie. He'd promised me it was a "clean" car, which I took to mean not stolen and properly registered. I looked at the dashboard clock for the hundredth time since I'd left Duckie's tidy two-bedroom row house this morning.

8:54 a.m. Dammit. I should have been at Balti-more/Washington International Airport by now. BWI was only thirty-seven miles north of DC, an easy fifty-minute drive under ideal circumstances. But nothing is ever ideal, especially when it comes to DC traffic. That was why I'd given myself a full two hours to make this trip.

I had hit a construction detour just as I left the District

and crossed into Maryland. Traffic squeezed down to one lane. It was Wednesday morning, and this was supposed to be reverse-commute rules. I headed out of the city on I-95 North, not part of that death march that slogged into DC on I-95 South. Where were all these stupid people going? They were all in my way, conspiring to ruin my life in some congestion cabal.

I was on my way to pick up Sarah. She had an 8:30 Southwest flight, nonstop out of Logan and scheduled to arrive at BWI at 10:10 a.m. Sarah had booked the flight as soon as I'd walked out of the courthouse. She'd insisted on coming down to see me, and I did not protest. I couldn't wait to see her. We decided it was safer for her to fly into Baltimore and stay out of DC altogether.

I could not—would not—be late for this airport pickup. I would not keep Sarah waiting. Today or ever again.

Mercifully, I got out of the construction zone past the 495 Beltway around Calverton, where traffic opened up to three lanes. I swerved into the far-left lane and hit the gas.

9:00 a.m. I had some time to make up.

It had been a helluva twenty-four hours since the guards had dragged me out of my top bunk. Gonzalez had been right about court. Duckie and I took the inmate transport and met our shared attorney in the courtroom in our orange jail scrubs. My case went first. Calderon looked like a little kid whose puppy had just been stolen. It was clear he was not in on this. I glared at him until Gonzalez leaned into me and whispered for me to knock it off.

Fairfax Circuit Court Judge Clayton Whitley appeared surprised by the commonwealth's attorney's motion to dismiss. He aggressively questioned Calderon. Calderon stammered through his responses, saying repeatedly that it was in the interests of justice that my case be dropped. The word *justice* coming out of that man's mouth grated on me. I wanted to punch his face until he stopped saying it.

Then my big moment arrived. With a subtle shake of his head and a look of disdain on his face, Judge Whitley slammed his gavel down and said those beautiful words that echoed in my head: Case dismissed; the defendant is free to go.

Gonzalez and I embraced, then Gonzalez had stepped to Calderon and extended his hand, which the deflated ACA refused to shake. I turned to look over my shoulder at Duckie, who sat behind me awaiting his turn. He had the biggest smile on his face, an expression of true joy that I had only seen these past twenty-four hours. I liked it.

Part of me still wanted Sarah and Quinn there with me in the courtroom to celebrate my freedom. They had both paid so dearly for it. In the end, we had all dismissed this option, not knowing if Prisha or her henchmen would show up. I knew from experience that she was a sore loser. She would strike back sooner rather than later.

I walked away from the defense table and took a seat on a nearly empty bench among the few spectators in the courtroom that morning. My first steps as a free man in almost half a year. I couldn't stop smiling.

Next, Duckie's case was called and he stepped up and took a seat next to Gonzalez. The judge reviewed the papers in front of him. He raised an eyebrow, gave Duckie a terse look, then glanced back at the paperwork. When Judge Whitley finally spoke, it was over quickly. Duckie had a drug possession case, a common occurrence in this courthouse. Gonzalez and Calderon went through the motions, and the gavel came down. The big man was free.

We all got the hell out of there as fast as we could. We had gotten what we came for, and any lingering or gloating might anger Lady Justice. We had put our fingers on her scale, tipped it just enough to make things right. But she could be a fickle, thickheaded woman, induced to specious action by apostates. I would resume my discussion with her at another time.

When I hit the courthouse steps, I did that most cliché of things: threw my head back, soaked in the blue sky and wispy white clouds, and drew my first deep breath of freedom. Duckie stood next to me, and I was pleased to see he did likewise. We embraced. Gonzalez gave us our moment, then insisted we go. He was on edge and wanted to be far away from the courthouse. That was just fine with Duckie and me.

We all piled into Gonzalez's Mercedes. I gave Duckie the front seat, as I wasn't sure he could even fit in the back. He climbed in and slid the seat all the way back. I sat behind Gonzalez, and as he pulled out into traffic, I turned in my seat and watched for anyone following us, all the way to his office. I didn't see a thing.

Nia met us at the office, and she and Duckie shared a tender moment before we all savored our victory over Prisha Baari. I used Gonzalez's secure line to speak briefly to Sarah and Quinn. Told them I loved them and would see them soon. Hearing the joy in their voices almost brought me to tears. I confirmed Sarah's flight information, then hung up and started counting the minutes until I would see her.

We said goodbye to Gonzalez, and then Duckie and I drove with Nia to their residence, the one they kept secret and separate from their criminal life. It was a historic nineteenth-century row house in the eastern section of Capitol

Hill. It was set on a narrow brick courtyard one block from sprawling Lincoln Park, the biggest urban park in the neighborhood and former site of the largest District hospital during the Civil War. Their row house was centrally located, a mile due east of the U.S. Capitol Dome, and only a mile southeast of Gonzalez's office, as it turned out.

We parked in a cramped covered garage across the courtyard and approached the row house on foot. It was two stories, narrow and tall, made of brick that had recently been painted a rich violet blue. The brickwork around the window molding and crown was ornate; the house's only modern concession was the black steel security bars on the front door and first-floor windows. Inside, the nine hundred square feet were well appointed, with honey oak floors and a gallery kitchen awash in stainless appliances. The two sunny bedrooms were both upstairs, separated by a full bath.

Duckie had insisted I stay with him and Nia that first night, before I headed up to Baltimore for my reunion with Sarah. I accepted their hospitality. They offered me the spare bedroom, but I insisted on taking the sofa downstairs. I wanted to afford them as much privacy as possible in their snug home, this being Duckie's first night out of jail and all.

We all enjoyed a fine meal of baked whitefish, fresh greens and sourdough bread. Nia was a great cook. She frequented Eastern Market, which was located only a few blocks away. It was a well-known foodie haven and the best place in the District to find farm-fresh produce and other gourmet foods. Conversation flowed easily, as did the wine Nia had paired with the fish. It was delicious. All of it.

We talked late into the night. I finally begged off, as I had to get up early the next morning. We said our goodnights, and Duckie and Nia went upstairs. I cleaned up in the downstairs bath and took my place on the sofa. It didn't take long for the muffled moans to drift downstairs. I dutifully buried my head in my pillow and tried not to hear. I dreamed of my own carnal reunion with Sarah less than twelve hours away. That beautiful thought lulled me to sleep in minutes.

I awoke just before daylight. I folded my bedding, stacked it neatly on the sofa, then quietly showered and shaved. Nia had thoughtfully provisioned the downstairs bathroom with toiletries, as well as a change of clothes for me. Sweet.

The two lovebirds sauntered downstairs a little after seven. They were both sleep weary; Duckie clomped down the stairs barefoot in his boxers and t-shirt. Nia made the coffee, which we took into the living room.

Duckie got down to business over our second cup. One of his guys was bringing over a car for me to drive to the airport. Something clean and cool, no problems. Nia retrieved a paper bag and handed it to Duckie. He pulled out a roll of bills and a cellphone. I protested his generosity, to no avail. He slid the money and phone over to me and told me to take them, that I'd need them. I blushed and thanked them both. Duckie instructed me to park the car at the airport garage, not on the top floor if I could help it. I was to leave the keys on the rear passenger tire and text Nia the stall number. He'd have one of his guys come and pick it up after Sarah and I had flown back to Boston.

We finished our coffee with small talk. All that was left was to say goodbye. I stood, and Nia gave me a big hug. Thanked me for getting her man out of jail. She told me I was welcome in her home anytime. I thanked her for everything and meant it.

I turned to Duckie, who towered over Nia and me both. His toffee eyes had softened. He smiled broadly, the little-boy smile I'd first seen yesterday morning when he realized we were both getting out of jail. I returned his smile and we hugged it out. I thanked him. He wished me luck and told me to be careful. He told me to call him if I ever needed anything. That was all that needed to be said.

I got in the dull gray sedan and drove off.

9:05 a.m. I was flying up I-95 North in the fast lane. Deep in thought. Will I be late? How will my reunion with Sarah go? Am I the same man she visited in DC Jail Christmas last? I was in twilight, that reptilian state where one does a rote task, like driving, unconsciously but proficiently. That was why I hadn't noticed my speed had crept up to eighty miles per hour.

The wail of a siren snapped me out of my trance. I looked in my rear-view mirror. A cop on my bumper.

9:11 a.m. read the dashboard clock. *Fuuuck.*

I pulled over to the side of the Interstate. The cop followed. Cars whizzed by me, their speed a reminder of how far behind schedule this little stop would put me. The cop just sat in his car. Forever. Checking the plates and warrants on my little Chevy. It was then I remembered I hadn't even checked the plate tab or glovebox for the car's registration. Nothing I could do about that now. I could only trust Duckie that this car was as clean as he said it was. I hoped the cop wouldn't ask to search it. My consent would allay suspicion and speed things along. My refusal would make him suspicious and he would start messing with me. Sobriety test, interrogation, and the like. Maybe even call a dog in. I would not only be late but entirely miss Sarah's pickup. I decided to play it breezy and let the cop search the car if he wanted. Roll the dice.

The cop finally left his patrol car and crept up to my driver's-side window, which I had already rolled down. Hands at ten and two on the steering wheel. John Q. Citizen here. Nothing to worry about.

The cop was short and stout, with buzzed hair and dark aviator glasses. Immaculate uniform, hat squared on head. Yeah, he was that cop. The one who enjoyed his job a little too much.

"Is this your car, sir?"

"No, Officer," I answered. "My car's in the shop. This is a friend of a friend's car. I'm on my way to pick up my mother at the airport. She just got out of the hospital and I'm taking care of her."

This guy looked like a momma's boy, so I took a shot.

"What's wrong with her?"

"Leukemia. I hope it don't run in the family," I responded with a shrug and thin smile.

The cop then asked for my license and registration. Gonzalez had given me my new false identification packet at his office. Quinn and Sarah had put it together and shipped it to him, and he had stored it in his office safe. This was my new persona, the name I would live under with Sarah when we went underground. It was the name on my one-way airline ticket back to Boston. I wasn't expecting to have it tested so soon.

I handed over my fake Virginia driver's license and sought the cop's permission to fish the registration out of the glove box. God, I hoped it was in there. He grunted his approval. I popped open the glove box and took out a handful of papers. I sorted through the napkins and assorted garbage, my stomach sinking. At the bottom of this pile I felt something rigid. I grabbed it and was relieved to see it was the registration, behind a see-through plastic window. I pulled it out and read it fast. It was current and it matched the car. I thanked Duckie under my breath and handed it over to the cop.

He took both license and registration back to his car for another long interlude. Cars whizzed by. Time whizzed by. I knew my new ID wouldn't have any warrants, but didn't know if it would pass scrutiny with this toy-soldier cop.

Finally, the cop paraded back to my car and handed me back my stuff. With dramatic flair, he removed his aviators, leaned into the window and thrust a speeding ticket at my face. I took the ticket from his hand with forced calm, adding a sincere apology for good measure. He gave me his best Clint Eastwood and told me to slow it down. I promised him I would. He straightened up, adjusted his aviators on the bridge of his pug nose, tugged at his cop hat and sauntered back to his car.

I eased back onto I-95 while I watched the cop in my rear-view mirror. He followed me for over two miles. Forced me to do a weak fifty-eight miles per hour the whole way. I milked the steering wheel hard and screamed under my breath. *C'mon!* If this jack-off paced me all the way to the airport, I was doomed. I cheered when the cop did a U-turn at one of those official-use-only turnarounds and headed in the opposite direction on I-95 South.

9:49 a.m. I crumpled the ticket into a ball and threw it on the floor. I had just passed the Guilford exit and a big bold sign that claimed that BWI was only twelve miles and eighteen minutes ahead. I knew better.

I pushed the pedal to the floor and watched the speedometer jump.

———

I stood inside BWI, in front of the big board for incoming flights. Southwest... 8:30 a.m.... from Logan... delayed! The new arrival time was 10:35 a.m.

I shook my fists in exaltation. I had sped all the way to BWI. Screeched tires in the parking garage. I'd found a spot, written the stall number in ink on my hand, then grabbed my bag and sprinted to baggage. I'd arrived at BWI at 10:22 a.m. Twelve minutes off schedule, but thanks to Southwest, thirteen minutes early.

I was keyed up, sweating and breathing heavily. I went to the bathroom, splashed cold water on my face and head. Tried to make myself presentable. I looked up at the mirror and the reflection smiling back at me. Sarah would be here soon. I shook out my hands, rolled my neck back and forth, and left the bathroom.

I walked through baggage, found the board and saw that her flight was assigned carousel eight. I took a nearby seat and waited.

I couldn't stop sweating. I dabbed my forehead with a length of paper towel I had taken from the bathroom. I was too wired to sit, so I stood off to the side, staring down the walkway beyond. I had a perfect spot for Sarah's arrival. So there I stood, bag at my feet, hands jammed into the front pockets of my stiff new jeans. I flicked my thumbs against the fingers inside my pockets, then thought better of it. I pulled both hands out and laced my twitchy fingers in front of me.

My excitement grew as I saw people start to gather

around carousel eight. Her flight had landed. More passengers arrived. More excitement.

I scanned the faces in the crowd. I couldn't stand still.

I saw her first. Sarah glided towards me, pulling her wheeled overnight bag behind her. Her head swiveled, looking for me. She was dressed in travel casual. A multicolored sundress with white cotton t-shirt and flat sandals. Her bright blonde hair was pulled back in a high ponytail. She looked tan and fit.

Sarah froze when she spotted me. A sea of faceless passengers flowed around her in shadow. I lost my breath. I heard nothing. Saw nothing but her face. She fought her emotions, then rallied and raised her chin to smile. I did the same. We ran towards each other. Magnetic pull.

We embraced, each of us gasping. Sarah trembled in my arms. She planted her head on my shoulder. I nuzzled my nose into her neck. The same orange jasmine scent I remembered from high school, a bouquet Sarah came by naturally. We kissed. Laughed nervously, breathlessly. Kissed again.

I took her bag, and we walked hand in hand to the taxi stand. We waited in line and engaged in the tentative small talk that couples do after a long separation. When our turn came, we took a taxi one mile to our hotel that Sarah had reserved in her false name.

We checked into our room on the eighth floor. I dropped our bags in the closet. Sarah drew the curtains closed. We met at the king-size bed.

"We made it," I told her incredulously.

We embraced; we laughed and cried together.

We made love on that king-size bed. Where I was rough, she was soft. Where I was hard, she was gentle. When I was eager, she was patient.

We ordered room service and made love again amid a tumult of bedding. This time slower and more deliberately. Afterwards, we lay back, spent.

We ordered room service and got caught up. Spoke of our future together. Our new life on the run. We vowed to be there for each other. Always. We nestled together in exquisite silence.

I studied Sarah's face, the half of it shown by the low bathroom light. For the first time, I saw what a toll all this had taken on her. I wondered if the fugitive life was best for Sarah. If it would slowly rub the shine off her. We didn't have any other option. I really wished we did.

Sarah was exhausted. We were meeting her sister Nicole, who also happened to be my ex-wife, tomorrow in downtown Baltimore for an early dinner. Both of us wanted to see her and say goodbye. Sarah fought to stay awake but soon surrendered. She slept with her head on my chest. I felt her warmth, heard the soft murmur of her rhythmic breathing as she slept.

I stared up through moist eyes. Followed the long wavering crack that ran across the ceiling in our room.

I was a better man at her side. I wanted to be a better man. Not for myself, but for her. I needed her respect. Her love. I was a different man without her: the drifter who had wandered aimlessly for five years; the angry, vengeful, dispirited man who longed to spill Prisha Baari's blood. Sarah elevated me above these alternate versions of myself.

Our bodies fit together as if by celestial design. Our coupling was as strong as gravity, as certain as time itself. I believed in us as strongly as I did these universal truths.

Sarah had me convinced that I lived in a world with some purpose. A purpose we would find together. With her, my life held a modicum of meaning, a sense that all this had been designed by some invisible and benevolent hand. And that some things, a precious few things, were pure truth and undeniable.

I could not recall when I had ever been this happy.

CHAPTER ELEVEN

SARAH AND I ENTERED THE RESTAURANT AND SCANNED the tables for Nicole while we allowed our eyes to adjust to the darkness. The cool blast of air conditioning felt great. It was early evening and holding steady at a humid eighty-six degrees. We had taken a twenty-minute taxi ride to Inner Harbor, Baltimore's major tourist hub, where locals and tourists come to eat, drink and be entertained. We wove through the throngs of people crowded along the brick promenade, taking in the ships and sights the harbor had to offer. It still felt weird being out in public after six months in captivity. I fought against a low-grade paranoia, against the uneasy sense that at any moment someone would swoop in and put me back behind bars. Crowds made me uncomfortable. I was glad when we arrived at the restaurant.

Baltimore was famous for its crab cakes, made from the local catch right from Chesapeake Bay. We'd let Nicole select the restaurant. I'd assumed she would go with seafood, as she loved crab cakes. I'd also hoped for someplace casual, but she'd chosen a five-star steakhouse instead; Sarah was paying, after all.

The hostess greeted us stiffly, then walked us to our table. The place was all polished mahogany and diffused lighting. The dining room had no exterior windows. I took in my fellow diners as we passed their tables. This was a khaki pants, Oxford buttoned shirt and loafers kind of place. All ironed. I had none of these things. All I had was the outfit the jail had returned to me and the jeans/shirt combo that Nia had provided and that I now wore. I had tucked in my shirt and made an honest effort at grooming. Sarah, by contrast, looked resplendent in her cream-colored capri pants and flowing silk top. She wore her sun-kissed blonde hair down, center parted and off her face. It fell to the middle of her back and shimmered when she moved. Sarah's beauty got us past the dress code.

Nicole was on one side of a high-backed booth. A near-empty glass of wine sat in front of her. She saw us approach and downed it. The hostess deposited us at our destination, and before we had a chance to sit down, Nicole asked her for another glass of wine. The hostess made a sour face and said she would pass her order on to our waitress. Nicole missed the dig and dismissed her.

We went through our greetings. Sarah kissed Nicole on the cheek. I did not. Nicole was dressed in a black jacket over a loose white t-shirt. She wore her dirty-blonde hair piled up on her head. Loose tendrils fell to frame her puffy face. She had little makeup, just rose lipstick and heavy mascara that darkened her cold blue eyes. Half-dollar-sized gold hoop earrings in both ears. She had a bar piercing through the top of her right ear, which hadn't been there the last time I had seen her.

Sarah slid onto the leather bench and took the seat directly across from Nicole, up against the mahogany panel at the back of the booth. I followed and sat to her left on the aisle. A small wall sconce with an upturned copper shade hung from the panel between the two sisters. Smooth jazz breathed in the background.

"Where's Teddy?" Sarah asked.

"Home with a sitter," Nicole responded. "The adults have to talk."

I recognized that look on Nicole's face. Had seen it many times when we were married. A storm was brewing. Sarah gave Nicole a stern big-sister look that she ignored. Thankfully, our waitress, a fresh-faced sorority girl, arrived and interrupted the mounting tension. She handed Nicole her glass of red wine; Nicole took a healthy swig before she placed it down on the table. The waitress then placed two plates between us: calamari, fried with sweet and spicy sauce, and broiled mushrooms caps stuffed with jumbo crab.

Nicole had taken the liberty of ordering appetizers for the table. She knew I found squid and mushrooms repulsive. I glanced at her and got a knowing smile. *Bon appétit*. Well played.

We made our entree choices: I ordered the twelve-ounce ribeye, medium, with a house salad. Sarah went against the grain and got the Chilean sea bass and steamed broccoli. We both chose water as our beverage. Nicole ordered two four-ounce beef medallions topped with six large shrimp, creamed spinach, and another glass of Pinot with her meal.

The sisters dug into the appetizers and struggled to find their equilibrium. I speared one of the stuffed mushrooms and picked the crab out of it. It still tasted of mushroom. I gagged and switched to the complimentary basket of wheat and sourdough rolls. Bread and water for the ex-con.

Despite it all Sarah and Nicole had remained close. Sarah had kept Nicole updated with just enough information to keep her satisfied. Nothing but the headlines. But now, emboldened by the wine, Nicole began to probe for details. Sarah parried and deflected. I mostly stayed out of it, with the exception of answering a few cancer questions. I said I felt fine, and that, now that I was exonerated and out of jail, I expected to get my first round of treatment soon. Most of that was true.

I continued picking at the appetizers, watching the sisters out of the corner of my eye. Nicole was a low-pressure system; Sarah was her opposite. I feared they might collide and wanted to avoid all that wind and rain. Sarah had insisted we see Nicole before we disappeared. I had protested mildly, but I also understood and supported her. Now that we were here, though, I just wanted this dinner to end.

The storm clouds appeared with the entrees. Nicole took a long drink from her Pinot, then thumped it back down on the table. She glowered at me while she cut her steak, then put a forkful in her mouth and turned her glare on Sarah.

"Sooo, you and Frank are eloping, is that it?" she said coolly. "That's why we're having this nice little dinner together? You had to tell me this in person?"

"No!" Sarah exclaimed. "Frank and I aren't eloping. Where did you get that idea?"

I must say I liked the thought of it. If Sarah had asked me to marry her, right now at this table, in front of her sister, I would've instantly said yes. I already had plans to propose marriage when the time was right, but I was ready now.

"Well," Nicole continued, swallowing a bite of steak, "you two are quite the happy couple now. Just like old times. And you mentioned you were going on a trip or something, so I just figured..."

"Not a trip, exactly." Sarah cut into her bass. "We have to go away for a while."

"Away, huh?" Nicole slurped her Pinot. "Like—get away from it all?" She hit me with a hard look. "You know, Frank, I would've gone with you when you took off last time. But you never asked me, did you? Remember that?"

I sat back against the bench seat and sighed. "That was a long time ago, Nicole." I dropped my right hand under the table and squeezed Sarah's thigh. "And this is totally different."

"Yeah." Nicole pulled a piece of steak off her fork with bared teeth. "That was a long time ago, Frank. Before you were homeless and a murderer." She smiled at her jab.

I didn't take the bait. I knew how that would end.

"Look," Sarah said, rising to my defense. "We're not here to relive the past. This is important and I need you to listen carefully." She leaned in and began. "Frank and I are going to be leaving in a few days. We'll be gone for a while. Maybe a long while."

"Where?" Nicole asked sullenly.

"I can't tell you. For your own safety. And ours. We'll

have to stay in touch on burner phones and such. Powerful people are after us, and—"

Nicole snorted. "Who? Who could possibly be after you, Sarah?"

"The same people who put both me and Frank in jail for crimes we didn't commit. That's who. I'm serious, Nicole."

Nicole appeared dubious. Indifferent. She continued attacking her steak with gusto. Sarah's and my entrees had gone cold. I sipped my water and waited out the silence. I was about to say something when Nicole started up again.

"Since we're all just talking here..." Nicole swirled her fork in the air, then popped a shrimp into her mouth. "You know," she leaned in, "just us girls." She looked between us. "I thought I'd mention that I told Teddy both of you were in jail." She gave us her what-do-you-think-of-that expression.

Sarah gasped and held a hand to her mouth.

"Why did you do that, Nicole?" I demanded.

"He asked me, Frank. He asked for you, and why he couldn't see his Auntie Sarah anymore. I couldn't lie to him. So I told him the truth. That you were both in jail."

"I can't believe you did that," Sarah murmured.

"And that's the real reason Teddy's not here. He was afraid. Afraid to see you both."

"Goddammit, Nicole," I growled. "You had no right to tell him that."

"No? He's my son. And he deserves to hear the truth."

The pain on Sarah's face was too much for me to bear. I said something I shouldn't have.

"Oh, yeah? Well, maybe it's time Teddy heard the whole truth."

I regretted it as soon as it flew out of my mouth. I had

just written a check I didn't want cashed. I tried to wave Nicole off with a desperate look, but it was too late.

Nicole took a long draw of wine. She threw her head back, eyes on the ceiling. Held this pose for a few beats, then leveled her eyes back on me. They were dark and stormy. She smacked her lips and leaned in for what I knew was her coup de grâce. "You know, Frank, maybe you're right." Her voice dripped with sarcasm. "Maybe your son is entitled to the whole truth."

It was a gut punch. I stopped breathing. I felt Sarah jolt next to me. I heard her dry-heave, then choke.

"Nicole..." I stammered.

"What?" Sarah shouted. Other diners turned to us, then looked away quickly.

Nicole appeared pleased with herself. She looked between us, then back to Sarah. "Frank never told you?" She paused a beat. "Teddy's our son. Frank's his father."

Sarah whimpered. She turned to me. I looked into her wide, questioning eyes and wanted to disappear. Wanted the earth to open up and swallow me whole.

"Sarah... I can explain... I..."

"Yeah, Frank, explain it to her. I want to hear this."

"Damn it. Shut up, Nicole."

"Is it true, Frank?" Sarah asked, hands trembling.

I nodded my head yes. Took her hands in mine and told her everything I was going to tell her after we got settled in our new life and past all this shit. I told her how Nicole's extramarital affair had ended our marriage, and how my one-night mistake with Prisha Baari had cost me my job and her everlasting enmity. I told her how all this had led me to leave Nicole for my five-year homeless odyssey. I swore to Sarah that I had had no idea that Nicole was pregnant when I left.

That I had found out only later, after I'd got out of the hospital and Teddy was already five years old. Nicole had convinced me that it was best that Teddy not know I was his father, and made me promise I would keep our secret. I'd kept this promise because I thought it best for Teddy right now, and because I feared Prisha might target him if this secret leaked out.

The look in Sarah's eyes made me want to crawl away and never return.

"I'm sorry, Sarah," I pleaded. "I hated keeping this from you. I swear I was going to tell you." I squinted at Nicole. "Later. And not like this."

Sarah pulled her hands from mine, accidentally sweeping the fork from her plate to the floor. The loud clank drew more looks from other diners at nearby tables. She fixed her younger sister with a fiery glare.

"You!" she said through gritted teeth, and pointed her finger. "You did this on purpose. You were always jealous of Frank and me. Never could stand us together. And now, this?" Her face was ashen with rage.

"I'm just trying to do what's best for you, Sarah. I thought you should know... before you two go riding off into the sunset together."

I slammed my fist on the table. Nicole jumped. Sarah didn't.

"You don't know what the hell you're talking about, Nicole," Sarah said firmly.

"Yeah?" Nicole crossed her arms tight to her chest. "Well—you're not as smart as you think you are..." she glanced at me "...getting involved with this fucking train wreck."

"And you're a princess, aren't you?" Sarah snapped.

"Always have been. Everything always had to revolve around little Princess Nicole, didn't it?"

Nicole's face flushed red. The storm was ready to break. Her lips curled back into a snarl. "Fuck both of you!" she shouted. "I hope you have a wonderful life together!"

She stood up, knocking her glass of water all over the table. I grabbed it and set it upright, but the damage had already been done. Nicole stormed out of the steak house, leaving a gawking audience in her wake. The manager came to our booth and asked if everything was all right. *Where to start with that one?* I asked for the check and refused doggie bags. Sarah sat next to me, stunned to silence. We paid the three-hundred-dollar tab and went outside.

It had begun to rain. Sarah told me to take her back to our room. We walked in silence through Inner Harbor to the nearest taxi stand. I held the door open for Sarah, who climbed in and refused to look at me. I slid in beside her, shut the door and gave the driver directions. We both stared out our windows, soaked by the rain and chilled by the space between us.

It was a long ride. I don't remember much of it.

———

When we got back to the hotel room, Sarah locked herself in the bathroom, and after a moment I heard the shower running. After a long few minutes, she emerged from the steaming bathroom with her hotel robe cinched tight. I showered next. Tried to scrub this night off me, without success. I emerged to a dark room. Sarah had closed the curtains and was lying in bed. She faced away from me. I lay down beside her.

Wrapped my arms around her. She didn't move away but didn't reciprocate. I apologized once more, and again ran through my reasons for not telling her about Teddy. She said she understood but didn't want to talk about it now. So we both silently lay there in the hotel bed. Two wounded animals.

Eventually Sarah's breathing changed and I knew she'd fallen asleep. She hadn't said goodnight.

———

I awoke to the sight of Sarah packing her overnight bag in the dim light of the room. The curtains were drawn, and I could see it was still dark outside. I rolled over towards the night-stand. The red numbers on the digital clock read 5:18. I jumped out of bed and went to her, I asked what she was doing. She gave me a weak smile and kept packing. Her eyes were puffy and red.

Our flight did not leave until ten a.m. I gently held her at the shoulders and asked her what was going on. She looked away to gather her emotions, then back at me with more tenderness than anger.

"I'm going back to Boston alone, Frank."

I just stood there, speechless. The floor began to move below my feet.

"I need some time alone to figure all this out."

Sarah zipped her overnight bag closed. It sounded to me like the clang of a jail cell door.

"My life has gotten so complicated since you came back," she said. "I just need to be sure before I leave everything behind to start a new one with you."

I asked her what she needed to be sure of.

"You just stay here," she said, not answering me. "I'll call you in a couple of days."

I protested. Said I'd accompany her to the airport. That I could be ready in five minutes.

"No, that's all right. I'll take a taxi to the airport. See if I can get an earlier flight. Quinn'll pick me up at Logan."

I begged her not to go.

She stepped to me and we kissed. She brushed my cheek with the back of her hand. Orange jasmine.

I followed her to the door in just my underwear, not quite believing what was happening. She opened the door and took a step into the hallway. I stood in the doorway, slack-jawed.

Sarah turned and tried to speak. No words came. Her eyes filled with tears. She gave me a peck of a kiss, then turned and started down the hallway, pulling her overnight bag behind her. The wheels squeaked on the carpet. I watched her walk down the hall. Then around the corner and out of sight. She never looked back.

My brain screamed *Run*. Run after her. Make her stay, make her understand. But my bare feet stayed planted in that doorway. On the sticky, maroon carpet.

I heard the distant ding of the elevator. The doors opened and closed.

She was gone.

CHAPTER TWELVE

May 26, 2017
Duckie's row house; East Capitol Hill
Washington, DC

I was back in the District early. Couldn't stay in that hotel room one minute longer.

Sarah had already checked us out. I took a taxi to the airport. I couldn't recall the parking garage stall number. Couldn't focus on much except for the fact that Sarah was gone. I thumbed through my texts with Nia and got the stall number. I shuffled through the parking garage, which was empty at this time of the morning. I didn't know if Duckie's men had already taken the car back to DC. I was relieved when I saw it in its rightful spot. Keys still on the rear passenger tire. I drove back to Duckie and Nia's row house, dark clouds swirling in my brain. Outside, the sun was rising on what promised to be a beautiful spring day.

I called Nia on the way. I told her something had happened and asked could I come back for the day. I had woken her up, but she told me I could come by. I wanted to give her and Duckie some time, so I parked by the Eastern Market and waited until just past 8:00 a.m. before I headed over there.

They were both up. They greeted me at the front door with tentative, inquisitive looks. I went in, and we all sat down in the living room. Instrumental music streamed from the Amazon Echo smart speaker, clad in the new oak wood-grain shell that matched their hardwood floors. It made me think of ODYSSEUS, then Prisha Baari, who had started to leech into my mind like a poison.

I wondered if Prisha could hear us. If she could, what would she think? I imagined her snickering at my breakup with Sarah—if that's what this was. The word *breakup* slammed around in my head. I sought a better euphemism—time apart, trial separation maybe—but given my dark mood, it felt more like a breakup. I saw Prisha's gloating, laughing face. My rage surged and roared in my ears. Let her listen. Let her stream her little hidden messages into this living room. Her time was coming.

Nia came in from the kitchen with coffee. They sipped at theirs while mine went cold. They asked me what happened. I told them. I relayed my story; it sounded curiously flat to me, the observations of an eyewitness to a cop. I heard the words I was saying but couldn't believe them somehow. Like I was talking about someone else's life.

I blamed Nicole. Her heedlessness and impetuous callowness. She and Sarah shared a complicated past, in which I was just one more complicating factor. Nicole cared more about losing me to Sarah than she cared about me. I was pissed at her now, but knew her well enough to know she'd blurted out our secret without any malice aforethought, as Gerry Gonzalez would say. I would forgive her for this someday. Not today, or tomorrow. But someday.

Prisha Baari was another story. I had parked much of my trouble at her door, ever since that one mistake late on a Friday night on her office couch. From this one event had sprung a ceaseless trail of miserable causal effects: loss of job, reputation, government benefits, self-worth, marriage. Then came homelessness and hopelessness, my son, redemption and restoration. Followed by false felony murder, jail, and two attempts on my life. Then my first homicide. And now Sarah was gone. I held Prisha accountable for all of it. She had become my unhealthy obsession. My hatred and rage were focused into a laser beam, the red dot right between her eyes. In my addled state, I decided it was Prisha who had caused the estrangement between Sarah and me. I had to do something about this.

I shared none of this with Duckie and Nia. Just stuck to the facts. I had already told them I had a son. And they knew about my short marriage to Nicole, the wrong sister.

After I finished my story, Nia walked over and gave me a hug. She and Duckie were both sympathetic and kind. Said all the right words one does when trying to support a friend through an emotional crisis such as this. But I had disconnected. A fallen leaf in a tempest. Unable to process that Sarah had walked out of our hotel room and out of my life. The sight of her slumped figure walking away from me down the hall played in a continuous loop in my mind.

Duckie and Nia stayed by my side the whole day. They said I should get outside and move, so we did the tourist thing. They dragged me to Eastern Market, where we ate breakfast and Nia gave me a tour of her favorite food vendors. Then off to the nearby U.S. Capitol Building. We took the official tour, which was a first for me. Everyone seemed to enjoy it. I smiled when prompted and didn't hear a thing. From there, it was the National Mall and the four-mile walk to the Lincoln Memorial and back. The sun was out. Federal office workers loitered as they took their lunches on park benches, only half a workday standing between them and their weekend. Tourist families ambled along, maps in hand. Children ran in circles. Dogs pulled on leashes. I took it all in behind dark sunglasses. Watched it like a movie. My heart skipped every time I saw a tall, fit blonde woman. And every time, the tiny spark of hope was smothered when the woman turned and it was not her.

We ended our day back at Eastern Market. Nia picked up a few things, and we went back to the row house and ate an early dinner. Duckie cleared the kitchen table and I did the dishes, and then we all sat back down. That was when we had our first beer. We toasted to better days ahead. Then the bourbon appeared. We all did a shot to Sarah and me. Or Romeo and Juliet, as Nia phrased it. I hoped our story would have a happier ending. Duckie brought out a few joints. I abstained while Duckie and Nia smoked up. I went in for another bourbon. My new Kentucky friend. I didn't have to explain or justify my distorted logic to him. The how or why of Prisha being the center of my universe. He got me. He sure did.

————

There's an old Irish proverb that says, "The truth comes out when the spirits go in." Any true Irishman knew the truth of it. I counted myself in their company.

That amber elixir stripped off my superficial filters. Got me down to the deep end of the pool. I now lay on the pool bottom, flat on my back, looking up at a distorted surface through ten feet of cold water. My scalding rage bubbled up. I clenched my rocks glass and followed those bubbles as they rose.

"We should smoke that bitch," Duckie said, exhaling a cloud of musky chronic smoke.

"What?" I stammered. I surfaced and sat on the edge of my pool, shivering.

"Your bitch. We should smoke her. Tonight. Grab my AK and take care of this right now. Bitch killed Jamal—and fucked your shit all up."

Duckie took another hit. Held it, then exhaled a cloud of smoke that smelled like sugar and burnt marshmallows.

"Let's do this," he said as he passed the joint to Nia.

Of course I should have told Duckie this was crazy. But my Kentucky friend didn't think so, and neither did I. I wanted to let my rage run. Have it take the wheel tonight. I stood at the edge and stared into my abyss. I rocked back and forth. Heel-to-toe, toe-to-heel. It was just like the pool. I fell in.

Tonight I would be behind the wheel for a drive-by shooting of Prisha Baari.

———

It was past midnight. Duckie and I sat in silence in the dull gray Chevy I'd brought back from the airport. I was behind the wheel. Duckie was in the passenger seat, which was reclined and pushed all the way back. AK-47 between his legs on the floor. Both front windows opened just a crack to listen to the night noise of the neighborhood. We were in Petworth NW, a few blocks over from the Parkview Bodega, where Prisha and her crew had set up shop to work on ODYSSEUS. Petworth was a good draw. The kind of neighborhood where Duckie and I could sit in a car unmolested. A place where shootings were not uncommon.

All I had to track Prisha down was her Lexus and this bodega. We weren't going to go to the CIA and knock on that front door after all. We cruised the streets around the bodega for hours until I spotted Prisha's shiny black Lexus. She had parked it on a residential side street and presumably walked the few blocks to the bodega. I found a parking spot a couple hundred feet away, on the same side of the street as the Lexus, with the bodega behind us. Prisha would have to walk right by us to get to her car. I cut the engine and we waited.

My elation at finding Prisha's Lexus slowly waned as the hours passed. The seriousness of my situation had completely sobered me up. My fickle Kentucky friend had moved on to other conquests. Duckie gave me a final chance to abort our mission. I declined his offer. He seemed pleased with my decision. Back at the row house, Nia had said if anyone, man or woman, had done her like Prisha had done me, she would light them up. True that, sister.

So that made our conspiracy unanimous. It's so easy to sell a man what he desperately wants.

We each watched our own side of the street. I'd parked away from the streetlights, and we both slouched down in our seats. The neighborhood was quiet. A few cars but little foot traffic. We sat in silence. Duckie gripped the AK. He nodded off a few times. I nudged him awake. I thought of Sarah and what she might think of me sitting here. Prisha's murder would be one final secret I would keep from her. Maybe the CIA would not publicize her death and Sarah would never learn of it. Prisha's death would be a good thing. For me and for us. Maybe it would even bring an end to all of this. Maybe her Viking and the rest of them would just melt away. Then Sarah and I could live our lives in the open. Not hiding behind false aliases and looking over our shoulders. That was what kept me behind the wheel. Hope's a powerful thing.

———

Duckie slapped my leg. "Hey! Check it out," he hissed.

I looked in the rear-view mirror and shot upright in my seat. I spun around and looked out the back window. It was her. Prisha Baari. Striding up the sidewalk. Approaching on Duckie's side. About fifty feet behind us.

"It's her!" I whispered. We exchanged nods and dropped as low as we could in our seats. My heart pounded in my chest so hard I feared the whole world could hear it. The click of Prisha's heels announced her approach. I heard the lilt of her voice, softly humming. My nostrils flared with her scent as she passed our parked car. No more than three feet from Duckie and his AK. My gut clenched. I awaited her scream and her fast-clicking heels that would signify our undoing. I counted out my breaths and waited. Nothing. Duckie raised his head and I followed his lead. We peeked over the dashboard and picked Prisha back up. She was two cars in front of us and walking without a care in the world.

We both crouched back down in our seats. I started to

turn the ignition. Duckie's huge hand grabbed mine. We watched Prisha saunter past three more parked cars. Duckie removed his hand. I started the car.

"Give her a minute," Duckie said softly.

I waited. Prisha put two more parked cars between us.

"Okay, go," Duckie instructed. "Nice and slow."

I eased the Chevy off the curb and began to creep up on Prisha, now about a hundred and fifty feet ahead of us. I heard the sharp clack of metal on metal as Duckie checked his AK.

"Nice and slow," he repeated.

My eyes locked onto the back of Prisha's head. Duckie's window squeaked as he lowered it all the way down. My eyes fixed on Prisha. Her mane of raven-black hair. I imagined her head exploding like a melon. Shards of skull and brains spraying all over the sidewalk.

"Slow down, man." Duckie raised the AK to his shoulder. Hung the rifle out the window and took his aim.

I slowed the car as instructed. I kept my eyes on our target. Couldn't help myself. A lapse of discipline. I was the driver, not the shooter. My eyes should have been on the road. They weren't.

A horn blared. I looked up. Blinding headlights. Coming straight at me. I had drifted into the opposite lane. In the path of an oncoming car headed straight for us at speed. I jerked the wheel to avoid a collision.

Pop! Pop! Pop!

The driver leaned on the horn as he passed our car. He screamed something out his side window.

"Fuck!" Duckie shouted.

I looked. His huge torso still hung out the window, rifle at the ready. I didn't see Prisha. Duckie bellowed and unleashed a salvo of rounds into a parked car directly opposite ours. Glass shattered. The *thwap* of a bullet on metal filled my ears. A car alarm began to wail. Headlights approached, getting bigger in my rear-view mirror.

I stomped on the gas. Duckie almost fell out the window before he managed to drop back into his seat. The whole car shook.

"What the fuck?"

"Car behind us!" I shouted, not taking my eyes off the rear-view mirror.

I sped down the residential street. Took the first left, tires screeching. Took a right, then another left. No more headlights in my rear-view. I slowed to the speed limit.

"You all right, man?" I asked.

Duckie nodded. He looked straight ahead.

"Did you get her?"

He grunted. Head still forward. "No."

CHAPTER THIRTEEN

MAY 27, 2017
DUCKIE'S ROW HOUSE; EAST CAPITOL HILL
WASHINGTON, DC

GRIEF: KEEN MENTAL SUFFERING OR PAINFUL REGRET.

I drove at Duckie's direction to St. Paul's Rock Creek Cemetery, a large swath of green on the eastern border of Petworth. We parked in front of a creepy statue of a shrouded, seated figure staring blankly ahead. We were to meet one of Duckie's guys here, to trade cars and dump the AK.

I learned much later that on this transformative night, we were parked in front of the Adams Memorial, commissioned in 1886 by poet Henry Adams in loving remembrance of his wife, who had committed suicide by cyanide a year prior. Adams was so stricken with grief he'd refused to have the memorial inscribed, or even speak her name after her death.

For many, the memorial had become the physical embodiment of grief, without form or expression. To others, it was simply terrifying and haunting. For me, on this night, it was both.

Years later I would mark this night as the beginning of my own grieving. My first tentative step on the tortured path to surrendering my rage-filled obsession with Prisha Baari. It would be a long journey with an unknown end. And it all started on this dark night, waiting with Duckie and his AK in front of the grief statue. Who said the universe doesn't have a sense of humor?

Duckie ran a tight crew. His man was right on time. We both jumped into the clean ride and turned over the AK. Duckie drove back to the row house, where we explained to Nia what had transpired. Shit happens, and everyone missed their shots now and again. To Duckie's credit, he didn't put the blame where it belonged: on me. Nia asked if there were any witnesses. We both said we didn't think so. Other than Prisha, who we assumed was still alive. She nodded and said, "Good." My enemy was their enemy now.

I had to drive up to Boston to see Sarah and Quinn. Tell them what had happened. What I'd done. Tell them that Prisha already knew, or would assume, that it had been me. It really didn't matter. She would retaliate either way. I had put all of us in imminent danger, and now I had to go to Boston and face the music. Confess my sin and ask forgiveness. Their answer would decide my fate.

Nia said I wasn't going anywhere tonight. It was too late and I needed some sleep. I protested. Said I shouldn't be under their roof, the shit magnet that I was. Nia told me I was staying the night. End of discussion.

We all went to bed. I darkened the living room and lay

down on the couch in my clothes. I had only been out of jail for eighty-four hours before I had re-offended, adding the attempted drive-by murder of Prisha Baari to my criminal resume. Good job, Frank. I tried to empty my mind. Listened to the ticking clock in the kitchen. Sleep found me after a long struggle.

————

I awoke with a start. Daylight streamed through closed blinds. I fumbled with my phone. 7:30 a.m. I jumped off the sofa and tidied up my sleep area. I took a five-minute shower, then put the same clothes back on and emerged from the downstairs bathroom. Duckie and Nia were in the kitchen. The aroma of ground coffee summoned me. I said good morning, and before I continued Nia said I would be staying for one cup of coffee before I left. I agreed.

We stood in the kitchen, mugs in hand, them leaning on the counter, me by the refrigerator. The coffee didn't disappoint.

"Heading up to Boston, huh?" Duckie asked.

I nodded.

"All right, then." He grabbed a set of keys off the counter and tossed them my way.

"Take the Olds. It's good." He took a long draw off his coffee. "Saturday traffic. Should be up there for dinner."

The thought of sitting down to dinner tonight with Sarah and Quinn seemed as alien to me as what had transpired last night.

"You go tell that girl you love her. Tell her what a goddam fool you've been," Nia said with a twinkle in her eye.

"Nia's right." Duckie drained his mug and rested it on the counter. "Go get your girl back, Frank. Make things right with her. All this gangster shit—this thug life—ain't for you two. Go find yourself someplace on a beach and chill."

I nodded.

"And take care of that motherfucking cancer too," Duckie said with a grim smile.

I choked out a laugh. Nia and Duckie joined me. You can only laugh about cancer with good friends.

Finally, I told them I had to go. Nia gave me a hug and peck on the cheek. Told me to drive safe. She smiled at Duckie and left us alone in the kitchen.

"Here's my new number." Duckie handed me a scrap of wrinkled paper.

I put it in my pocket.

"Anything you need," he said.

"I know."

"And buy yourself some clothes when you get up there. You look like shit."

"Okay then," I said.

I crossed the kitchen to him and we embraced. A beat longer than before. I knew it might be a long time before we saw each other again. I sure hoped I'd see this man again.

Duckie walked me to the door and I left. Got in the white Olds and headed north.

I had some explaining to do.

CHAPTER FOURTEEN

May 27, 2017
Quinn Doyle's Beacon Hill condo
Boston, Massachusetts

Buzzz. I took my finger off the call button for Unit 606.

"Yeah?" Quinn Doyle asked.

"It's me. Frank."

A long pause.

Buzzz. The lobby door clicked open. Inside, I passed up the elevator and searched for the stairwell. I had just spent nine hours in the car, and I did not want to be in another claustrophobic box.

I had called Sarah after I passed through New York City and told her that I was on my way up to see her and Quinn. That I had to talk to them both. She'd pressed me for details. I told her what I needed to say was better discussed in person. She asked if I was all right. I said I was. I don't think she believed me. I told her I'd be there sometime after six p.m. She said okay, but her voice said otherwise. She'd given me the address to Quinn's condo, speaking slowly and choosing her words carefully. Our conversation was halting, punctuated by awkward gaps of silence. I hung up with a bad feeling.

I took those six flights like a man walking to the hangman's noose and hoping for salvation on the other side. On the sixth floor, I stopped two doors down from Quinn's place to gather myself. I ran through what I'd say. I wiped my hands on my jeans. A couple of deep breaths and off I went.

I knocked on the door. Quinn answered. He greeted me coolly. I dropped my eyes. He told me to come in. I followed him through the entry and into the main room, where I halted at the sight of her. Sarah had her hair down, framing her face. She wore large-framed glasses, the same shade of blue as her eyes. A worn, fitted gray t-shirt, long khaki shorts and sandals finished her look. She stood tall, hands thrust in pockets, and looked at me quizzically. I tried to speak. To breathe. Nothing came. The speech I had prepared on the road for the past nine hours had abandoned me. I just stood there, more frightened than I'd ever been in my life.

I'm not a crying man. Hadn't shed nary a tear despite all the shit that had happened to me since I left the army. Didn't cry in the army, either. Even at the memorial services for the men I lost in Afghanistan. No tears as an eight-year-old boy at my father's funeral, a performance that had caused some hand-wringing among the few relatives who'd bothered to attend. Now, I'm not proud of this. Quite the contrary. I felt all the emotion, but the tears never came. That's what made what happened next so extraordinary.

I lost it. Standing at the entry to Quinn's living room, my eyes fixed on Sarah's face. I just lost it. I mean totally lost it. Tsunami lost it. One second okay. The next, sobbing like a baby. Once it started, I couldn't stop it. Ugly crying. Wailing. Shaking. I fell to my knees. Hands over my face. The torrent of tears wouldn't stop.

After a time, I felt a gentle hand on my head. I looked up through my hands. It was Sarah, her face soft, eyes welling up. I grabbed for her like I was scrambling into a life raft. She stroked my hair. My dam had broken. I let it all out. Sarah sat down next to me on the floor. I buried my head into her neck. Sweet orange jasmine. I told her I loved her. She said she knew. I told her I was sorry. She knew that too.

Quinn had left the room and given us our privacy. An act of politeness he could have dispensed with. He was family, and I didn't care if he bore witness to my purification. Sarah and I stood and embraced. We kissed. We wiped the tears from each other's eyes. She had forgiven me. Without hearing a word of my stupid speech.

———

We were all sitting at the kitchen table. The same table, they tell me, that Gerry Gonzalez sat at two months ago when he'd told them about how Duckie had saved me from Prisha's Israeli assassin.

The time had come to spill my beans. I went straight at it. I told them everything. No excuses. Just like it was. I took full responsibility. Admitted the drive-by was a stupid thing to do. Reckless. My actions had put us all in danger. Not from the cops, as I still believed there were no bystander witnesses to the shooting. Our danger would come from Prisha and her group. I apologized with all my heart and asked for their forgiveness, my heart in my mouth. Quinn Doyle was not known to be a particularly forgiving man.

Quinn scowled at me. "What a stupid thing to do, Frankie." He shook his head. Bit his lip. "You trying to get us all killed?"

Nothing I could say to that.

"Jesus, Frankie!" Quinn raked a hand through his unruly mop of salt-and-pepper hair. "This really puts our balls in a vise." He rose from his chair. "Shit." He paced. "She'll send that Viking after us. Sure of it."

"That's why I drove right up here," I said. "We need a plan."

That set Quinn off. "Oh, now you want a plan!" He tapped his finger against his temple. "You don't think sometimes, Frankie. Just charge right up that hill."

"Quinn," Sarah interjected, "Frank's here to make things right. We need your help."

This calmed him a bit. He spun away from us, then stood with his arms braced on the counter, facing the kitchen sink and wall beyond. I held my breath. And my tongue. Finally, Quinn turned back to face us.

"You!" Quinn took a step towards me, wagging a finger. "Last time I say this. No more of this solo operator shit, Frankie. I see this one more time from you and we're through. You'll never see either one of us again. You understand?" He was glaring at me.

I understood. What I really understood was that Quinn spoke not only for himself but for Sarah too. I had to find a way to keep a lid on this rage I carried within me. Otherwise I would lose them both. For good.

"You're right, Quinn," I said quietly. "No more. I give you my word."

That was what Quinn needed to hear. Quinn had offered me one last chance, and I had taken it. Most men didn't get this generosity from him. I was grateful for it. Now, there was no need for any more discussion on this point. Quinn loped across the kitchen and stood over me. I thought he was going to hit me. Instead, he grabbed my face in both hands and roughly kissed the top of my head. All was forgiven. Then he gave me a hard slap in the same spot he had just kissed. There it was.

"And we three tell the truth to each other—always. You understand?" he said. I turned and looked up at him. "Sarah told me about Teddy. What were you thinking, Frankie?"

"I had my reasons for not telling you both about Teddy," I said. "Shitty reasons, but reasons."

"No, I understand, Frank," Sarah said. She reached over and covered my hand with hers. "I was a little harsh on you in Baltimore. I'm sorry. Nicole got me spun up. She's good at that."

"I know," I said. "It's one of her special gifts."

"How old's that boy now?" Quinn asked.

"He's six. Starting first grade in the fall," I responded.

Quinn drew in a long breath through his teeth. "He's almost the same age you were when your father passed, Frank."

"You mean when he was murdered?" I retorted. Quinn took a step away from me and fell silent. "Arthur died when I was eight and in the third grade," I reminded him.

Quinn's eyes were downcast. He stroked his chin and then spoke in a quiet voice, as if he was talking only to himself. "A boy that age needs a father." He looked up at me. "You need to tell him, Frank. The boy deserves to know."

I let that sit there. One major problem at a time. There were probably people on their way to kill us right now.

"What are we going to do, Quinn?" I asked.

Quinn backpedaled to the edge of the kitchen counter-top. He leaned on it and folded his arms across his chest. He held the room.

"We're going to have to kill her," Quinn said flatly.

"No!" Sarah shouted. "I'm not going to live like this anymore. I can't do this. Not knowing if we're all going to live another day. I'm tired of it. All of it. We need to run. Far away. Now."

"It's not that easy, Sarah," Quinn said.

Sarah turned to fully face me. Took both my hands in hers. "Run away with me, Frank. Let's go tonight. Some-where on the West Coast. Where we can walk to the Pacific Ocean each morning. Watch the sun set each day. Hear the gulls squawk." She was breathless now, her eyes wide and searching mine. "What do you say?"

I loved this plan. But Quinn was right. Being a fugitive is expensive. And not as romantic and easy as Sarah made it out to be.

"That sounds great, sweetheart, it really does. But do you really want to live our lives as fugitives? No more contact with friends? Family? Looking over our shoulders the rest of our lives?"

"We have that now!" Sarah jerked her hands from mine and slammed back in her chair. "You've got two women in your life, Frank. Prisha Baari and me. And it's time you choose. I'm going to find a sleepy little town and start my life over. I want you to come with me, Frank. I really do. But you have to come alone. Leave Prisha behind. I need an answer from you." She glanced at Quinn and back to me. "Right now."

It was clear to me that Sarah had reached her limit. Her capacity for this life. She had done her best, given her all. And she was done. She was going to the West Coast, with or without me.

Sarah had given me my ultimatum. Love or hate. Her or Prisha.

I looked deep into Sarah's sad blue eyes for a long moment. She held my gaze.

I chose love.

PART II

To live is to suffer. To survive is to find some meaning in the suffering.
　—Friedrich Nietzsche

CHAPTER FIFTEEN

THE ELECTRIC CLIPPER WHINED AS I RAKED IT OVER MY
bald head. I then trimmed my stubbly beard. I missed my
shoulder-length hair, but missed my jail cell less, so I went
through this ritual twice a week. The dark chocolate contacts
had been harder to get used to. Add a pair of non-prescrip-
tion matte-black frames and my own mother wouldn't recognize me. Or maybe she wouldn't care to. I had not contacted
her once in the eight months Sarah and I had been on the
lam. I was sure Prisha, or the FBI, or someone was monitoring her phone. I would not give them that easy lay-up.

I splashed cold water on my face and dabbed it dry with
a towel I pulled off the rack. Part of the matching set of green
towels and floor rugs and runners Sarah had bought for the

bathroom in our rented condo. The place was seriously dated. White ceramic countertops, pressboard cabinets and scuffed linoleum that had surely seen the Reagan administration. It was too dark, despite the round globe light bar over the sink. The exhaust fan clanged, so I never used it, which gave the small space a damp feeling.

I slid my hand over my nearly bald head, then said goodbye to the stranger in the mirror. I walked through our one bedroom to get out to the main living area. It had been finished as a rental unit. High-pile baby-blue carpeting and knockdown drywall texture on all the walls and ceilings. Everything that could hold a coat of paint was covered in flat dove white. We hadn't done much to decorate the place, not knowing if we would have to bug out in the middle of the night. Sarah had put a few things up on the bare walls to brighten up the place a bit.

On the plus side, it came fully furnished (think 1980s) and the owner lived out of state and never bothered us. I walked past the U-shaped kitchen counter and checked the time on the microwave clock. Sarah would be home soon. She was going to be pissed. I'd had a bad day at work and the boss had sent me home early.

I plopped down on the beige faux-leather sofa in a sitting area that faced a large rectangular window and took in the view. It was sublime. This view was why we'd chosen this place. Or more accurately, why Sarah had insisted we choose this place. It was right on the coast, with an unobstructed view of the Pacific Ocean across an expanse of green lawn. The shore was not more than two hundred and fifty feet from where I sat. Sarah and I often relaxed out on our third-floor balcony at night and listened to the waves.

We'd left within forty-eight hours of my arrival at

Quinn's Beacon Hill condo. We'd driven south to Florida, then straight west on I-10 all the way to Los Angeles. We'd stayed in LA for a week, then driven up the coast on US-101 North, searching for Sarah's happy place. We'd crossed the California border and driven six miles more. Across the Chetco River Bridge and into downtown Brookings, Oregon, and Sarah had known instantly she'd found her sleepy West Coast town.

Brookings, a town of under seven thousand, was nestled into the southern corner of Oregon's coastline, about three hundred and fifty miles south of Portland. It had golden sand beaches, seaside cliffs, and a laid-back vibe. Daytime temperatures rarely dipped below fifty-five degrees, and there was enough sunshine to stay bronzed all year round.

We checked into a hotel and got word to Quinn. He flew out to Oregon to help us get established in our new life. He stayed for three months in the nearby town of Gold Beach, twenty-eight miles north of us. He visited most days and helped keep our nerves in check. We found ourselves the condo, and Sarah and I both found employment at the local food co-op. She worked on the register and food counter, and I stocked shelves. Even after the bribe payment that had got me sprung from jail, Sarah still had over one million dollars' worth of investments from her career as a senior executive at the prestigious consulting firm of White Rogers Young. We picked up the jobs mainly for the full medical benefits: Sarah was committed to getting me into treatment for my leukemia ASAP. We now punched the clock forty hours a week for twelve dollars an hour. Two bucks over minimum wage and three hundred dollars less per hour than Sarah used to earn. She was never happier. She loved the earthy bohemian groove in Brookings. And she liked her job at the co-op. Me, not so much. That is, if I still had a job after today.

The front door opened. Sarah locked and bolted it behind her and stomped into the room. She pulled up in front of where I was sitting on the sofa. Her hands were on her hips, eyes afire. I knew I had this coming.

"What the hell's wrong with you?" she shouted.

I absorbed that body blow in silence.

"What were you thinking, Frank? Are you actually trying to get us fired? We need this job."

Sarah raised both hands to her face, then ran her hands through her long hair, which was now colored velvet plum and shaded darker at the tips in a style she called ombre, whatever that meant. I caught a glimpse of the tattoo she'd got our first month here. It was a dark, one-inch butterfly on the inside of her wrist. She wore a loose flowered sundress that was fitted at the waist and fell below the knee. Toe and thumb rings, and a bar piercing through her upper right ear, had quickly followed the butterfly. Sarah had really embraced the boho life here in Brookings. She said she was just trying to blend in, but I knew different. This was her true self, much more so than the Beltway corporate bandit she had been most of her adult life.

"Byron was mouthing off again, and you know I can't stand—"

"Your boss said you shoved him against a wall! That you were choking him!"

"Lily's overdramatic. And she wasn't there anyway."

"She said they have a zero-tolerance policy. I talked her out of firing you. All you have to do is go back in tomorrow and apologize to Byron."

"What!"

"And that's what you're gonna do tomorrow. Tell Byron how sorry you are and that it will never happen again."

"But—"

"I don't want to hear another word about it." Sarah hovered over me as I sank into the sofa. "Understood?"

I opened my mouth to protest. Sarah fixed me with a stern look, and I thought better of it. I nodded yes and slid over on the sofa to give her a seat. She dropped down next to me. The sofa cushions exhaled. She took in the Pacific Ocean for a long moment, then sighed and turned to me.

"You're gonna have to get a better hold on your temper." She placed a hand on my leg. "Seriously, Frank. I know you're trying, but you've got to stop snapping on people. I like work. Like the people there. And we need the health benefits."

"I know," I said. "But Byron's such a fucking tool."

"I don't care. And that doesn't mean you get to strangle him to death."

"Dare to dream," I responded with a chuckle.

Sarah slapped my leg, then nuzzled into me. I wrapped my arm around her. We sat and watched the Pacific Ocean in silence.

My simmering rage for Prisha Baari had prevented me from letting her go for good. She was a scab I couldn't help picking. An old wound that wouldn't quite heal. I was doing my best, but I'd have to do better. Sarah deserved better.

We ate in, an early dinner of baked salmon, rice and asparagus with lemon butter sauce. Over dinner, Sarah again gently brought up the topic of my going to see a therapist. We had talked about it before, and I had dismissed the idea. I didn't think I needed one, and feared that it might lead to a compromise in our false identities. Sarah had protested, saying it would do me a world of good and was worth the risk. That was where we had left it.

Sarah thankfully changed topics now and said she had heard from Nicole today. She and Nicole had mostly patched things up since their blow-out in Baltimore. Both of Sarah's parents were dead, and she was not close with the rest of her family. Nicole was all she had. But Quinn had stressed the importance of leaving our old lives behind. Clinging to old friends and family was how they caught fugitives.

A few exceptions were made, but exacting protocols had to be followed. Someone in Quinn's old crew knew a guy who knew a guy who was a brilliant techie at MIT, and the guy had created some secure communications protocols for us. Nothing too complicated for us to use, but it demanded diligence and focus. Not two of Nicole's strongest points. Neither Quinn nor I had the heart to sever Sarah from her little sister, so we held our breath and hoped for the best. I kept in contact with Duckie and Nia this way, and we both stayed in touch with Quinn and Gerry Gonzalez as well. I spoke to my mother Emily through Gonzalez, who now represented her and cloaked my messages in attorney–client privilege. Only Quinn knew where we were and what we now looked like.

I cleaned up after dinner. Sarah poured a glass of wine and went upstairs for a soak in the tub. I yelled after her that I was going for a quick walk on the beach. She told me not to go too far. I said I wouldn't.

I took the stairs and walked the three flights down to the lobby of our building. I paused to catch my breath before pushing through the front door. A gust of wind hit me in the face, and I cinched my hoodie tight over my head. I went around the side the building and took the steep gravel path to the beach. It was twilight, my favorite time of day. That time between daylight and darkness when anything seems possible. The sun was setting over the Pacific, all aglow in red and orange. I gingerly made my way down to the rocky beach, where I stood in front of a string of hundred-foot-high sea stack rocks just offshore. The grayish sand was loose here, and I sank to the top of my boot soles. I turned into the wind and tasted its salty breath on the back of my throat. I coughed. That familiar dull ache in my bones was still there.

I had had five courses of chemotherapy over an intense four-month period from early August up to Thanksgiving of last year. Lots of chemo. And blood and platelet transfusions to prevent bleeding, antibiotics for infection, and handfuls of other medications to control the side effects. We'd got an early Christmas present when we learned my leukemia was in remission and my blood counts were back to normal levels. They call this "no evidence of disease," or NED. Meet NED. My new best friend.

My doctors had cautioned me, however, that my remission might be temporary. That the leukemia might come back and that I might need intermittent treatments for up to two more years. That was all fine with me. I'd had just a one-in-four chance, and I'd beaten the odds. I would live to fight another day.

Sarah had handled all the paperwork for my treatments. She was a wizard. She wrestled with our insurance company and located state resources to lessen our out-of-pocket expenses. We were both concerned that the hospital, the insurance company, or the state might stumble upon our real identities, but our false IDs passed their first big test without a hitch. The co-op and even my boss Lily were generous with me during my treatments and gave me as much time off as I needed. I had been slowly regaining strength the past two months and actually felt pretty good most days. Sarah still doted on me a little more than she should, like when she told me not to walk too far tonight. I groused but silently loved her for it. I hoped this was what we would be like in our old age.

The reds and oranges had faded now as the sun receded below the horizon. The wind picked up and the temperature dropped. I jammed my fists into the front pockets of my hoodie. Toed the lapping waves with the tip of my boot. I stared into the dark water. I would have to go into work tomorrow and eat shit. Apologize to pissant Byron. Fedora-wearing, ironic frames Byron.

I thought of Prisha Baari. Why couldn't I just let it go—let *her* go? For Sarah. For us. Prisha was my dark mistress. The silent third party in my relationship with Sarah. I felt an adulterer's shame. I had tried to declare a ceasefire, but I was a soldier at heart. And soldiers fight. It's what we do.

I needed to get Prisha out of me. An exorcism to evict the demon and end her possession of me.

I looked across the vast, dark ocean and screamed into the crashing waves. A primal scream from deep within me. An eye-bulging, teeth-flashing, spit-spewing roar.

The violence of my outburst triggered a hard coughing attack. I bent over, hands on knees, choking and hacking at the water's edge. The sun had dropped below the horizon. It was now almost dark. I heard a sharp squawking overhead. I straightened and looked up.

Three seagulls flew low and out to sea.

CHAPTER SIXTEEN

MARCH 27, 2018
BROOKINGS FOOD CO-OP
BROOKINGS, OREGON

I WORKED IN THE BACK OF THE STORE NOW. SHIPPING and receiving and such. Away from the customers and sheltered from most of my co-workers. My punishment for the Byron incident. I gritted through my apology and got put on ninety days' probation. I had been an ideal employee the past two months. One more month to go. I actually liked it back there. I had more privacy and people left me alone. Bryon could have his produce, stock his shelves, deal with the customers. I'd spend my days unloading trucks and stacking boxes.

It was Sarah's day off. She was at the salon getting her velvet plum touched up. I was off early today, and we had a hiking date in Boardman State Scenic Corridor, twelve ocean-hugging miles of state parkland located between Brookings and Gold Beach along Highway 101. We'd stop by to see Quinn in Gold Beach, and he'd make us one of his spectacular dinners.

The park began just three miles north of Brookings. We loved the forested trails and steep and rugged coastline views. I felt much stronger now. Maybe it was unloading all those boxes from the food truck deliveries. I'd even got back into the gym recently.

Sarah was a bright light at the co-op and everyone loved her there. She made friends easily—well, acquaintances, as we called them. We were still fugitives living under false identities, and establishing close relationships was how you got caught. I was more of a loner, which suited me. Sarah took co-op food and wine classes with her "acquaintances" and tended her vegetables and flowers at our community gardening plot downtown. I helped sometimes, but mostly read commercial fiction on our little patio overlooking the Pacific. I did start to learn Montenegrin, the official Balkan language of the Republic of Montenegro, a small country in southeast Europe along the Adriatic coast that broke from Yugoslavia in 2006. Montenegro was not part of the EU and had no extradition treaty with the U.S. That's where we would bug out if things went to shit.

I had not embraced our new boho life as Sarah had, but all in all in. And I was happy. I loved being with Sarah and seeing her blossom. On my good days, I just smiled and nodded and watched the world go by. On my worst days, I'd pick my Prisha scab and bleed anger at her and resentment towards myself. I'd haul myself out of the abyss by remembering my Medal of Honor and fighting back the shame and the pangs of cowardice. Thankfully, these dark days were getting less and less frequent. I was getting stronger. Better.

I was unloading fruit crates from a truck that had just pulled up to the loading dock at the back of the store. My phone vibrated inside my side cargo pants pocket. I stacked the dolly full of crates, then wheeled it out of the truck and into the dock area. I had more trips back into the truck but decided to check my phone. I thought it was Sarah telling me she was running late at the salon.

I pulled my phone from my pocket and inhaled sharply. It was a Google Alert I had set up for Prisha Baari. I read the headline.

PRISHA BAARI, EX-CIA DEPUTY, ANNOUNCES BID FOR VACATED U.S. SENATE SEAT IN NEW YORK.

———

PRISHA BAARI, EX-CIA DEPUTY, ANNOUNCES BID FOR VACATED U.S. SENATE SEAT IN NEW YORK.

At the same moment, three thousand miles away in Kingstowne, Virginia, a slovenly woman was reading the same headline. She too had a Google Alert for Prisha Baari, but for very different reasons.

Linda Webb stood gobsmacked among the broccoli and cucumbers at the Safeway grocery store at which she now worked. The store was located less than two miles from her townhouse. It was her first full week of work and she hated it. She stood frozen in the middle of the aisle, eyes fixed on her phone. She didn't see the annoyed looks or hear the grumbling of other customers as they maneuvered their shopping carts around her.

Webb clicked the email and read the linked article. It contained a small image of Prisha, with her big fake smile, behind a podium that had her red, white, and blue campaign logo slapped on it. Webb focused on Prisha and that big-toothed smile of hers and felt the familiar sting deep in her gut. God damn her! This was why Prisha had left the CIA without looking back. Why she had abandoned Webb to fend for herself amid a sea of enemies at CIA. Enemies she had cultivated over the years at Prisha's behest.

Prisha Baari had resigned as deputy director of the CIA without notice on a Friday afternoon. March 9, 2018, to be precise. For the first time in years, Webb did not have Prisha's long shadow to hide behind. Her enemies came for her quickly. They put her on administrative leave without pay, which would eventually become a dismissal for cause after they manufactured a bogus security violation and circled the wagons. The sweet irony that her demise was based on false testimony—just like she had lied to convict Frank in Hewitt's murder—was lost on her. Webb had frantically tried to contact Prisha to solicit her assistance, but she had changed her numbers. Prisha had hung her out to dry. Webb had always suspected she would. Desperate and disgraced, and without any income or her security clearance, Webb had grabbed the first job she could find.

She shoved her phone back in her pocket and shuffled her little cart down the aisle to add two boxes of fresh toma-toes to the display. Webb worked at a leisurely pace, inten-tionally placing the tomatoes with the stickers facing out, against the explicit instructions of Nate, her nineteen-year-old wannabe boss. Piss off, Nate.

Webb stacked the tomatoes and schemed. Her first impulse was treachery. She could ruin Prisha's Senate campaign before it even got off the ground. Anonymously provide the media with all the dirt she had, which would certainly be enough to drive a stake through the heart of the campaign. Webb basked in the warm glow of this, then saw Charles Hewitt's face. A chill ran through her. Prisha would know it was Webb who was behind the leak, and she would make a move on her. If Webb killed Prisha's campaign, Prisha would kill her. Of this she was certain.

"Hey, Linda," Nate said in a singsongy voice.

Webb hated how he was always creeping up on her. Watching.

"Now, we talked about this before." Nate stood too close to her. His arms hung straight down over his crotch, fingers laced. "We don't display the tomatoes with the sticker showing. It's against company policy. Remember we talked about this, Linda?"

Nate's head leaned to one side as he repeated himself. Which he did all the time. Webb wondered if it was a verbal tic. If he even knew he did this. It made him come off as condescending. She didn't answer him out of spite.

Nate huffed and slid past her. He spun one of the tomatoes around, sticker to the rear.

"See, Linda? That's not so hard, is it? And doesn't it look better for the customer?"

Webb smiled with sarcasm sharp enough to cut diamond.

"Good. Now fix the rest of those tomatoes. And let's try to do better next time—okay?" Nate drew out the cadence of that final "okay." Another trademark of his.

Webb watched him leave. She scanned the vegetable

bins she had just loaded for any additional violations. She had to get the hell out of here. Now.

She thought hard while turning tomatoes around. She stuck a thumb into a few at random. Just because.

Why not do the opposite? she thought. Keep her enemy close? *Yes!* Her heart leapt. She'd approach Prisha for a job as a staffer for her Senate campaign. Hadn't she been Prisha's (mostly) loyal administrative assistant for much of Project ODYSSEUS? Hadn't she shown herself to be a useful asset? Webb would contact Prisha's campaign manager or chief of staff and grovel for an interview. Maybe even use subtle blackmail if needed. Although she would have to do this with a light hand. Why not? The pay would be much better than what she got now. And she would get the satisfaction of quitting on Nate. Webb was even open to traveling to New York if need be. It wasn't like she had much of a life left in Virginia anymore. Webb made up her mind. Better the devil you know than the devil you don't.

She finished her shift under the watchful eye of the omnipresent Nate. She picked up a few items after she clocked out, taking advantage of her store discount while it lasted. Webb worked in the fresh produce section, but actually hated fruits and vegetables. She stuck to the center aisles of the store and bought only things that came in a bag, box, or can. Manufactured food with long lists of long-worded ingredients. She finished her shopping with a one-liter bottle of bargain brandy. Her eyes lingered on it in her cart and again sitting on the conveyor belt as it moved towards the register. The cashier, a cheery part-time college girl, scanned the brandy. Fifteen dollars. Webb ground her teeth and grimaced. Shame and anger battled for supremacy.

Webb loaded her four plastic grocery bags into the trunk

of her aged blue Honda Accord. The inside of the car was cluttered with enough garbage that any passerby would rightly think she lived in it. Webb was deep in thought as she drove the two miles to her townhouse. She brought the mail in and threw everything on the kitchen counter. The townhouse was dark and dank. Webb didn't like to open her windows, or her curtains for that matter. She preferred her solitude since her daughter Anna had left to live with her ex-husband two towns over. Anna had had to change high schools in her senior year, a hardship she'd gladly endured to be rid of her mother.

Still, and despite their dysfunction, Webb loved and missed her daughter. In her own way. The place felt empty without her.

Webb put away her groceries and opened her mail. Bills and junk mail, except for the last item she opened. It was a letter from her ex-husband's attorney regarding an upcoming child custody hearing. Apparently, Anna had decided to go through with it and make her estrangement from her mother permanent and legal.

Webb pulled a dirty water glass from the dishwater, the same glass she had used last night at about this time. She rinsed it with warm tap water and grabbed her liter bottle of hooch. She poured a full glass, neat, and swirled it in her hand. She thought of better nights. Nights when she'd returned from her job at CIA. On those nights she would sip her beloved Remy Martin 1738 Accord Royal, at one hundred dollars per liter, and savor the butterscotch notes and dark chocolate finish. In those days, she had drunk cognac, not brandy. And bought her spirts at an upscale liquor store and not a grocery store.

Webb would look up Prisha Baari tomorrow. Tonight, as most nights, she would drink.

She leaned against the kitchen island, studied the glass in her hand. Screw it. Webb took a long pull. Felt the familiar sting on the back of her throat. She took another.

If she couldn't be with the one she loved, she would damn well love the one she was with.

CHAPTER SEVENTEEN

APRIL 4, 2018
PRISHA'S GEORGETOWN TOWNHOUSE
WASHINGTON, DC

PRISHA HATED THE SOUND OF THIS WOMAN'S VOICE. HER
thick accent, that high-pitched rapid cadence. Her speech
peppered with non sequiturs, repetitive invocations of Allah.
Inshallah this and *Al-hamdu-lillah* that. Hated the loose cut
of her robe-like abaya dress. Hated the sharp features and
deep lines of her weathered face. The stink of ammonia and
cumin she left behind after each visit. Prisha hadn't even
bothered to wear her hijab head scarf for this visit. A grave
offense to the old woman, as was the Adele soundtrack
streaming through Prisha's new Apple HomePod speaker,
which she had just purchased two months ago.

Both women sat stiffly in their seats at the cafe table in

the kitchen nook of Prisha's Georgetown townhouse. The old woman refused to sit in the living room, where Adele and the HomePod resided. She was a strict Wahabi Muslim and disapproved of many social practices widely enjoyed by the rest of the developed world—and her daughter, Prisha Baari.

Meera Naqui Baari had often sparred with her daughter during her quarterly visits to the U.S. Today, though, Meera was willing to overlook the disrespect shown her by Prisha's bare head and Adele's soulful emotive voice. They had bigger problems to discuss on this visit.

It had been less than one month since Prisha's sudden resignation from CIA, and a mere week since her Senate campaign announcement. Prisha's Saudi benefactors, the true owners of ODYSSEUS, were very unhappy with these decisions. As they saw it, they owned Prisha as well. They had placed her in the U.S. as a young teenage bride to a gung-ho Marine. Paid big money to purchase her full American citizenship. Funded her undergrad and graduate degrees. Placed her on the staff of an influential congresswoman, and nurtured her rise to the top at CIA.

These benefactors, oil tycoons and Islamic extremists all, were inextricably tied to the Saudi government, and to the Saudi royal family and its 1.4-trillion-dollar net worth. The benefactors had a plan, and they expected Prisha to do as she was told. And for years she did, as far as they knew. At their direction she had gained dominion over ODYSSEUS as CIA Deputy Director, then had stolen the technology and spun off a secret side project led by Khabir Ahmad. Ahmad led the technical part of the secret project and reported back to the benefactors, while Prisha had played her double-agent role at CIA. She'd maintained full Saudi access to ODYSSEUS as the Americans poured billions into its development. The benefactors had their own ideas about how they would use this wide-scale brainwashing tool, but they'd kept these ideas to themselves. Prisha had a pretty good idea what the benefactors were up to. And as it turned out, she had a few ideas of her own.

The fiasco in the bodega basement involving Frank Luce had set ODYSSEUS back, no question. Ahmad and his team had worked nonstop for over a month to fix the damage done to ODYSSEUS by Darryl Robinson's virus. What had emerged was ODYSSEUS 2.0, a more stable, robust version of the original. Ahmad needed one more year to get ODYSSEUS to Saudi standards. Everyone at the inner circle of this secret project knew this timeline, Prisha Baari most of all.

Prisha had always seen the political potential of ODYSSEUS. She craved it for herself and awaited her opportunity. It had come earlier than expected.

First, the New York U.S. Senate was vacated by the resignation of the incumbent due to a debilitating health condition.

Then, something more intriguing. Current president Mo Udell, in his second and final presidential term, had initiated an effort to repeal the Twenty-Second Amendment, which limited presidents to two terms in office. Udell's effort had gathered momentum. The latest polls showed Americans approved of the measure by a small majority. Not enough to force thirty-eight state legislatures to action just yet, but a dramatic change from its beginning, when the measure's popularity had polled in single digits.

Prisha thought she might know why the American people had had such a change of heart.

She had briefed ODYSSEUS to Udell at the White

House. He'd consistently acted uninterested, but Prisha now believed this to be a feint. Old Mo Udell was perhaps more cunning than he appeared. The way she saw it, it was more than plausible that he was using ODYSSEUS to manipulate support from the American public to repeal the Twenty-Second Amendment—a move that would conveniently allow him to remain in the Oval Office for a third term. Was this too far-fetched? Could she be the only one to see the political potential of ODYSSEUS? Prisha thought not.

ODYSSEUS was like the atomic bomb. No one could maintain a monopoly on this explosive technology. It was just a matter of time before someone stole it (besides her and the Saudis, of course) and it proliferated around the world. As the bomb had. And so it came down to who would use it first, who could get it to market and make the biggest impact fastest.

In her mind, the puzzle pieces fell into place: the New York U.S. Senate seat had unexpectedly come open. Prisha had attended college at Barnard in New York City and loved Manhattan. It appeared Udell was making his move for a third presidential term in 2020. Why not give ODYSSEUS a trial run in New York, then put it to the ultimate test when she ran for president herself in 2020?

Prisha knew the capabilities of ODYSSEUS 2.0. It was not yet fully developed to Saudi specifications, but Prisha bet it would be good enough for her needs. Fortune favors the bold. She decided to roll the dice and test ODYSSEUS on the voters of New York. She would try to beat Udell to market.

Now she just had to beat her mother.

Prisha knew the risk she took in betraying the benefactors. She would never be beyond their reach, even as a CIA executive. On their whim, she knew, she could be abducted and taken back to Saudi Arabia for some advanced interrogation and torture. Until she welcomed death. But kidnapping and killing a sitting U.S. senator was an entirely different matter. She would wrap herself in the star-spangled banner and be untouchable. She was willing to bet her life on this assumption. Her gamble was that she could stall her Saudi benefactors for six months. Enough time for her and ODYSSEUS to win her Senate seat. If she won, she'd be untouchable.

Prisha pushed her raven hair off her face and took a deep breath. She regarded her mother's scowling, withered face and gave her best submissive smile.

Prisha had fully expected this visit. That the benefactors would send her mother to scare her back into line. Prisha was their long-term asset. She sat and listened dutifully as her mother relayed their message. They had invested decades of hard work and millions of dollars in her. How dare she go against their wishes. They demanded Prisha get back on script. Renounce her Senate bid and go back to CIA. CIA was the only place where their investment could fully mature into ODYSSEUS 3.0. Then and only then would they consider Prisha's future. A future they, not she, would decide.

Time to lie. Which Prisha did as easily as others changed their socks.

Prisha looked her mother in the eye. "Mother, you know I have remained faithful to our benefactors. Our project will continue on course, and I will deliver ODYSSEUS 3.0 to our benefactors as promised."

"Do not lie to me, Prisha. They tell me you have fired Khabir Ahmad and denied him access to our project."

This was in fact true. In anticipation of her resignation from CIA, Prisha had hired Ahmad's replacement, a Slovenian named Ziga Oblak. Oblak, a man of Prisha's own choosing, had assembled an entirely new ODYSSEUS 2.0 team. A team independent of the Saudis and that reported only to Prisha. This new team had stripped the bodega basement bare of all ODYSSEUS property and relocated it to a secret location in New York. Prisha had not only fired Ahmad and denied him access, she had ordered Karlsson to kill him. It was an assignment he had gladly accepted, as Karlsson had never liked Ahmad much. Karlsson was tracking Ahmad down as Prisha spoke to her mother in her kitchen.

"With respect, Mother, they are mistaken," Prisha lied. "I fired Khabir Ahmad for incompetence and insubordination. I moved ODYSSEUS from the bodega to secure it from him. He was trying to steal ODYSSEUS and sell it to the highest bidder."

Prisha studied her mother's face. It didn't appear she was buying it.

"The benefactors are livid. They demand our complete loyalty. You have betrayed very powerful people, daughter. They will wipe our family from the earth if something is not done to make this right and restore their honor." Meera fidgeted with her hands. "Will you meet with Abo?" she asked.

Fares Abo was an undeclared deep-cover representative of the Saudi intelligence agency, General Intelligence Presidency, or GIP. He was attached to the Saudi Embassy in Washington, DC. Prisha had sporadically met with Abo and his predecessors for many years, beginning in 2000 when she had become a congressional intern.

Prisha didn't like the sound of this. Abo was a serious and scary man. She did not want to be alone with him right now. Or ever again, for that matter.

"I am always pleased to meet with Abo, of course," Prisha said with as much sincerity as she could convey. "But I'm afraid I'm very busy right now, as you can imagine. Perhaps in a month or so?"

Meera's face flushed and her eyes narrowed. She jabbed a gnarled finger at her daughter. "You!" she shouted. "You were always a disrespectful, spiteful child." She dry-spat for punctuation. "Praise Allah your father is not alive to see what has become of you."

Prisha's temper flared at the mention of her father. She held her tongue with difficulty.

"We have done everything for you, Prisha. And this is how we are repaid?"

"*Everything*? You've done *everything* for me?" Prisha said incredulously.

"You disrespect me, daughter. Your father as well."

"Respect?" Prisha spat. "Like how Father respected me? Pimping out his fifteen-year-old daughter to the Americans? You call that respect?"

Meera's face darkened. "You know that was for the best. Inshallah."

Prisha's mouth dropped open. "For the best, Mother? And was Father raping me for the best?"

Meera issued a weak denial and looked away.

"Yes, Mother. Father said I had to know how to please a man for our little plan to succeed. So he raped me. Many times. Until I pleased him."

Meera raised her head to address her daughter. There was fire in her eyes.

"How dare you speak of such things!" She rocked in her seat. "We all did what had to be done." She flipped her hand at Prisha. "And look at you now. A big, important American woman. You would have none of this but for me and your father."

"So you want a thank-you?" Prisha screamed.

"I want you to do as the benefactors command. What I ask of you. Beg them for mercy and you shall have it. Save your reputation, and those of me and your entire family. I can't go back to Saudi Arabia without your oath to submit to our patrons. Anything less will mean my death, and the death of our family. Do you understand this?"

"Death?" Prisha laughed. "I don't care about death. Do you know I killed Tommy Boone? The American you gave me to?"

Meera gasped, her hand over her mouth.

"Yes, Mother. I killed Tommy. Last year. I made him blow his brains out. Had my hands in his skull. What would our benefactors think of that?"

Meera's face turned ash gray. She leaned away from Prisha.

"My daughter," Meera said in a whispering, pleading voice. "We must do what is asked of us now. Do you understand this?"

Prisha smiled inwardly and assumed a submissive posture. Her face softened. Eyes downcast.

Meera reached across the table and took Prisha's hands in hers. Prisha squeezed her mother's hands. Meera gave her daughter a thin-lipped smile, which Prisha returned.

Meera sighed heavily; her shoulders and face relaxed. "That's good, daughter."

Prisha rose from the table and walked silently into the

other room. Out of sight of her mother. She switched Adele out for some hardcore American country music, then raised the volume and leaned against the credenza. A big smile broke across her face. She lingered. Waited for the loud music to find its mark.

Prisha returned to the kitchen wearing the same smile. She brought two crystal wineglasses and her best bottle of Bordeaux. A look of confusion appeared on Meera's face. She started to speak. Prisha held one finger to her lips and shushed her mother silent. Confusion turned to apprehension. Prisha popped the cork and placed the two wineglasses down. One for her, one directly in front of Meera. Prisha slowly poured Meera a glass of red wine, her eyes fixed on her mother's face. She filled her own glass and took her seat.

For Meera, a strict Wahabi, the consumption of wine was expressly forbidden and considered a grave sin. The very presentation of wine to her, by her own daughter no less, was the height of heresy. Meera looked angrily at Prisha.

"Mother," Prisha said in a playful voice. She raised her glass. "Join me in a toast. To the next senator from the great state of New York!"

Meera glowered and mumbled something in Arabic.

Prisha took another mouthful. "You are a guest in my home, Mother. I have offered a toast. You have disrespected me with your refusal."

Prisha slugged down the rest of her wine and placed the glass back on the table. She wiped her lips, then fixed her mother with an icy stare.

"Now get out of my house."

Prisha held her gaze until her mother rose from the table and shuffled to the door. Meera turned and glanced back at her daughter. Prisha smiled and held her silence. Meera turned and left. They would never speak a civil word again.

Prisha reached across the table and grabbed the old woman's full wineglass.

She had another toast to make.

CHAPTER EIGHTEEN

APRIL 10, 2018
WHITE HOUSE ROSE GARDEN
WASHINGTON, DC

SPRING WAS PRESIDENT MO UDELL'S FAVORITE TIME of year in the nation's capital. Gone were the snow and slush of winter, the oppressive heat and humidity of summer still months away. He stepped from the Oval Office onto the covered portico. He took a deep breath and held it, eyes closed. The garden was just now coming into bloom. He turned to his left and walked down the white colonnade. He stopped at the top of the wide four-step stone staircase, which led down to the Rose Garden lawn. The lawn resembled a small football field, 125 feet long and half as wide. It was a deep, rich green and mani-cured to championship golf course standards. Flower beds and ornamental trees flanked the lawn on each side, just awakened from their winter slumber and awash in pale whites and vibrant reds and golds. At the far end of the lawn, a small patio area with white lawn chairs sat under a spreading shade tree. It was Udell's presidential pocket garden. It was also his favorite spot on the White House grounds.

The cherry trees were now in full bloom, drawing millions of tourists to the Tidal Basin and Jefferson Memorial. Udell thought of how Thomas Jefferson, the Sage of Monticello, had loathed the presidency. He, by contrast, loved being president, embracing it with a zeal not seen since Theodore Roosevelt had occupied the office. The presidency wore most men down, as evidenced by their before-and-after photos. Lincoln had aged twenty years during his four years in office—or a score, as he would so eloquently have put it. Not Udell. He still looked the same as he had when he'd first stepped foot in the White House. He was now halfway through his second term and didn't want to leave anytime soon.

Udell was a populist president with an approval rating that consistently hovered in the sixtieth percentile. His party held a strong majority in both houses. He was having a great time, and the American people weren't complaining. So why not let the good times roll?

Franklin Delano Roosevelt. That was why. His unprecedented four consecutive presidential terms had led to the ratification of the Twenty-Second Amendment in 1951, which limited presidents to a maximum of two four-year terms. One rotten apple spoils the bunch.

Or maybe not. Udell thought it might be time to repeal the Twenty-Second Amendment. Give the American people the freedom to select the president of their choosing: him, of course. So what if he had already served two terms? Good enough for FDR, good enough for him.

Amending the U.S. Constitution was difficult by design, however. It took the approval of two-thirds of the House and Senate, and three-fourths, or thirty-eight, of the state legislatures.

To date, twenty-seven amendments had been approved, six disapproved, and over twelve thousand proposed and considered. Only one amendment, the Eighteenth, which established Prohibition, had ever been repealed. The chance of any constitutional amendment being repealed would be roughly the same as a person living to be eighty years old after being struck by lightning. Still, Udell liked those odds.

He decided to explore the viability of the Twenty-Eight Amendment to the Constitution, a repeal of the Twenty-Second Amendment and presidential term limits. Udell owned majorities in both the House and Senate. He was confident he could bend enough arms and provide enough pork to get his two-thirds votes. It wouldn't be pretty, he knew, but politics is an ugly business.

Udell's problem would lie with the state legislatures. He did not have the political reach to convince thirty-eight state legislatures to ratify. In the current climate, no one had that kind of weight. Udell would never sit for a third term playing by the rules. But rules were only for people who followed rules. Udell did not count himself in that flock of sheep. He was a wolf. And wolves get the job done.

The solution came to him slowly, but Udell seized it once he saw it. ODYSSEUS. He would use it to buttress his existing popular support and stir up such a frenzy for his Twenty-Eighth Amendment that the state legislatures would have to bow to public pressure and ratification.

It could work. In fact, it *was* working. Or it had been, until recently. And that was why Udell had summoned CIA Director Robert Johnson to the Oval Office today. Johnson had better have some answers. Udell's time and temper were running short.

———

"Look, Bob, we don't have a lot of time," Udell said, glancing at his wristwatch. "I've got a meeting in a few minutes, so I'll get right to the point."

That was a lie. At least the meeting part. What was true was that Udell didn't have much time for CIA Director Robert Johnson, who was currently sitting across the vast presidential desk in a plain upholstered side chair. He was a short, pudgy man in an ill-fitting suit. He incessantly stroked his unkempt goatee, a tic that infuriated Udell. Both men were in their mid-sixties. Johnson looked it.

"You were here in the Oval eighteen months ago, with your girl there, when she promised me she'd deliver me ODYSSEUS by February last. Remember that?"

Johnson cleared his throat. Took a swipe at his goatee. "Yes, Mr. President. We worked through the issues we had in December. And we delivered ODY 2.0 to you in February... Yes."

"Two weeks late and two hundred million over budget. But that's not why you're here. My guy tells me that ODYSSEUS isn't working anymore. That right?"

Udell had from the start embedded a trusted man from his White House staff on the CIA ODYSSEUS team. He didn't trust the agency with this kind of technology. His mole was an effective back door for Udell and the White House to keep watch on both the CIA and the project. At first, Udell had feared ODYSSEUS would be used by deep-staters for domestic surveillance or some other unconstitutional end. Then came his own ODYSSEUS epiphany. Udell now believed it could give him a few more springs in his beloved Rose Garden.

"Uhm, yes, sir."

"My guy tells me the thing isn't working worth a damn. What the hell's going on over there at CIA, Bob?"

"Well, as you know, sir, my deputy suddenly resigned last month, and she—"

"The girl?"

"Yes, sir. My deputy—former deputy. Prisha Baari. She resigned suddenly and she was head of the project. That left us in a bit of a bind. But I've got a new acting deputy, and he's getting up to speed fast, and—"

"I'm asking you what's wrong with it," Udell pressed.

"My tech people tell me it's a little buggy."

"What the hell's 'buggy' mean?"

"Buggy. You know. It's not working quite right now, but I'm confident we'll have it back online soon."

"It's been down about a month, is that correct?" Udell leaned over his desk, elbows on the blotter, both fists jammed under his chin.

"I believe so, yes." Johnson shifted uneasily in his seat.

"About the time your girl deputy quit on you. That about right?"

Johnson's eyes widened at the implication. Another nervous goatee stroke.

"I don't think she did... No... she wouldn't..."

"Which is it, Bob? She didn't do it or wouldn't do it?"

Johnson's fat face blushed; beads of sweat sprang to his forehead. He swallowed twice before answering.

"No, Mr. President. I don't believe Ms. Baari sabotaged ODYSSEUS before she left CIA. If that's what you're asking. Sir."

"Well, that's one hell of a coincidence, then, wouldn't you say?"

Johnson didn't say. Couldn't say. He held his silence.

"So when am I going to get this thing back?" Udell said. He tapped the face of his wristwatch. Tick-tock.

Like Prisha, Udell had put together his own off-the-books ODYSSEUS team at a secure dark site in southern Maryland. Johnson knew nothing of this. Prisha had a U.S. Senate seat to win. Udell had a U.S. Constitutional amendment to ratify. ODYSSEUS was now a three-headed hydra.

Johnson tilted his head back and stroked his goatee as he tried to come up with an answer that Udell wanted to hear.

"Stop it!" Udell shouted.

Johnson's hand shot from his face to his lap. He dropped his eyes and rolled his shoulders forward.

"I need ODY back up now. Not next week. Not next month. Now! Is that understood?"

"Yes, Mr. President." Johnson bolted upright in his seat.

"I'm going to send a few more men over to you... to make sure there are no further problems with this."

"Yes, sir. Thank you, sir." Johnson nodded. His fat face was the shade of watermelon.

Udell dismissed Johnson, and he took his leave. The president left his desk and returned to the Rose Garden. The midday sun had begun to burn off the morning cloud cover. Udell squinted into the glare.

He didn't trust Robert Johnson; nor did he fear him. He

could manage and manipulate Johnson. They were both in it up to their eyeballs with ODYSSEUS. Each knew they could bring the other down. Mutually assured destruction. Udell was a good judge of people. Johnson was no ideologue or moral avenger. He was a coward at his core and would not risk his own well-being to reveal Udell's involvement with ODYSSEUS. His secret would be safe with Johnson.

Udell was not so sure about Prisha Baari. He did not believe in coincidences. The timing of her leaving CIA and ODYSSEUS going down made his ass itch. He thought it possible that she had spiked ODYSSEUS on her way out the door. But to what end? And then there was her Senate campaign announcement two weeks ago. Why now? Was he the only one who saw the political potential of ODYSSEUS? Perhaps he had underestimated the girl with the nice rack.

Udell would follow the U.S. Senate race in New York very closely. Prisha Baari now had his full attention.

CHAPTER NINETEEN

October 23, 2018
WABC-TV Eyewitness News 7 Studio; Manhattan
New York, New York

"Good evening, everyone. I'm Walt Harris, Channel Seven Eyewitness News, WABC-TV New York. Thank you for being with us tonight, two weeks before election day, Tuesday November sixth, for the one and only debate between the candidates for the vacated U.S. Senate seat in New York. And let's welcome the candidates tonight: the Democratic candidate, Edward Reeves, and the independent candidate, Prisha Baari."

Prisha looked at the camera, saw the red light and smiled her big, toothy smile into the lens. She had recently drawn even with her opponent in the polls and had come to win tonight.

"This will be a thirty-minute debate and may be viewed

live or streamed on our news app and on all our social media outlets. It will also be rebroadcast in its entirety this Sunday on our morning news program, NYnews. The rules for tonight's debate are simple. Each candidate will have forty-five seconds to answer questions, and thirty seconds for any rebuttal. A coin toss decides who gets the first question."

Prisha had come a long way to be on this stage tonight. She was one of two candidates remaining after seven months of bloody skirmishing. No one had expected her to be dead even with her well-financed Democratic opponent two weeks out. Not even Prisha. Early on in the race, she had been polling dead last. But ODYSSEUS had taken care of all that. Well, ODYSSEUS and Leo Rekker, Prisha's cutthroat campaign manager and former CIA colleague, whom she laughingly referred to as her "prince of darkness."

Prisha had failed to earn the backing of either major political party; as a result, she had been forced to run as an independent. In those early days, she had had limited funds as well. She had sweet-talked former college boy-toy and current Wall Street billionaire Thatcher Kenworthy out of five million dollars, but that was a pittance for a U.S. senator campaign. Her lack of funds had forced Prisha to go to ODYSSEUS early.

Ziga Oblak, her aggressive new ODYSSEUS project lead, had started out by bombarding New York voters, unbeknownst to them, with ODY audio messages. This onslaught of political propaganda was hidden and attached to their favorite streaming music. The results were instant and impressive. In a field of eleven candidates, Prisha went from an unknown to the new shiny object voters couldn't stop talking about. This led to more campaign donations, which led to more open doors, and her candidacy had gained real momentum. One of the beauties of ODYSSEUS in the political sphere was that it worm-holed a candidate's message right into voters' brains, greatly reducing the money a candidate needed to run a viable campaign. Prisha spent most of her campaign funds on herself, on opposition research and operations, and on bribes made by Leo Rekker to secure the favors and promises one needs to win a U.S. Senate seat.

"By coin toss, the first question goes to the Democratic candidate, Edward Reeves," Harris said. "So let's get right to it."

Walt Harris, a smooth and dapper fifty-something African-American man, turned to face the candidates across the news studio. Each candidate sat on a high stool behind a glass-top table, which made them visible to the television audience from the waist up.

Prisha sizzled in front of the camera. She wore a form-fitting scarlet blouse and matching lipstick. The silk top showcased Prisha's augmented breasts and long raven hair, which she wore down. It was her lucky blouse and had worked before in situations such as this. Prisha was betting everything it would work on Reeves tonight.

Reeves wore the dark suit, white shirt, light blue tie and flag lapel pin uniform that was standard issue at party headquarters. He was a tall white man in his late fifties, with fair hair and complexion. His fixed nose and capped teeth smoothed out his otherwise hard-edged facial features. Reeves was already sweating through his pancake makeup. His navy-blue eyes darted around the studio. He appeared to know that this was not going to be a fair fight.

Harris asked Reeves a long-winded, rambling question about terrorism. In the past month in the city, there had been two bombs found in the subway. And just last week, a

Pakistani national had shot up a mall upstate. The question came down to what Reeves proposed be done about this.

Reeves was the current attorney general for New York and had run on his record as a strident law-and-order man. He reminded the voters of this now. He said that, as their senator, he would increase funding for law enforcement and sponsor bills that increased the penalties for terrorists. There followed a few minutes of empty promises and sound bites about the scourge of terrorism, and how he was the only candidate qualified to keep New Yorkers safe.

Reeves had overplayed his hand, and Prisha knew it. She rebutted with her resume as deputy director of the CIA: at age thirty-four she had been the youngest person to hold this office, and also the first woman and non-white; as DD/CIA she had played an integral role in the war on terror in the United States; her various successes in her nine-year tenure included the killing or capture of several top-ten terrorists worldwide.

Prisha turned to face Reeves. Gave him a good full-frontal view of the lucky blouse. She claimed she would be the tough-on-terrorism candidate. That as an Arab woman of Saudi birth, she was the candidate who best understood the issue. That Reeves was ignorant of the cultural issues under-lying Islamic extremism, and that his plan was anti-Arab and bad for America.

Prisha finished with a flourish. She turned away from Reeves and looked through the camera lens and into the living rooms of the millions of New York voters watching tonight. Prisha, with all the sincerity she could muster, told the voters she was an American, not a Saudi, and that she saluted the American flag just as they did.

Getting her U.S. citizenship out in the open early was a

calculated risk, but one Prisha had to take. She wanted to address this early. Put Reeves off-balance and on the defensive. It was Prisha's only landmine in this debate, so she would make it *her* landmine. She would lead Reeves right to it and hoped he mis-stepped.

Prisha's Saudi benefactors had been a problem throughout her campaign. They had first tried to intimidate her into returning to the CIA. When this tactic failed, and—thanks to ODYSSEUS—her campaign had taken off, they had leaked details of Prisha's green card fraud with Tommy Boone and the subsequent bribery that had resulted in her naturalized U.S. citizenship. This bombshell had dropped Prisha's poll numbers and shaken her campaign for a news cycle or two. Only a heavy barrage of ODYSSEUS messaging had righted the ship.

Next, the benefactors had tried surveillance, harassment, and outright physical threats. Prisha had responded by hiring a second team of top-notch bodyguards. By this time, however, Prisha was a national media darling and too conspicuous to abduct. She knew the Saudis lacked the assets inside the United Sates for such an operation, and bringing in a Saudi team to snatch her on U.S. soil was now too risky. Prisha's deft maneuvering had forced the benefactors to stalemate.

Reeves didn't disappoint. He stepped on the landmine.

"The *New York Times* has reported various improprieties surrounding the circumstances by which you obtained your United States citizenship," he said. "Allegations of immigration fraud and outright bribery. Would you care to explain this to the voters watching tonight?"

"If I may, Mr. Reeves," Harris interrupted. "You and Ms. Baari have both exceeded your time on the first question."

He paused a moment to allow the candidates to unclinch. "As my first question to Ms. Baari was to be on the immigration bill currently before Congress, allow me to rephrase." Harris lowered his eyes to the papers in front of him, then jotted something. He looked up at Prisha. His eyes took a quick detour over the red blouse before reaching her face.

"Ms. Baari. The immigration issue is on the minds of all Americans, from a border security and human rights perspective. Congress is debating a foundational immigration bill as we speak. Your opponent Mr. Reeves has cited allegations of immigration fraud attributed to you by the *New York Times* and other national publications. Would you care to address this?"

"Yes I would, Walt," Prisha responded.

Come to mama. Reeves had stepped on the landmine, and now it was time for the explosion and the flying body parts.

Prisha again addressed the camera lens. She first categorically denied the allegations. These were allegations she knew to be true, of course, but truth was but a minor obstacle for Prisha, one she easily sidestepped. She pandered to a feelings-over-facts America. This was a fundamental principle of ODYSSEUS. One of the reasons why it worked so well: it was much easier to nudge people into darkness than to pull them into the light.

After her denial, Prisha took the offensive. She accused Reeves of manufacturing the allegations against her. Next, she slipped on the mantle of victimhood. Said Reeves's attacks were anti-Arab and anti-woman. She labeled him a racist and a misogynist. A white, privileged, out-of-touch, unwoke, establishment man. Prisha was fifteen years younger than her opponent. She was the progressive reform candidate. She would go to Washington and fight for change. Her opponent was the status quo.

Reeves stammered a rebuttal. He had thrown his haymaker and missed. Prisha had slipped his knock-out punch and kicked him hard in the groin. He had been badly shaken in the exchange, and now he would never recover. They traded questions and rebuttals, and then Prisha switched to a coquettish style and toyed with him. Turned towards him, full-frontal, as she addressed him. Smiled her big-toothed smile and softened him up with her dark chocolate eyes.

Prisha's sudden shift confused and disarmed Reeves. Prisha felt his eyes on her. And her lucky scarlet blouse. Prisha warmed at the realization. She had him. Time to go in for the kill.

The final question went to Reeves. It should have been a softball for him. The question was how he would address the inherent corruption in the financial markets. Reeves straightened and spoke into the camera. He reminded voters of his crusade against crooked Wall Street financiers and hedge fund managers, and pledged to continue this fight in Washington. He reasserted his brand as the law-and-order candidate.

The camera lens zoomed in on Prisha as she prepared for her final rebuttal. She turned to Reeves, smiling.

"You say, Mr. Reeves, that you are the law-and-order candidate. And I concede that your conviction record as attorney general is laudable. But gender discrimination is also a crime, is it not?" Prisha paused to enjoy the look of confusion that washed over Reeves's face. "Why is it, Mr. Reeves, that under your administration as New York

Attorney General, you hired twenty percent fewer women than your predecessor?"

"That's not true—" Reeves interrupted, his eyes wide and roaming.

"Is it because you don't respect women?" Prisha asked, raising her hands to chest height.

"Of course not!" Reeves looked towards Harris, who offered no relief. This was good television. He was not about to stop this train.

"Mr. Reeves, I have depositions from three different women who have each sworn under oath that you have made unwanted sexual advances towards them during your tenure as attorney general. What is your response to these women?"

"That's a lie!" Reeves shouted.

And it was. Prisha and Leo Rekker, her dark prince, had handsomely paid three women Reeves had never met to fabricate their accusations. Each account was a vaguely crafted fable that Reeves, though innocent, could never wholly refute.

"Are you calling these three women—these three brave survivors—liars?" Prisha asked.

Reeves broke out in flop sweat. His eyes darted. His hands gesticulated helplessly.

"No! I respect all women. I—"

"Like you have respected me here tonight, Mr. Reeves?"

Reeves choked and swallowed. Deer in headlights.

"You have been staring at my chest the whole night, haven't you, Mr. Reeves?"

"I have not!" Reeves roared.

"You're doing it right now!" Prisha chuckled, then turned to face the camera.

"I'll let you, the viewers and voters of New York, decide.

I ask you to review the video of our debate tonight and count the number of times Mr. Reeves looks directly at my chest."

Walt Harris gasped. He sputtered his way through the debate wrap-up and then bid the viewers a hasty good evening.

The cameras went dark. The crew broke into spontaneous applause for Prisha, which she acknowledged with a head nod. Walt Harris was bent over, giggling.

Prisha turned to face Reeves. She smirked and raised both her hands to her breasts. Gave them a good squeeze.

She stared deep into Reeves's eyes and saw his fear. Her ambrosia. In that moment, they both understood who would be the new U.S. senator from New York.

———

The Reeves–Baari 2018 debate video was viewed over one hundred million times on YouTube in the twenty-four hours following the debate, smashing the record previously held by the South Korean boy band BTS for the music video to their song "Idol." It went on to become the first-ever YouTube video to top ten billon views worldwide.

The Reeves–Baari debate became the most studied video since the Zapruder film. Based on the millions of comments left by viewers, the consensus was nine: Reeves had inappropriately glanced at Prisha's breasts nine times during their debate.

The lucky blouse had claimed another victim.

CHAPTER TWENTY

November 6, 2018
The Chatwal Hotel; Producer Suite; Manhattan
New York, New York

THE CRISP NIGHT AIR PINGED HER LUNGS LIKE peppermint. Prisha took a long draw off her 2008 Dom Pérignon. She closed her eyes as the gold silky champagne hit the back of her throat in an eruption of spices. Her mind drifted back twenty-five years to her freshman dorm at Barnard College. Six miles and a million years from where she now sat.

Earlier this evening, Prisha had stood on a makeshift stage at historical Washington Square, under the iconic 124-year-old marble arch and in front of a huge American flag, and had given her acceptance speech to a throng of forty-five thousand screaming supporters. Prisha electrified her audience. She spoke of humility and service. Of how they had sent her to Washington. And how she would fight for them. She told them how proud she was to be their senator. The crowd loved her for it.

None of this was true, of course. Prisha planned on holding her Senate seat for no more than two years. A mere third of her elected term. She had other ideas, ones that didn't involve the cheering idiots in front of her.

Prisha had easily defeated Edward Reeves with sixty-three percent of the vote, becoming the first independent candidate to hold a major federal elected office. She had captured the national spotlight and become a political sensation. The new "it" girl. An intelligent, exotic Arab woman who shone in front of a camera or a crowd. Prisha intended to take full advantage of their ignorance.

Prisha would travel to Washington, DC, next week. Her first order of business would be to make surreptitious contact with Fares Abo and deliver her ultimatum to the Saudis. Prisha had documented all she had done at the direction of the benefactors, from her immigration fraud through ODYSSEUS and everything in between. This dossier was more than enough to cause an international incident of epic proportions. Surely enough to ruin Saudi–American relations and possibly start a wet war between the two countries. Prisha had already provided this dossier to a few trusted people, with instructions to publish it should anything happen to her. It was her dead man's switch, which she hoped would neutralize the Saudi benefactors and keep her alive. A high-stakes gamble, to be sure, but one Prisha felt she had to make.

All that could wait, however. Tonight she would savor her success and scheme with her head of security. Prisha had noted a coolness between her and Karlsson of late. She wanted to take his temperature tonight.

They arrived at the elegant Chatwal Hotel directly after her acceptance speech and took the private elevator to the Producer Suite on the penthouse floor. Prisha was famished and summoned the room butler. She ordered petit filet mignon, medium rare, with a radicchio and soppressata salad. Karlsson got the Faroe Island salmon and winter salad.

The Producer Suite was magnificent. Seven hundred square feet of chic cinnamon opulence and spice-hued leather furnishings. They sat at a dark oak table in the dining area, which was adjacent to the living room and fireplace. Prisha popped the first magnum of 2008 Dom Pérignon before dinner. She and Karlsson clinked glasses and toasted her victory.

Prisha ate all her meal. Karlsson picked at his. They left the dishes for the room butler and took the magnum bottle up a spiral staircase leading to a large roof deck. The view over 44th Street and the Manhattan skyline was spectacular.

The roof deck was long and narrow, the three-foot railing at its edge the only thing between them and a death plummet to 44th Street, hundreds of feet below. The stone and concrete deck was softened by potted trees and flowers. Two wide chairs with plump art deco cushions were separated by a low, square cocktail table. Another magnum of Dom sat on the table chilling. Skyscrapers soared all around them.

Prisha drew another breath of crisp peppermint air. The bustle of Manhattan murmured far below. She opened her eyes and turned to Karlsson. His eyes were fixed on his champagne flute. He had barely touched it.

"Quite a day, huh?" Prisha said.

"Yup."

"We did it, Henrik."

"You did." Karlsson took a sip of his champagne.

"You could act a little more excited about it," Prisha said with a snort.

"No, I'm excited. Really, I am. Congratulations." Karlsson turned to Prisha. He looked tired, distracted. He raised his flute but did not drink.

Prisha attempted to engage Karlsson in conversation. She asked him what he thought about her new ODYSSEUS tech, Ziga Oblak, and the dark prince, Leo Rekker. Prisha also asked Karlsson some personal questions about his second-in-command, Darius Pierre, who had recently caught Prisha's eye. Karlsson responded with monosyllabic answers. It vexed Prisha and she called him out on it. Karlsson responded languidly that he didn't want to talk business tonight.

"What's our situation with Ahmad?" Prisha asked.

Karlsson sighed loudly. "I told you. I'm doing all I can to find him. I think he's back in Saudi."

"We should have killed him."

"Well, I would have if I could've found him, Prisha. You pulled all our equipment out of the bodega before I could grab him. It spooked him."

Prisha didn't like to be criticized. Even by Karlsson. And particularly not tonight, after her coronation.

"Luce, his girlfriend, and that mobster are still loose out there too. What are you doing about that?"

"What do you mean, what am I doing?"

"I have to start preparations for my POTUS 2020 run, and those three are loose ends that have to be dealt with."

"They're underground, Prisha! We're monitoring all

their friends and families. One of them will slip up. We'll get 'em."

"I am not a patient woman, Henrik. You know that."

"I don't know why you're so stuck on this. If they were going to expose you, they would have done it by now. I'll bet Luce is living a quiet life somewhere with no intention of getting involved with you or me ever again." Karlsson was drinking now. He poured himself some more champagne and shot some back. "My advice is that you leave all three of them alone."

"You're going soft on me, Henrik."

Karlsson leveled Prisha with a look that indicated otherwise.

"I'm the one Luce shot, not you. I have no problem killing him, or his girlfriend either. But the mobster is a problem. Killing him would likely start a blood feud. And anyway, if we kill Luce, that would probably bring in the Irish mob anyway. Not worth it."

"I still want them found," Prisha ordered.

"I'm looking, Prisha," Karlsson said irritably, then broke off and brooded in silence.

Prisha regarded him thoughtfully; she was growing more uncomfortable with her head of security by the minute. She poured herself another glass and drained half of it.

"Henrik, I'd like you to bring Darius Pierre in on this. I want him on-point for Luce."

"Prisha, I—"

"Look. I think you're doing a great job. And we wouldn't be where we are today without you." Prisha flashed Karlsson her big-toothed smile and wondered if it still worked on him. "I know you've got a lot on your plate right now. Darius can handle Luce. Okay?" She reached over and placed her hand on Karlsson's arm.

Karlsson stared at her hand. He looked away and nodded.

Prisha's stomach dropped as a sudden realization hit her. Was her Viking through? This would be a problem. He knew way too much. And you couldn't just fire a man like Karlsson. She thought of Darius Pierre. Wondered if he was ready to step up. Prisha would speak to him tomorrow. Take his temperature too.

Prisha studied Karlsson's face as he gazed up at the night sky.

She pictured him stripped naked and on his back. Laid out on a boat surrounded by his meager belongings. The boat is launched off a rocky beach and into the frigid water. It drifts offshore into the dark. Under a full moon. The thwish of a bow release. The arch of a solitary flaming arrow overhead as it seeks out the funeral pyre. A bright flash. A distant fire burns. Her Viking, on his way to Valhalla.

An honest tear formed and fell to her cheek. Prisha Baari brushed it away before Karlsson could see.

CHAPTER TWENTY-ONE

JANUARY 9, 2019
FERRY BUILDING; EMBARCADERO
SAN FRANCISCO, CALIFORNIA

WE EMERGED FROM THE UNDERGROUND SUBWAY station at Embarcadero and twirled around to get our bearings. Neither Sarah nor I had ever been to San Francisco before. We'd never even been west of the Mississippi before we went underground a year and a half ago. Given our circumstances, we hadn't traveled much outside of southern Oregon. This would be our first road trip.

Quinn was right. We couldn't miss it. The Ferry Building and its 245-foot-tall clock tower was at the foot of Market Street, right where it was supposed to be. It was a five-minute walk east of where we now stood. We started out for it, blinking against the late morning sunlight. It promised to be a beautiful day. The temperature inched towards sixty degrees, with clouds forecasted to roll in later this afternoon. Maybe we'd see some of that famous San Francisco fog we'd heard so much about.

The clock tower was modeled after the twelfth-century Giralda bell tower in Seville, Spain. The clock dial itself was a full twenty-two feet across. The clock bell chimed portions of the Westminster Quarters on every full and half hour during daylight hours. I checked my watch. We were to meet Quinn and Gerry Gonzalez under the clock at 11:00 a.m. I looked forward to the show.

Quinn had contacted me on our prepaid disposable phones and said he had to see us. I'd immediately asked what was wrong. Sarah and I had not seen Quinn in over nine months, since he'd left Oregon to go back to Boston. We all stayed in regular contact but eschewed face-to-face visiting for security reasons. Quinn said he had spoken with Gerry Gonzalez and that we all had to meet. Under the clock. I asked Quinn if this was good or bad, and he said we'd talk at the clock. Sounded bad to me.

Everything was more complicated when you lived the fugitive life. You had to assume you were being watched all the time. And keep the lurking paranoia at bay. Not an easy trick.

This meeting took extensive planning. Gonzalez flew to Las Vegas (because he was a Vegas guy), gambled a few days, then rented a car and drove nine hours to San Francisco. He cleaned himself the whole next day, walking and taking taxis all over the city while looking for surveillance. He called Quinn the next day to report he was good. The following day, Quinn flew from Boston to Oakland and booked into a hotel in the Lake Merritt area. That night he gave me the green light, and Sarah and I left Brookings at 3:30 the next morning. We drove seven hours south on US-101 to the East Bay, where we parked at the North Berkeley BART station and took a twenty-five-minute subway ride into the city and got off at Embarcadero. Then, finally, we'd taken the five-minute walk to the clock.

Sarah and I crossed Embarcadero Plaza and approached the two men standing under the big clock. It had been a long time since we had seen Quinn. Gonzalez longer still. We hugged as the chimes rang out overhead. Gonzalez marveled at Sarah's velvet plum hair and bohemian conversion. He didn't comment on my stubbly head and beard. We all wore some variation of hats and sunglasses. Gonzalez's and Quinn's appearance had not much changed since we'd last seen them.

We walked through the Ferry Building Marketplace, which was crowded with tourists milling about the food and souvenir shops. We went out the other side and walked along the outdoor plaza, San Francisco Bay fifty feet to our right. We stopped at the far end, where we all got a cup of Blue Bottle coffee. Organic fair-trade Yemeni pour-over coffee, served in a clear glass mug with a two-bite seeded cardamom cookie. Sixteen bucks. Welcome to San Francisco.

Our green-haired server with the nose piercings said they had heated outdoor seating to help take the chill off the Bay breezes. We took our heated seats away from the waterfront crowd. I sampled my sixteen-dollar cup of coffee. Not bad, but maybe not sixteen dollars' worth of good.

We were all delighted to be together again. We sipped our coffee and got caught up as the ferries glided by. I gave my cancer update. I'd had my last intermittent treatment three months ago and I was now NED again—no evidence of disease. I had regained my strength and stamina too.

And things had settled down after Prisha's shocking Senate bid announcement. In fact, the past nine months had been the best time Sarah and I had ever spent together. I had reconciled myself to work at the food co-op. I didn't mind working on the loading dock, where I passed most of my shift with earbuds in, listening to podcasts. Sarah still loved her job and her work friends. We'd spent the summer hiking and exploring the coastline of southern Oregon. We laughed more. Sometimes I went whole stretches in a day without thinking about our old identities and life back in DC. Overall, Sarah and I were happy. Content, even. That is, until Quinn called.

We had all finished our coffee. None of us opted for another sixteen-dollar round. It was time to get to business. Gonzalez glanced over both shoulders and began to explain why we were all here.

He told us that last week, just after Christmas, a sleek reptile of a man had visited him unannounced at his law office. Gonzalez didn't want to see him, but he was most insistent. There was an intensity to the man that made Gonzalez nervous. He thought the best way to get rid of him would be to grant him a quick meeting. So he brought the man into his office, which was empty due to the holiday. The man carried with him a huge black leather doctor-bag briefcase that appeared heavy.

Gonzalez said the man was about my age, early forties. A dark-skinned Arab man with perfectly combed black hair and wide hazel eyes. He was impeccably dressed in an expensive suit and open-collar shirt. He spoke crisp English with just a trace of accent and sat with his legs crossed at the knee, hands neatly folded in his lap.

The man had introduced himself as Fares Abo and

explained that he spoke on behalf of a very powerful consortium of men from the Middle East. He stated that his main purpose was to seek Gonzalez's assistance in scheduling a meeting with Quinn and me. He refused to state the purpose of this meeting. He then unlatched his briefcase, which was resting on the chair next to him, reached in, and pulled out stacks of clean one-hundred-dollar bills. Ten thousand dollars in all. He solemnly arranged these thick stacks of bills in front of Gonzalez on his desk. The man told Gonzalez it was his finder's fee. This growing stack of bills became the third party in their conversation.

Gonzalez had wavered a moment, then politely declined. This guy gave him chills and he wanted no part of him.

Abo had then asked Gonzalez if he would pass a message to us. He'd added another ten thousand to the pile on the desk. Gonzalez had considered the stacks of cash; he was only human. He told the man he would hear him out.

Abo said the men he represented were from Saudi Arabia and exceedingly wealthy. They were all also exceedingly unhappy with Prisha Baari. Abo said Prisha had betrayed these men, and they wanted something done about it. She had stolen something from them. Something very valuable that they wanted back. These men had tried to reason with her, but Prisha would not listen to reason. She had severed contact and was now blackmailing them. This they could not tolerate.

Abo claimed all he wanted was a private audience with Prisha. He explained that he was regrettably unable to do this himself. Prisha was now a sitting U.S. senator, which made things more delicate for him and his friends. They did not have any deniable assets currently in place in the U.S.

who had the ability to impact Baari as they wished. After some delicate questioning by Gonzalez, it became clear that these men aimed to kidnap Prisha, and that they wanted to hire Quinn and me to do their dirty work.

Gonzalez tried his best to hide his shock and fear. He said that even if he could contact Quinn and me, we would have no interest in this. Abo said a man named Khabir Ahmad had indicated that we would, in fact, be interested and were capable of doing the work required. Gonzalez said he didn't know any Khabir Ahmad (which was true) and that his clients were still not interested.

Abo gave Gonzalez a reptilian grin and once more reached into his bottomless briefcase. Another ten thousand dollars hit the desk. Gonzalez tried to stifle a smile but failed.

Abo reminded Gonzalez that he had not yet asked about the fee. Gonzalez held his ground and responded there was no amount of money that could get his clients interested in this sort of thing. Abo had then leaned forward and offered his terms: thirty million U.S., tax-free; five million up front, as a show of good faith; twenty-five million on delivery of Prisha Baari to him. Alive.

I laughed out loud. So loud I covered my mouth with my hand.

"Are you kidding me, Gerry?"

"I wouldn't be here if I didn't think this guy was serious."

Both Sarah and I turned to Quinn.

Quinn shrugged. "From what I heard from Gerry, the guy could be legit. We did as much checking as we could. Hard to tell. Maybe Prisha's setting a trap. Or the feds. We won't know for sure until he wires the five million."

"No!" Sarah shouted. "No one is wiring anything!" She clamped her hand on my forearm. "We're not doing this."

Gonzalez apologized to Sarah. Said he understood, but as our attorney he thought he was duty bound to convey this most unusual offer.

I exchanged looks with Quinn.

"That's a lot of money, Sarah," Quinn said. "We wouldn't have to kill her. Just hand her over."

"I don't give a shit about her! I don't want that woman back in our lives. Things are good here." Sarah threw her head back, flipped her hair violently. "No. We won't do it."

"Frank?" Gonzalez asked.

Sarah shot daggers at me. I slumped in my seat.

"Uhm, well," I stammered. "Is this even possible?"

Gonzalez and I looked to Quinn. I felt Sarah's eyes on me.

"Well, sure, I guess," Quinn said, avoiding Sarah. "I'm sure I could put a crew together. It'd be risky, but for thirty mil there'd be no shortage of volunteers."

"No!" Sarah said again, face reddening.

Thirty million tax-free dollars was a shitload of money. It would set Sarah and me up for life. No more working for Lily at the food co-op. Maybe we'd move to Hawaii. Or Fiji. Buy a bungalow. Live on the beach and drink from coconuts. Plus, Prisha would get what was coming to her. I didn't know exactly what these Saudis had in store for Prisha, but it would be bad. Really bad. And that was good enough for me.

Quinn's eyes softened. I followed them to Sarah. She was shaking with emotion and a building rage. Her fingernails dug into my arm.

Quinn and I both shook our heads. We were really all in this together. The three musketeers. It had to be unanimous. Quinn and I had already forsaken our vendetta against Prisha for Sarah. Now, I was back to the binary choice I'd made in Boston a year and a half ago: Sarah or Prisha; love or hate. Simple choices can be hard.

"We're not interested, Gerry," I said.

"Yeah, me neither," Quinn said. "Thirty mil is lot of money, but it ain't worth stepping back into this pile of shit."

Sarah exhaled in relief. It sounded like a moan. She wrapped me up in a big hug. She felt so good.

So that was the end of it.

Sarah and I spent the rest of the afternoon walking to Crissy Field and across the Golden Gate Bridge. Hand in hand. We stayed the night in the city and drove back to Oregon the following morning. Quinn and Gonzalez both flew back to the East Coast that night. And Prisha continued to serve her term as the junior U.S. senator from New York.

Athos. Porthos. Aramis. The three musketeers had held rank.

All for one. And one for all.

CHAPTER TWENTY-TWO

January 24, 2019
Walmart Superstore 5580; Parking Lot
Fairfax, Virginia

"He gonna show?" Darius Pierre asked in a deep baritone voice from the driver's seat of the dark-gray Chevy Tahoe LT.

Prisha checked her watch. "He'll be here."

Prisha, now U.S. Senator Baari, had barely spoken with ACA Calderon in the twenty months since their tense meeting at Gravelly Point. A lot had transpired since Gravelly Point, and Prisha was now in a position where she needed Calderon's help one last time. He repulsed her, and she him. She had had to cajole him to take this meeting with veiled promises of riches. That was what motivated Calderon, she knew, and that was what would bring him to the back corner of this busy parking lot at Walmart Superstore 5580, two miles from where he plied his trade as a felony prosecutor at the Fairfax Commonwealth's Attorney's Office.

Prisha sat directly behind Pierre in the rear passenger seat of the Tahoe. The crown of his shaven head, a shiny hazelnut brown, protruded above the seat rest. He was a large African-American ex-cop in his early thirties. He had a good twenty pounds and two inches on his boss Henrik Karlsson, but Prisha had seen Karlsson toss Pierre around like a rag doll on more than one occasion. She and Pierre had grown familiar with one another in the two months since her Senate victory and his taking over for Karlsson as the lead on the Luce operation. Pierre lacked Karlsson's intelligence and cunning. He was more malleable, less sophisticated. He responded well to Prisha's bit in his mouth. They had sex at Prisha's whim. Pierre was an unimaginative lover, but serviceable enough and eager to please.

"We should shoot over to his office," Pierre said. "I'll go in and grab him."

"Patience." Prisha nudged the headrest in front of her, which caused Pierre's head to bob.

"Hey!"

"Here he is," Prisha said.

The back passenger door opened and Calderon tumbled in, breathing hard. He wore a heavy wool coat and a fleece watch cap pulled down over his ears. He pulled off his oversized sunglasses after he slammed and locked the door.

"Andrew, what a pleasure to see you again," Prisha said.

Calderon had put on another forty pounds. He was beginning to lose his hair; it made his forehead look big and splotchy. His jowly neck prevented the top button on his white Oxford shirt from buttoning, so he wore his tie knotted loosely around his neck. His dull eyes had receded into his fleshy face.

Calderon looked between Prisha and Pierre, who had turned in his seat. "Who's this? Where's the other guy?"

"Never mind that," Prisha responded. "We have some things to talk about."

She had grown impatient with Karlsson and his handling of the Luce matter and suspected he was slow-rolling her on the whole affair. Karlsson had been a vocal critic of her termination strategy, which was why she'd brought Pierre in. Pierre had quickly confirmed her suspicions about Karlsson, still technically his boss. For now. Prisha would keep Karlsson around until he was no longer useful. Pierre hadn't located Luce or his friends either, but had proved himself in gathering dirt on Calderon. Dirt she would use now.

"I see your boss Aaron Geller has a real Democratic challenger this year," Prisha said. "And that the governor is backing the guy. Word is Geller is out in November."

"Yeah, he's toast," Calderon said. He fidgeted in his seat. "I don't have much time, Prisha. You're a big senator now. I don't see what you could possibly want from me."

Prisha wanted plenty. She was running out of time, and 2020 was a presidential election year. She intended to announce her candidacy in nine months, October of this year at the latest. Prisha's U.S. citizenship would be a significant obstacle to her presidential aspirations, but not anything she couldn't overcome.

Article II, Section 1, Clause 5 of the U.S. Constitution stated that the president must be a "natural-born citizen" but failed to define this term. Prisha intended to use this to her advantage.

The consensus of constitutional scholars and relevant

case law was that, subject to exceptions, "natural-born citizens" were those citizens born in the United States. Prisha had been born in Saudi Arabia, which on its face eliminated her from serving as U.S. president.

Prisha intended to claim that birthright citizenship made her the exception to this rule.

Birthright citizenship arose from the first part of the Citizenship Clause in the Fourteenth Amendment to the U.S. Constitution. Accordingly, U.S. birthright citizenship was acquired by any person automatically, by operation of law, when one or both parents were U.S. citizens. Birth country did not matter. Prisha's father was a U.S. citizen, albeit fraudulently. No matter. This made Prisha a birthright U.S. citizen.

Years ago, the Saudi benefactors had chosen not to bring young Prisha Baari into the U.S. based on her father's false U.S. citizenship, judging it safer to do a straight run-of-the-mill green-card-to-naturalized-citizenship fraud. It had worked flawlessly, and even allowed Prisha to be a U.S. senator. But the fact remained: only "natural-born citizens" could be president.

There had never been a birthright citizenship president, but such a president was not precluded by the U.S. Constitution. Prisha planned on being the first. She would state that birthright and natural-born citizens were the same vis-à-vis constitutional presidential requirements. Prisha would exclaim that any other interpretation was xenophobic and racist. She would bait the courts and Congress. Dare them to stand between her and the voters. And to seal the deal, she would use ODYSSEUS to make this an issue of freedom and democracy. Prisha was betting that no politician or judge would have the guts to stand in her way. It was a safe bet.

However, October would be here before she knew it, and she needed Frank, Sarah, and Quinn dead and buried by then. Preferably both. To increase her odds, she'd have them all re-indicted for the murder of Charles Hewitt. That would get the FBI looking for them as well. And that was where Calderon came in.

"I need your help, Andrew," Prisha said, her voice dripping with honey. "I just can't sleep at night anymore, knowing the killers of my friend and colleague will not pay for their crime. It's time the Hewitt family had some closure with this." Prisha searched Calderon's fleshy face for her entry point. "I need you to help me help Lady Justice to get this one right."

"I'm not interested in helping that whore Lady Justice," Calderon scoffed. "And besides, the Hewitt homicide case is dead. There are no witnesses left, and my boss already had the case dismissed. It's done... and so am I."

"I can produce Linda Webb as a witness," Prisha offered. Calderon rolled his eyes.

"I can provide a second witness, too. C'mon, Andrew. The case forensics are solid, enough for an arrest warrant at least. And you know... homicide cases take time. Delays are common. With luck, the case won't be tried by the end of the year."

Calderon slouched, disappeared into his big wool coat. Sweat was beading on his expansive forehead. His flat eyes shifted between Prisha and Pierre in the front seat. He thrust his head from side to side, making his fleshy face and neck wobble.

"No," he said through pursed lips. "This is crazy. I don't want any part of it."

Pierre reached into the back seat and placed a huge right

hand on Calderon's shoulder. Calderon jumped as if shocked by electricity.

"You sure about that, Andy?" Pierre said, squeezing down hard. "From what I can see, you could really use the money, man. Cheap suit, bad haircut. And you got divorced last year, right? Alimony... and child support for little Allison? Old lady's got your balls in her hand and she's squeezing hard. Am I right? And you're a county prosecutor on a fixed income. Living in a divorced-dad studio apartment off the highway and driving that shit 2004 puke-green Honda Accord—"

"Hey, what...?" Calderon mumbled. "How do you know all this? Have you been following me or something?"

"That's not important, Andrew," Prisha said. "What is important is, what's the number?"

"What?"

"We both know Geller took a payoff to dismiss the Luce case," Prisha said. "He did it once, he'll do it again. For the right number. I need you to find out what that number is."

Calderon leaned against the car door, away from Prisha and Pierre. His eyes bulged; his mouth hung agape. His face flushed red. He shook his head hypnotically.

"You like the ladies, don't ya, Andy?" Pierre asked.

Calderon turned to face Pierre; his eyes were now squinted almost shut. He started to speak, then stopped.

Pierre raised his hands in mock surrender. "Hey, man. No judgment. I like pretty ladies myself. But I don't have to pay for them like you do, Andy. What do ya think your boss, the commonwealth's attorney for the largest county in Virginia, would have to say about one of his homicide prosecutors entertaining escorts while his sweet little three-year-old daughter is sleeping across the hall?" Pierre's hand went back onto Calderon's shoulder. "That doesn't end well for you, Andy."

Calderon sputtered. No words came.

"All we need is the number," Prisha said. She placed her hand gently on his leg. "And a finder's fee for you, of course. I want this to work for everyone involved."

"I can't," Calderon mumbled. "I... I can't."

"Sure you can, Andrew," Prisha said with a bright smile. "Same as before. Luce goes down for the homicide. Doyle's his accomplice, and the woman—put something on her, too. Accessory after the fact or something. Use your imagination. I need arrest warrants on all of them, and we need them all in custody. Understand?"

Calderon held his face in his hands. Blew out a long breath.

"I don't know Geller that well. Not like this," Calderon said.

"Feel him out," Prisha said.

"He'll never go for it."

Prisha reached into her bag and pulled out a fat envelope. She handed it to Calderon. He hesitated but took it.

"What's this?" Calderon asked. He opened the flap and fingered the stack of one-hundred-dollar bills stuffed inside. Five thousand dollars in all.

"Just a little show of good faith," Prisha said with her open, big-toothed smile. "I know you can do this, Andrew."

Calderon lowered his head and tucked the envelope into the inside pocket of his jacket. He grabbed at the door handle and made to leave.

Prisha squeezed his leg tight. Calderon jumped.

"Don't let me down, Andrew." The big-toothed smile was gone. "I need the number. And I need it now."

CHAPTER TWENTY-THREE

MARCH 19, 2019
FRANK AND SARAH'S RENTED CONDO
BROOKINGS, OREGON

THE PIERCING RING OF A TELEPHONE WOKE ME FROM A deep sleep. I kept my secure phone on full volume on the nightstand next to the unregistered Glock 9mm in case they came for us in the middle of the night. I rubbed my eyes and grabbed it. 12:21 a.m. Sarah and I had been hiding out in Oregon for two years now, and the phone never rang this late at night. I knew before I even answered the call.

"Yeah," I answered. I sat up in bed and switched on the light. Sarah sat up too, wide-eyed and alert.

"You all right, Frankie?"

Quinn spoke in a rushed, breathless cadence I'd not heard from him before. My stomach clenched into a fist.

"Yeah, we're okay—"

"Sarah? She with you?" Quinn asked.

I glanced at Sarah. She had grabbed hold of my leg over the thin polyester blanket. She mouthed "Who is it?" several times.

"We're both here. What's wrong?"

"Quick. Put me on speaker."

I activated the speakerphone and held the cellphone between us, up by our heads.

"We're on speaker. Can you hear me, Quinn?" I asked.

"Sarah, you there?"

"I'm here, Quinn. What's going on?"

Quinn was breathing heavily. I heard the slam of a car door. An engine roared to life.

"Where are you?" I asked.

"On the road," Quinn said tersely. "We don't have much time, so I need you both to listen to me very closely—"

"Are you okay, Quinn?" Sarah asked, panic in her voice.

"They've got warrants on all of us!" I heard the screech of rubber on road. Sarah's fingernails dug into my leg. "The cops could be there any minute. You two have to get outta there. Now!"

"What?" Sarah stammered. "How?"

"Hewitt's murder," Quinn said. He grunted and cursed.

Sarah pulled her knees to her chest, wrapped her arms tight around her legs. "No... No..."

"Are you sure, Quinn?" I asked.

"Yes!" Quinn shouted. "We gotta go. Now."

"No..." Sarah repeated, shaking her head.

"A guy I know has a brother who's a BPD detective. He just called and told me his brother was at a cop bar tonight... They all got shit-faced, and another cop told him they had a murder warrant out for me."

"He was drunk," Sarah protested. "Maybe this guy got it wrong?"

"No," Quinn responded sharply. "The cop works with the FBI on the fugitive task force."

I turned to Sarah. She was shaking with fear, a look of wild desperation on her face.

"Maybe they don't know where we are?" I offered. "Maybe our IDs are still good?"

"They know where I live, Frankie!" Quinn shouted. "The cop told my friend the address and fucking number of my place in Beacon Hill. No one knew I was there. Just you two and a few of my guys."

I wondered if one of Quinn's guys had ratted him out.

"They got us on the phones," Quinn said before I could ask. "I think Nicole got sloppy. Which means they got Sarah's phone. Which means they got ours, Frankie."

The color drained from Sarah's face. Her mouth opened and closed like a guppy out of its bowl.

"Fuck," I mumbled. I knew they had us.

"No..." Sarah stammered again. "Can't be. We told Nicole to switch phones every month, just like us. I thought she was doing it."

"Yeah, well, she didn't," Quinn said. I gave Sarah's shoulder a squeeze. She needed it. "Burn your phones—both of you—after we hang up."

I told him we would.

"It's time to go," Quinn said. "Meet me in the new place at the spot. In the sun. Got it?"

We had worked out this plan in the event we ever had to bug out on short notice. An occasion just like this. It was coded such that anyone listening to our conversation, which I now had no doubt the FBI were, would have no idea what we were talking about. What Quinn had just told me was that we were to meet him in the new place (New York City) at the spot (Central Park, in front of the Shakespeare statue at mid-park at 66th Street) in the sun (at noon).

Quinn was on his way now. He had to drive four hours south from Boston, and he would be in Manhattan before sunrise. We had to drive the full three thousand miles across the country. And we had to start this drive now. Tonight. Quinn would give us a few days to get to New York, then take his place on a park bench at the Shakespeare statue every day at noon. He would wait exactly fifteen minutes and leave if we didn't show. Quinn would repeat this every day until our reunion. We would have no telephonic contact with him until then.

I told Quinn we understood.

"Got everything you need?" he asked.

Our bug-out bags were packed and stashed in the back of our closet. They were actually large-capacity backpacks. Mine black, hers teal green. Each contained a full set of new false ID, several prepaid cellphones and SIM cards, fifty thousand dollars in cash (small denominations and street-worn), one change of clothes, toiletries, light disguise (wigs, colored contacts, hat and dark glasses), and enough food and water for seventy-two hours. My pack also had a tactical knife, a baby Glock, and 9mm ammo.

"Yeah," I told Quinn, "we're good."

But we weren't good. Particularly Sarah.

Sarah took the phone from my hand. She spoke in a soft, hesitant voice.

"Are you sure, Quinn?" she asked. "Do we have to do this?"

Silence for a moment. Quinn cleared his throat.

"Yes, sweetheart," he said, his words slow and affectionate. "I'm afraid we do."

That ended the call.

I leapt out of bed and threw on some clothes. Sarah followed, moving slowly and robotically. We retrieved our backpacks from the back of the closet. I stepped to the bedroom window and fingered back the curtain a sliver. I searched the darkness for any signs of our enemy. All quiet.

I turned and saw Sarah shuffling towards the master bathroom, head down, dragging her backpack on the floor behind her. I reminded her we had toiletries in our packs. She kept going and trudged into the bathroom and out of sight. I told her to leave everything. That we had to go. Now. Sarah ran the bathroom faucet. Splashing sounds. I repeated my admonition. Told her we were out the door in three minutes.

I went into the living room, pack slung over one shoulder, my Glock tucked into my waistband. I flattened myself against the wall and peeked out the side window at the well-lit parking lot. I always parked our Volkswagen Passat under the lights and within view of this window. Everything looked normal. Nothing felt that way.

I took one final quick look around the condo that had been our home for two years. We had made a lot of good memories here. I knew how hard it would be for Sarah to leave this life. My eyes were momentarily drawn to a watercolor that hung slightly askew on the opposite wall, at the entry to the master bedroom. It was one of the few items Sarah had insisted we hang to brighten up the place. The painting depicted a sailboat in a sunny harbor, circled by seagulls. I had never really looked at it. The boat was sailing out of the harbor. Away from land and out to the open sea beyond.

A wave of anger flashed through me as I stared at the painting. Prisha Baari. She had been here all along, but I'd failed to see it. Oregon was never to be our safe harbor.

Sarah emerged from the bathroom, backpack slung over one shoulder. I stepped over to her and squeezed her shoulders with two outstretched arms. I studied her face and saw resignation. I asked her if she was ready to go and she nodded, head bowed.

I checked the door peephole, then opened the door a crack. Nothing. I stuck my head out and scanned the hallway. All clear. I grabbed Sarah's hand and led her down the hall to the stairwell. We swept down the three flights of stairs.

I hesitated at the solid metal exterior door. No way of knowing if a SWAT team stood, weapons drawn, on the other side. I took a deep breath and gripped Sarah's hand tightly. This was our Bonnie-and-Clyde moment. I threw the heavy door open and paused, shielding Sarah behind me. No gunshots. I scanned the parking lot and saw nothing.

I pulled Sarah across the pavement to our car. We tossed the backpacks into the back seat and jumped in. Our VW was registered in Sarah's old and now compromised false ID. We would have to replace it as soon as possible. For now, it would be our ride to freedom. I pulled out of the parking lot and checked my mirrors for headlights behind us. Nothing. We had bugged out clean.

Sarah released her seatbelt and turned completely around in her seat. Her face clouded as she watched the lights of our oceanside condo fade from view. She rolled back into her seat, eyes facing forward at what lay in the dark night beyond.

"I knew it wouldn't last." Sarah's voice was soft and flat. She would never see Oregon again.

New York City felt a long way away.

PART III

———

What does your conscience say?—'You should become the person you are.'
   —Friedrich Nietzsche

CHAPTER TWENTY-FOUR

MARCH 23, 2019
CENTRAL PARK; SHAKESPEARE STATUE
NEW YORK, NEW YORK

FRANK PAID THE CABBIE THE FIFTY-DOLLAR FARE, AND they both stepped out of the fetid back seat and into the din of Central Park East.

Sarah grimaced as she caught a glimpse of her reflection in the back window of the cab as it pulled away from the curb. Oregon Sarah, happy bohemian Sarah, was now dead. She looked down at her khaki slacks and sensible shoes and frowned. Gone were the flowing sundresses, velvet plum hair, and the bar piercing in her ear. Her new New York identity would not abide such whimsy. This new persona would be more mainstream, less memorable. Less Sarah. Her new identity separated her from Oregon more than did the three thousand miles they had traversed over the past three days.

The trip had pushed both Sarah and Frank to their limit. One drove while the other slept. East on I-80 most of the way. Sixteen hours a day. Interstate hotels at night. They'd reached Cheyenne, Wyoming, that first night. Twelve hundred miles from Brookings. The next morning, they'd found a local ask-no-questions used car dealership and bought a new car, a white 2015 Mazda 6. They'd spent fifteen grand cash for it. They couldn't risk trading in the VW, so they'd abandoned it, stripped off the plates, and left the keys in the ignition. They were confident the local car thieves would find it a good home.

Day two took them another twelve hundred miles. They'd collapsed late at night at a Days Inn outside Toledo, Ohio. Then on to New Jersey City, just outside of Manhattan, where they'd spent the night last night. They had been able to sleep past sunrise this morning before catching a PATH Red Line train to the World Trade Center Station. Then their fifty-dollar cab ride to Central Park.

The long drive was passed mostly in silence, interspersed with small talk. Neither Sarah nor Frank were prepared to discuss what had happened. Sarah grieved the loss of her Oregon life and the death of bohemian Sarah. The Kübler-Ross model provided for five stages of grief, popularly known by the acronym DABDA: denial, anger, bargaining, depression, and acceptance. Sarah had been in full denial when she'd received the late-night news from Quinn. This denial had given way to anger on the second day of their journey, somewhere outside Des Moines, Iowa. That anger had festered, then escalated all the way to New York. The woman who stood outside Central Park on this brisk spring morning was righteously pissed off.

Sarah slipped her new clean phone from her bag and checked it. They had plenty of time to reach the Shakespeare statue by noon. They walked north on Fifth Avenue, then turned in to Central Park just short of E 67th Street. She and Frank walked side by side in silence. Frank's hands were jammed deep in his jeans front pockets, hers in the pockets of her waist-length black leather jacket. They passed through the Olmstead Flower Bed, just south of Literary Walk. The tulips, pansies, and azaleas were not yet in bloom.

They found the statue of Shakespeare. It had been the first sculpture placed in the southern end of the park, to commemorate the 300th birthday of the Bard in 1864. Sarah and Frank stood before him now. He wore pantaloons and gazed down upon them from his high pedestal. Sarah had read most of Shakespeare's popular works and held him in reverence. This morning she felt nothing. She turned from him to find a bench and await the arrival of Quinn Doyle.

The biting wind and overcast skies kept most Manhattanites out of the park this morning. But with 1.6 million people stuffed into just twenty-two square miles of island, it was not as empty as Sarah had hoped. They found an empty bench thirty feet from the statue, close enough to observe Quinn's arrival, should he turn up as expected. For all she and Frank knew, Quinn was now in jail. Or worse.

Frank had his phone out, checking the time. He noticed Sarah looking over his shoulder and tilted the screen towards her. 11:51 a.m.

Sarah scanned the surrounding area and saw no sign of Quinn. She did notice an elderly woman alone on a bench, twenty feet opposite her in the shady vale. She had long silver hair and alabaster skin. Her lipstick was perhaps a shade too bright for a woman of her advanced age. She sat with perfect posture, gloved hands folded in her lap. The old woman stared right through Sarah. It made her uneasy, but she could not turn away from the old woman. She was dignified, shrouded in melancholy. Her loneliness palpable. Sarah gave the woman a polite, thin-lipped smile. The old woman acknowledged the gesture but failed to return it. Sarah looked down at her own hands, clasped in her lap.

She shuddered, pictured herself sitting on this same bench, forty years hence. Alone, and with her own shade of inappropriate red lipstick. Frank was not beside her, as he was now. He had been taken from her, and she had spent her last forty years mourning a life without him. It was Prisha Baari who would take Frank from her. Quinn, too. It was Prisha who would not stop until she took everything that mattered most to Sarah. She saw this clearly now. It was a personal violation. An unendurable defilement.

Sarah now felt what Frank felt. The weight he had carried these past two years for her. In haste, she had blamed Frank for the loss of their Oregon life. Punished him with her silence on their cross-country road trip. But now she understood. It wasn't Frank. He loved her. It was Prisha Baari. But for Prisha, none of this would have happened. But for Prisha, Frank would be next to her on that bench forty years from now. But for Prisha, she and Frank would walk hand in hand on the beach. In the sunshine, unafraid.

Sarah knew what she had to do.

She turned towards Frank on the bench. She took his face in her hands, looked deep into his green eyes. She kissed him.

"What was that for?" Frank said, and gave her a tentative smile.

"Thank you, Frank." She dropped her hands from his face and took tight hold of his hands. "Thank you for loving me. For choosing me over her."

Frank paused, cocked his head to one side. "You don't have to thank me for that."

"Yes, I do," Sarah said.

"Get a room, you two!" a voice called out.

Sarah looked, and there stood Quinn, smiling under sunglasses and a gray herringbone flat cap and matching scarf. Sarah bounced off the bench and into his arms. Quinn held her tight. Kissed her forehead when she finally released him. Frank and Quinn embraced, backslapping and grinning.

They took their seats on the bench. Quinn sat between Frank and Sarah. Sarah was glad to see the old woman had left. Perhaps their emotional reunion had been too much for her tired eyes.

Frank updated Quinn on their cross-country odyssey, and then Quinn filled them in on his own trip. As expected, he had been in New York for several days, staying at a hotel on the Upper East Side. He told them that the Boston Police and FBI had come for him the morning after he'd called them. Their arrest warrants were not yet public record, so as best Quinn could tell they were still sealed. He had paid his friend handsomely to keep his eyes and ears open for anything new. Quinn said he thought he was clean in New York, and then asked about them. Frank said they had spent the night in Jersey and taken a train and cab to this meet. Quinn nodded and said "Good."

That business concluded, they turned their attention to

the matter of Prisha Baari and what the available options might be. Quinn said there were only three things they could do now: one, go underground again, back into another fugitive life; two, turn themselves in to face their charges and fight their case; three, fight back.

He asked Frank and Sarah what they wanted to do. Both Quinn and Frank looked at Sarah. She held their eyes.

"We're gonna fight back," Sarah declared.

"We?" Frank asked.

"Yeah," Sarah responded. "All three of us."

The two men sat in stunned silence. Neither of them had expected that response. They tried to talk Sarah out of her decision. Laid out all the risks. Said if they went after Prisha there was no turning back. That it'd be either her or them. Someone was going to die.

Sarah listened politely, her lips pursed, resolute in her position. She had had enough.

Finally, she turned to Quinn. "So, what's next?" she asked matter-of-factly. "How're we gonna do this bitch?"

Frank's mouth fell open.

"Are you sure about this, Sarah?" Frank asked.

"Positive."

"Well, it's settled, then," Quinn said, wiping his hands. "I'm ready for this. And we both know Frank here's been pulling on his leash for two years." Quinn paused and turned to Sarah. "Now, Sarah. If you're gonna be involved in this, you'll have to do what I say. You got that?"

She nodded. Quinn accepted that as her word.

Over the next few minutes, Quinn laid out the plan. He would contact Gonzalez and have him contact Fares Abo to gauge whether the Saudis were still interested in their services. In the meantime, they would all rent apartments in

Manhattan and hide in plain sight among the masses. Finally, they all exchanged telephone numbers for their new clean phones, and Quinn reminded them to be extra careful. It wasn't just Prisha and her goons looking for them. The FBI was hunting them down now too.

They said their goodbyes, and then Quinn got to his feet, stretched, and strolled off into Central Park. Sarah and Frank watched him go in silence.

Frank turned on the bench to face Sarah.

"Where did all this come from?" he said gently. "We don't have to do this, you know." He took her hands. "I don't want you to do this for me, Sarah. It's too dangerous."

"I understand how hard it was for you to walk away from who you are," Sarah said. "And from what needed to be done. For a long time, I thought running away was the best thing for us. But I know now it was only the best thing for *me*. Running is rarely the right answer." She paused and looked at her lap. "I don't want to run anymore, Frank." She looked back up at him, met his gaze. "And I don't want you to either."

The emancipation of Frank Luce had begun.

Frank and Sarah left Central Park arm in arm. Sarah looked up at the Bard as they passed and recalled a line from one of her favorites, *The Merchant of Venice*:

I beseech you,
Wrest once the law to your authority:
To do a great right, do a little wrong.

CHAPTER TWENTY-FIVE

MARCH 26, 2019
PRISHA'S CONDO; MANHATTAN (UNION SQUARE)
NEW YORK, NEW YORK

KARLSSON RODE THE ELEVATOR UP TO THE THIRTY-fourth floor. The doors opened. He gritted his teeth and stepped out onto the plush blue-green carpet. He walked the length of the hallway, catching snippets of conversations and whiffs of fried food from behind the locked doors he passed. He arrived at the corner unit and knocked. Shifted his weight and waited.

Prisha greeted him in flannel drawstring pants and a white sweatshirt, a coffee mug in her hand. Her hair was up, and she wore big black-framed eyeglasses that softened her face. Karlsson followed her inside and double-locked the door behind him.

The condo was a corner unit that offered long skyline

views to the south, east, and north. It was appointed with flaxen oak hardwood floors and white plastered walls. The floor plan was basic: one long living room on one side, a master and a spare bedroom on the other side, and a small galley kitchen and foyer in between. Its key attraction was that it was centrally located in the heart of downtown Manhattan, a stone's throw from coveted neighborhoods like Chelsea and Greenwich Village. To Karlsson, though, the condo itself was unimpressive. In any other city in the USA, a place like this would have been occupied by a young blue-collar family just starting out. Here in Manhattan, these twelve hundred square feet of nothing special cost 2.25 million dollars.

Prisha could have her condo. Manhattan, too. Karlsson loathed the city as much as Prisha loved it.

He followed Prisha through the foyer and into the large rectangular living room. At the far end of the rectangle sat a deep blue sofa and patterned upholstered chairs arranged opposite in a sitting area. The other end, nearest the kitchen, had a four-top dark oak dining table that Prisha was now using as a work station. Floor-to-ceiling windows covered the east and south walls.

Prisha sat down at the table behind her open MacBook and gathered up her papers, which were scattered across the table. Karlsson sat in the chair opposite her and pushed back from the table to give himself more distance from his boss. Prisha ignored him as she finished scribbling something on a legal pad. She tore the page loose and stuffed it inside a red folder, which she slid to one side of the table. Only then did she address her visitor.

"So... Henrik." Prisha slammed her MacBook shut. "Tell me what happened with the arrests the other night."

The sarcasm and icy stare told Karlsson this conversation would not go well. Fuck it. He would tell Prisha the truth. Something she didn't want to hear right now.

"You partnered up with that dipshit Calderon and Darius behind my back. That's what happened."

Prisha's face flushed, and she squinted her eyes half-closed as she absorbed Karlsson's response. She swallowed her anger and responded.

"Perhaps I wouldn't have had to do this if you had been more successful in finding Luce and his two amigos," Prisha said, her voice dripping with sarcasm.

Karlsson didn't answer this salvo. Prisha brushed his silence aside with a sweep of her hand and changed tack.

"But I didn't call you up here to fix blame, Henrik." Prisha gave him her shy, conciliatory smile. He'd seen that smile work on others many times before. He wasn't buying it now.

"We have to find these three."

Karlsson nodded.

"Where do you think they are now?"

"I don't know." Karlsson shrugged. "The FBI hit both their places but got nothing. They're all in the wind. Under new aliases by now."

"What happened?"

"My guess is a leak. Someone on the task force probably told Doyle we were coming. He was in Boston with them, and he's got the most connections. Or it could have been your boy Calderon or someone in the Commonwealth's Attorney's Office." Karlsson shrugged again. "Could've been anyone."

Prisha shot to her feet. She banged the table as she rose, sloshing coffee over the rim of her mug and onto the tabletop.

She snatched her mug and strode into the living room, where she stood silent in front of the east-facing window. She sipped her coffee, her back to Karlsson, who remained seated. He leaned back in his chair and studied Prisha. She had lost some weight since last he'd seen her. Her raven hair was piled on top of her head. A couple of long strands had unraveled and fallen loose down her back.

Prisha turned on him, her eyes wild. "I want you to kidnap Luce's mother. That'll flush him out."

"Prisha—I'm not going to kidnap anyone's mother."

"His fucking ex-wife, then! Or his little jail buddy. I don't care who. Someone that'll make him stick his head above ground." Prisha eyed him coldly. "Then we cut it off!"

"The FBI's involved now. They found Luce's car in Wyoming, which means they crossed state lines. Unlawful flight to avoid prosecution. UFAP." Karlsson shook his head. "We can't just go kidnapping people, Prisha. You're a senator now, remember?"

Prisha grimaced, flared her nostrils.

"What about Doyle? Maybe we go after some of his crew in Boston? Smoke him out. We get him, and Luce and his girlfriend will follow. What about that?"

Karlsson chuckled to himself. His boss was unraveling.

"We're not going to start a war with the Irish mob in Boston, Prisha. That's worse than your kidnap-the-mother idea."

"Well," Prisha snapped, "what the hell do you propose we do? You're my head of security, Henrik. Do your job!"

Karlsson bit his tongue and let this insult go unanswered. He paused until he saw Prisha was ready to listen.

"We stay the course," he said. "Use your influence at FBI to get them to prioritize the UFAP case against Luce. We'll keep monitoring the friends and family. The ex-wife got lazy the first time. She'll do it again. Or someone else will. They can't hide forever. Either we'll get 'em, or the FBI will. Now's not the time to panic, Prisha."

Prisha responded to this chastisement with an icy stare, then excused herself and whisked past him and into the kitchen.

Karlsson listened. Running water, the slosh of a coffee pot being rinsed and refilled. He reached across the table and slid Prisha's red folder in front of him. Kitchen drawers sliding open. Karlsson opened the folder. On top lay the paper Prisha had been scribbling on when he'd arrived. Refrigerator door opening. His eyes quickly scanned the notes, written on lined yellow paper in blue pen. Looping, large, printed letters distinctive to Prisha. Refrigerator door slamming shut. Cream pouring. Karlsson's stomach knotted as he read down the page:

- POTUS 2020 (me and ODY)
- control SCOTUS; ignore Congress
- fascism; secularism
- Saudi = 51st state; nationalize oil; punish
- National Theater; Nero
- Catherine the Great
- my time is now!
- Luce? Henrik?

Coffee grinder. Karlsson's eyes lingered on his name, particularly the question mark that followed it. Gurgle of coffee maker. Karlsson closed the folder, then spun it around and slid it back to its original spot on the table. It clipped the edge of the puddle of spilled coffee, and he watched with dismay as the corner of the red folder went dark. He straightened the folder and pulled his arms back as Prisha emerged from the kitchen holding a fresh mug of coffee; she didn't offer him any. She gave him a what-are-you-up-to look, which Karlsson returned with a tight smile. He laced his fingers together in his lap under the table. Squeezed hard and held his breath.

Prisha resumed her seat at the table opposite Karlsson. She pulled out a dish towel and wiped up the coffee spill. She was slow and methodical, swirling the towel in a clock-wise motion as if polishing the table.

"Okay, Henrik. We do it your way." Prisha spoke into the dish towel, eyes downcast. She folded the towel into a tight square and placed it at the corner of the table, then straight-ened her red folder. Karlsson thought Prisha looked at it a beat too long. The small dark spot appeared enormous and seemed to be growing.

At last, she looked up at him. Gave him her big, toothy smile—a smile with a big question mark at the end of it. Karlsson wondered whether the question mark beside his name referred to the matter at hand, as in what were they to do about Frank Luce. Or whether it was his alone, as in what was Prisha to do with Henrik Karlsson.

His ears filled with a ringing like tinnitus. His vision narrowed on the smiling woman across the table from him. A woman he had known for many years but had now truly seen for the first time. He saw that the smile did not reach Prisha's cold, dark eyes. The pitiless, flat eyes of a shark. These shark eyes were now on him. Karlsson would never again be at ease in Prisha's presence. A line had been crossed.

He kept his expression carefully neutral as she scrutinized him. Had Prisha read his mind? Did she know his doubts? Had she noticed the stain on her red folder? That it hadn't been in the exact same place when she returned from the kitchen? And what would she do if she knew his heart? This was the only question he did not have to ponder: Prisha would kill him without hesitation, he knew, if his death best suited her interests.

Karlsson felt the weight of the Glock in his waistband. Maybe he should beat her to it.

"What's wrong, Henrik?" Prisha asked, a quizzical look on her face. "You look like you've seen a ghost."

Not a ghost. A monster.

CHAPTER TWENTY-SIX

April 17, 2019
Saudi Arabian Consulate General
New York, New York

I reached for the heavy glass door and held it open for Quinn. He entered the building and I followed. We took the stairs to the fifth floor and found the suite that housed the Saudi Arabian Consulate General.

The consulate was located on Second Avenue at East 46th Street, one block from United Nations Headquarters. The glass and steel high-rise in which it sat was nondescript enough. The only indications of its diplomatic tenant were the vehicle barriers that ringed the building.

Gerry Gonzalez had arranged this meeting. Neither Quinn nor I were happy about the venue, but he said the Saudis would only meet with us at their consulate.

A beautiful Arab woman in hybrid-Western dress met us

at the consulate door and escorted us to our seats in the waiting room. Then she took our driver's licenses. She excused herself and disappeared with our identification behind a fortified, locked door. I felt naked sitting in this place. Quinn game me a reassuring nod. It didn't help much.

We had arrived at the designated time, 9:00 a.m. The Saudis kept us on ice in the waiting room for almost thirty minutes. Doing who knows what with our IDs. Finally, the same beautiful woman emerged from the door and summoned us into the inner sanctum of the consulate. She put us in a small, windowless office with a single table and chairs. I couldn't see the cameras but felt their presence. She asked us if we wanted anything. We politely declined her hospitality. The last thing we intended to do was drink from any open container in this place. The Saudis were not our drinking buddies just yet.

We sat silent for another twenty minutes before the door again opened. A sleek Arab man, about my age and size, entered the room and took a seat opposite us at the small round table. The man was impeccably dressed and groomed. His wide-set eyes flicked like a snake's tongue between me and Quinn.

The man handed each of us back our false driver's licenses and introduced himself as Fares Abo. He said he was billeted to the consulate and that on the matter under discussion today he was authorized to speak on behalf of the Kingdom of Saudi Arabia and the Saudi Royal Family. Abo folded his hands on the table. He moved and spoke with an elegance that I found disquieting.

"Gentlemen, what brings you to our consulate today?" Abo asked.

"Concrete," Quinn responded.

"Concrete" was the code word Abo had provided Gonzalez for us to use for this initial meeting. Gonzalez had instructed us to extend the metaphor, so now we were both simple concrete men seeking contract work in the Kingdom. This meeting was being captured on high-resolution audio and video by the Saudis—their insurance policy, I guessed. The tradecraft was necessary for plausible deniability. And simply good etiquette and hygiene among criminal conspirators just getting acquainted.

The corners of Abo's mouth curled ever so slightly. He motioned with his eyes for Quinn to continue.

"I heard there was good concrete work to be done," Quinn said.

"There may be such work," Abo replied. "For the right person. The Kingdom is a vibrant place, and there is always much work to be done."

"Good," Quinn said. "We're ready to work."

Abo leaned back in his seat. He studied both of us. His little smirk returned.

"We had need of some concrete work this January past. Regrettably, you failed to bid on that job."

"Yeah, about that," Quinn said. "We considered submitting a bid on the project, but the timing just wasn't right."

"What has changed?"

"Well... my nephew here," Quinn jerked a thumb at me, "thought he might be out of the concrete business. But it's in our blood."

"Ah, but men have many passions, do they not?" Abo asked.

"Not me," Quinn said. "I've only ever been good at one thing. Concrete. Been doing it now for over fifty years. It's all I've ever known."

"And what of you?" Abo turned to me. "Do you love concrete as your uncle does?"

"I've recently reacquired my taste for it," I said.

"And your experience?"

"I worked at another big concrete company, learned the trade, before I came back to my uncle's shop," I said.

"How long?" Abo asked me.

"I apprenticed for four years. OJT. Then five years full-time in the field." He got my West Point and Afghanistan combat tour references. Or at least he appeared to.

"And then?"

"I took a few years off," I said. I thought it best to leave my homeless wanderings off my resume.

"I see." Abo stroked his chin. "But now I see you have returned to the concrete business. Maybe it's in your blood as well. As with your uncle."

"Maybe," I said.

"A chip off the old block," Quinn said.

"Yes—indeed." Abo smiled openly. His teeth were tobacco stained and too small for his mouth. He leaned towards me. "We are still in need of good concrete men. But tell me—why do you want this contract?"

"I know the project very well," I said. "I've studied the plans and have become quite enamored with this particular project."

"It's a big job. The consortium I represent is very anxious for this work to be done quickly. And to perfection. Are you sure you have the resources and personnel to fulfill the terms of such a contract?"

"My company's reputation speaks for itself. We'll get the job done," Quinn said. "I'm sure we wouldn't be here speaking with you if the gentlemen you represent didn't think us up to the job."

"I vetted you both, and your company, in January last. During our exploratory period pursuant to the previous contract—for which you chose not to submit." Abo recrossed his legs under the table. "As you stated. Your bona fides are impeccable. Your company's history and experience are impressive. We have no doubt of your ability to complete the contract to our mutual satisfaction."

"Same terms?" Quinn asked.

"Of course."

"When do you need your concrete poured?" I asked.

"Ah," Abo said. "Unfortunately, we are behind schedule with this particular project, I'm afraid. All our efforts to date have failed. We would need you to complete the contract at once." He looked us both dead in the eye. "Time is of the essence. Do you understand?"

Quinn and I said we did.

"So, gentlemen, are you once again interested in this contract?"

"Yes," I blurted out.

Abo then looked to Quinn. He nodded.

"Very good." Abo clasped his hands together. "A man will contact you with further details. He has been working on this project since its inception and has gathered much information that I am sure you will find invaluable." Abo rose to his feet and straightened, then buttoned his suit jacket. "We shall not meet again, gentlemen. Do you have any further questions of me?"

Quinn and I shook our heads no.

"Very well, then," Abo said.

He extended his hand. We both stood and shook it in turn.

"I wish you both well." We nodded. "And may I remind you, gentlemen—concrete waits for no one."

With that parting wisdom, Abo turned on his heel and left the room.

The beautiful woman returned and escorted us out, down the corridor, and to a private elevator. She inserted a key card, and the doors opened with a ding. She waved us into the elevator like a game show hostess, then stepped inside after us. We rode down to the ground floor in silence.

My knees buckled as the weight of what we had just done settled on my shoulders. We had just agreed to kidnap a sitting U.S. senator and deliver her to a hostile foreign power for thirty million tax-free dollars. Although tax evasion would be the least of my worries from here on out. A good part of me wished this contract called for Prisha's execution, not abduction. I took solace knowing that what the Saudis had in mind for Prisha would be much worse than the quick death a few merciful bullets to the head would provide. I was surprised to feel no joy or euphoria at finally being unleashed to seek my retribution. All I felt was a stead-fast resolve to get the job done. My aim was to keep Sarah safe, and to ride off into the sunset with our cut of the thirty million in our pocket.

I checked Quinn out of the corner of my eye. He stared up at the elevator numbers. His face bore no evidence of what he might be thinking.

The elevator thumped to a stop. Our escort keyed the door open, thanked us for our visit and gestured us out of her elevator. We strolled across the lobby and onto Second Avenue, into the din of the city. I squinted against the morning sun. Flinched at the blaring of taxicab horns. I fought for balance on rubbery legs.

Quinn and I walked briskly a couple of blocks north up Second Avenue. I started to settle down a bit. We exchanged looks at a cross-street at the end of a long city block and burst into nervous laughter.

"Well, that's fucking that, Frankie," Quinn said with a chuckle.

"Yup," I responded. "We're in it now."

Quinn nodded; the smile slid from his face.

"You think they're serious?" I asked.

"Gerry got them to pay five mil up front. That should happen by close of business today. When that five mil hits our bank account, then they're serious."

"You think they will?"

Quinn paused and considered it. "Yeah, I do."

We slowed to let the two people striding up behind us pass.

"Thirty million is pocket change to these guys," Quinn said in a hushed voice. "And they sure want Prisha bad. That much is clear."

"You think we can trust them?"

"I don't know," Quinn said. "They could try to screw us out of the rest of the twenty-five mil. We'll wait on our five today. If they send it, they'll probably pay us the remaining twenty-five when we turn Prisha over. And if they don't, we'll kill her." Quinn turned to me and smiled wide. "Course, we do that, they'll likely kill us too."

"Nice," I said.

I wondered if the Saudis wanted Prisha or ODYSSEUS. Probably both, based on the timing of their original approach to Gonzalez. It appeared they were certainly unhappy with

Prisha leaving CIA for the Senate. The partnership of convenience we had just consummated with the Saudis felt dirty. A wave of patriotism washed over me. Thinking of Prisha Baari not as a sitting U.S. senator but as the psychopathic pile of shit she was made me feel better.

And what of ODYSSEUS? Prisha had weaponized it, not me. That type of thing can't be kept secret forever. The ODYSSEUS genie was already out of her bottle. And she was never going back in.

"You think the Saudis already have ODYSSEUS?" I asked.

"Some version of it, anyway," Quinn speculated. "No telling who has it by now. Prisha. The U.S. The Saudis. Shit, even we have a copy of it."

"Think the Saudis will use it?" I asked.

"ODYSSEUS?"

"Yeah."

"Sure."

"Against the U.S.?"

Quinn nodded. "Probably. Yeah." He cleared his throat and spat. "Countries, like men, are ultimately guided by self-interest."

I cursed under my breath.

"Remember, Frankie. The enemy of our enemy is our friend."

CHAPTER TWENTY-SEVEN

April 24, 2019–July 24, 2019
Prisha Baari abduction preparations
New York, New York

The five million dollars was deposited as instructed in the account Sarah had set up in the Cayman Islands. The Saudis were serious. It was time to get to work.

Sarah, Quinn and I drove to Boston to recruit our team. We used all Quinn's guys, people he knew and trusted. Handshakes were made and money was passed. Quinn, his right-hand man, Finn O'Neill, and I would be the abduction team. Quinn and I would be the gunmen. O'Neill, being the biggest and strongest, would go hands-on with Prisha when the time came. The driver would be the same Philly guy we had used for the bodega job, the night I'd shot Henrik Karlsson. That had been a hot extraction, and Philly guy had got all of us out of there alive. Quinn said he was the best in the business.

Within two days of the deposit, a man did contact Quinn via Gerry Gonzalez. Just as Fares Abo had said he would. Quinn and I met the man at a midtown deli. He was in the Saudi Arabian Army and carried himself with the quiet confidence of a special operator. He was tall and lanky, with a dour countenance. He had lost his right eye in combat and had a dark prosthetic eye in its place, which caused him to blink compulsively. The man's Saudi name was too long and difficult to pronounce. I nicknamed him Dead Eye.

It turned out Dead Eye had been surveilling Prisha in the States for months. He was a wealth of information. He provided us with addresses for Prisha's Georgetown townhouse and New York condo, as well as her New York and DC Senate offices. He also gave us copies of his detailed surveillance logs. We used these to establish Prisha's discernible patterns.

In early May 2019, while the rest of the world was distracted by Baby Archie, Prince Harry and Meghan Markle's first child, Quinn's team had started their own surveillance of U.S. Senator Prisha Baari. The surveillance team comprised Quinn, O'Neill, me and a handful of O'Neill's guys. At her insistence, Sarah did some shifts as well. Mostly in New York. I even called on Duckie a few times when we were in a pinch and needed a quick eyes-on-target in the District.

As a U.S. senator, Prisha traveled frequently between Washington, DC, and New York City. She traveled by various modes of transportation: commercial airlines; Amtrak Acela trains; private vehicle and driver. As a minor congressional member, Prisha was not entitled to a government security detail. She had hired a private five-man security detail as soon as she announced her Senate bid, and had added to this team when she won her seat. And these guys were good. Mostly former Israeli and Eastern European ex–special forces types.

By mid-June there were one million protestors in the streets of Hong Kong. And we had all the intelligence we needed for Prisha's abduction. From June forward we mostly used the advanced electronic equipment already put in place by the Saudis to monitor Prisha's movements, augmented with sporadic hands-on work.

Analyzing Dead Eye's surveillance logs and comparing them to our own proved illuminating. First, the logs were largely consistent and demonstrated Prisha to be a woman of habit. A bad habit we planned to exploit. Next, Prisha's security detail was tighter and more aggressive both in Washington, DC, and when she was on official travel. The best opportunity for us to abduct her would be during one of her personal trips to New York City; she took along only three security staff for such trips—two body men and a driver. And oftentimes it was a mix of men who had not previously worked together as a cohesive team. These New York trips were supposed to be fun. Prisha relaxed on these trips, and this relaxed attitude infected her security detail.

Dead Eye had emphasized that Prisha liked to attend a Broadway musical about once a month and that she appeared most at ease at the theater. And sure enough, we had tailed her to a musical in May, and again in late June. On both these occasions Prisha had entered the theater alone while her detail waited outside. This waiting dulled their senses just enough. We noticed they got a little lackadaisical on her pickup after the show. This would be our best opportunity.

It was decided. We would abduct Prisha Baari when she attended her next Broadway musical.

CHAPTER TWENTY-EIGHT

July 25, 2019
The Al Hirschfeld Theatre; Broadway
New York, New York

Quinn Doyle's phone vibrated in his hand. He looked at it and his face went dark.

"She's coming out. Let's go."

I rode an adrenaline spike as I slapped at the door handle of the late-model silver Ford Taurus. Philly guy had us parked on West 44th Street, one block south of our target and facing east. Finn O'Neill was in the front seat and was the first one out of the car. Quinn and I were both in the back and we bailed out in unison, me into West 44th Street and Quinn curbside. The three of us grouped up and marched down West 44th. Then a left onto Eighth Avenue.

I slipped my hand under my shirt and felt the weapon snugged into the holster tight against my abdomen. I had chosen a SIG Sauer P365 9mm with three extended twelve-round magazines. One in the gun, the other two clanging together in the left front pocket of my cargo pants. I figured one way or another I'd never make it to that thirty-sixth round tonight. I was a better shot than that and suspected my adversaries were as well. It takes only one well-placed round to kill a man. Or a woman.

O'Neill and Quinn swept the sidewalk clean as they walked shoulder to shoulder, people giving way as they approached. I followed tight to their rear and covered our backs. We continued a hundred feet north on Eighth Avenue. Then a quick left onto West 45th Street, where all the drama would unfold. Our strides quickened as we neared the target. Apex predators on the hunt.

Tonight was the Broadway opening for *Moulin Rouge* at the Al Hirschfeld Theatre on West 45th Street in midtown Manhattan. Prisha couldn't resist. *Moulin Rouge* was one of the most highly regarded Broadway musicals of the season. It would go on to outsell *Hamilton* and become one of the most popular Broadway musicals of all time. She had to be here tonight. Which meant we did too.

Two members of our team, a man and woman posing as a couple, had followed Prisha into the theater. They watched her watching the musical, then text-messaged Quinn and put us on the move. The couple were armed but instructed to stay in the background. The plan was for Quinn, O'Neill and me to approach Prisha. Quinn and I would take out the security team, and O'Neill had Prisha. I had learned in Afghanistan that simple, audacious plans, aggressively executed without hesitation, were often what won the battle. I hoped that would be the case tonight.

Opening night was packed, as we had expected. Parked

cars flanked either side of the one-way street, which left only a narrow strip of pavement in the center of the street for moving traffic. We approached the theater from the opposite side of the street. It came into view at mid-block. A marquee over the theater's awning had been constructed for opening night and proclaimed "Moulin Rouge!" in big red letters. Below this and running horizontal along the bottom of the awning were the words "Truth—Beauty—Freedom—Love."

"Truth—Beauty—Freedom—Love." I vividly remembered reading this to myself as we approached the theater. As things turned out, those words would consecrate this ground. And I would honor them for the rest of my life.

We fanned out three abreast and crossed West 45th Street at the Japanese sushi restaurant. Much of the crowd had already left the theater and were making their way down the sidewalk, which was lined with large oak trees. People were smiling and happy, chattering about the musical. No one paid any attention to the three of us.

It was a sweltering, overcast night. A three-quarter moon hid behind dark clouds. A single bead of sweat ran down my spine. I wiped my forehead with the back of my hand. The street stink fermented in the humidity. The air was heavy and odorous as a soiled blanket. We reached the other side of the street and took our positions just west of the theater. We stood, Quinn at our center, in front of a comedy club as we awaited our quarry. Our night began in front of a damn comedy club. Another thing I'll always remember.

We stood in silence, each of us knowing what had to be done. I wondered how I would feel being three feet from Prisha with a loaded gun in my hands. We had promised the Saudis we would abduct Prisha, not kill her, and that we would hand her over very much alive. Not my preference.

Quinn knew this, and this was the real reason he'd put O'Neill on Prisha. Sure, O'Neill was bigger and stronger than me, but neither one of us would have any problem subduing Prisha. I'd guessed, though, that no one on the team was willing to risk the remaining twenty-five million by putting me in direct contact with her.

Quinn and I were the guns tonight. We each had our assigned detail member to worry about. I glanced at Quinn. He gave me a tight smile and said we had this. I nodded back. O'Neill was dialed in, eyes forward, fingers twitching. I went back inside my head and mouthed the words to myself: no hesitation; element of surprise; execute.

Prisha appeared out of nowhere. Standing outside the theater under the awning, her two body men at her side. *Shit.* On her other two Broadway nights, she had walked out of the theater alone and her detail had picked her up curbside. This was what we had expected tonight. We had counted on that few-second delay between her exit and pickup.

O'Neill and I looked to Quinn for his call. He didn't hesitate. He simply said "Let's do it."

We strode up to Prisha. My hand slid under my shirt, and I secured my grip on my gun. Pulled it a half-inch out of the bottom of my holster. I had the guy to Prisha's left. Quinn had the guy on her right. The black Suburban had not yet arrived curbside.

My guy saw me at about ten feet. His eyes widened, his mouth a big round circle. He was screaming. I heard nothing. I drew my weapon from my waistband. Raised it as I closed the distance between us. He was drawing now too, from a side belt holster he wore under his sports jacket. He canted his torso and swept his jacket clear with his shooting hand. That gave me all the time I needed.

No hesitation. Execute. I took another step forward and shot him twice. First shot to the chest. The second shot to the face at point blank range. He dropped to the sidewalk. Dead.

A muffled shot. Not mine. Prisha's second bodyguard dropped to the sidewalk. Quinn's guy.

O'Neill leapt forward and snatched Prisha with two strong arms. He lifted her off the ground by the shoulders. I remember her feet fluttering in the air. Raven hair flying as she thrashed.

I saw movement in my peripheral vision. People fleeing, dropping to the ground. Slow motion. The same O-ringed mouths as the man I'd just killed.

It was my own private ballet. Silent and slow.

That all ended with a piercing crack. The report of a rifle. I heard this clearly. Amplified. Like I was standing right next to the shooter.

A flash to my left. I whirled around. Quinn dropped to the sidewalk. A high-velocity rifle round had sliced dead center through Quinn's Level IIIa ballistic vest. The same one O'Neill and I wore.

O'Neill screamed for Quinn. My hearing had fully returned now. O'Neill spun like a top as I heard the second sniper's round explode. We learned later that this shot impacted O'Neill's vest at a life-saving angle—high, at shoulder level. It was a grazing wound that would heal in time.

Prisha squirmed from O'Neil's grasp after he'd been shot. I helplessly watched her scramble away down the sidewalk.

I dropped to my knees at Quinn's side, my own screaming in my ears now. Blood flowed freely from his chest wound. His eyes were wide. He tried to speak but was choking up blood. I raised his head off the sidewalk.

O'Neill swooped in and scooped Quinn up in his arms.

Another sniper's shot. It kicked up a cloud of concrete dust six inches to my left. We were taking rounds from across the street, atop a fifteen-foot brick platform in the cut between the sushi place and the adjoining high-rise next door. The platform where the building's ventilation systems were located. The shooter was using it as concealment.

The black Suburban sped past me down West 45th Street, careening off parked cars. Metal screeched. People were screaming, running. The Suburban skidded to a stop in the middle of the street. Prisha jumped in and it sped off, engine roaring.

I pointed across the street and pushed O'Neill in that direction. I slipped in the large slick of Quinn's blood and almost went down. I remember how neon-red it looked. Glowing. Lifeless.

We crossed the street to neutralize the sniper's line of fire. I heard sirens in the distance, approaching rapidly. I told O'Neill we had to get the hell out of here.

We ran down the sidewalk towards where we had left Philly guy and the car. O'Neill was in front, Quinn cradled in his arms. His head was hanging and bobbing to one side.

I covered our retreat. More cracks of the sniper's rifle. We were running away from the sniper on his side of the street, partially obscured by those large oak trees. I returned suppression fire to keep him pinned down. I did two magazine changes and shot my last mag empty to lock back. All thirty-six rounds down range. Rifle rounds thudded into the parked cars on either side of 45th Street. Car alarms wailed behind us. We kept running.

The Ford Taurus screeched around the corner as we approached Eighth Avenue. Philly guy screamed for us to get in. I popped the back door of the sedan open. O'Neill laid Quinn in the back, then went to get in beside him. I grabbed his shoulder. Told him to take the front seat. He did. I slid into the back with Quinn. I lifted his head up. Placed it in my lap. We sped down the street. Philly guy stared in his rear-view mirror as the sirens approached.

We took a few sharp turns that banged me and Quinn around in the back seat. I cursed Philly guy. He cursed me back.

Finn spun in his seat and looked at Quinn. We both knew it was bad.

"They had a fucking sniper!" O'Neill screamed. "A fucking *sniper!*"

"We gotta get him to a hospital," I shouted. "Now."

O'Neill nodded. "Quinn. Hang in there. We're gonna get you to a hospital."

I yelled at Philly guy to step on it.

Silence.

I yelled it again. Louder.

Quinn's face was ashen. I touched it with the back of my hand. His skin was cold and clammy. He was in and out of consciousness.

I pulled my gun and pointed it at Philly guy. I told him to drive to the hospital or I'd kill him. He turned his head right into the barrel of my 9mm. He didn't know it was empty. He gave Quinn a quick look and kept driving. We all knew the hospitals were the first place the cops would check. O'Neill and I didn't care. It was apparent to me that Philly guy did.

Quinn started to sputter and choke. He was trying to

speak. I told him to keep quiet, that we'd be at the hospital soon. He ignored me and continued to choke on his own blood. I raised his head up off my lap as high as I could. He cleared his passage with a big spew of bright red blood.

Quinn said something, in a raspy voice barely above a whisper. I couldn't hear over the yelling from the front seat. O'Neill telling Philly guy to go to the hospital. Philly guy saying they can't.

I dropped my ear as close to Quinn's mouth as I could. His head was still in my hands, raised on my lap.

I heard Quinn swallow. Gasp in pain.

"I... I love you Frankie," Quinn stammered. "You've been like a son to me. I..." Quinn went silent.

"I love you too," I whispered to him. Choking on my own words. Tears streaming down my face.

"I never meant..." Quinn spit up. Tried to get a breath to continue. "...never meant to hurt you." His eyes rolled shut.

"What? What do you mean, Quinn?" I shook him gently.

Quinn's eyes slowly opened. He raised his head with his last ounce of strength and locked eyes with me.

"Arthur!" Quinn bellowed. The exertion caused his head to slump in my hands.

A hot blade sliced though my gut at the sound of my father's name. He had been a member of Quinn's crew many years ago. Quinn and I had not spoken of him since he was murdered in the streets of Boston when I was eight years old.

Quinn reached up and gripped my wrist with his right hand. He spat up more blood and was trying to clear his throat. Raspy coughing. I elevated his head some more.

Quinn looked at me for the last time.

"I had to, Frankie." A tear leaked from the corner of his eye. "I'm sorry." His voice trailed off to a whisper.

Quinn exhaled abruptly. His eyes went wide. His body went slack, and his head lolled to one side. I laid his head back in my lap. Gently closed his eyes. Eyes that had seen enough for one lifetime.

Quinn Aidan Doyle, a son of South Boston, died in the back seat of a silver Ford Taurus on a hot summer night in New York City. Two weeks shy of his seventy-first birthday.

CHAPTER TWENTY-NINE

July 26, 2019
Gallagher Funeral Home
South Boston, Massachusetts

I cradled Quinn in my arms. Finn O'Neill lifted the Hyundai's trunk and I placed him in. I positioned him on his side facing away from me, in the fetal position. I wished I had something to cover his body with. We stood looking down at the man we'd both loved as a father. O'Neill stiffened and made the sign of the cross, then slammed the trunk shut and cursed under his breath. We would avenge what had happened tonight. But we couldn't do that from prison. Or the grave.

We had staged the second car, a black Hyundai Sonata, in Midtown, six blocks south of the theater on West 38th Street. Good thing too. There had been plenty of witnesses to the bloodbath tonight. The cops were surely already looking for a late-model silver Ford Taurus. Inside the Hyundai were more ammo, a change of clothes, and light disguises. Anything to throw off eyewitness descriptions.

We changed clothes. Reloaded and hid our guns under the seats. We ditched our body armor and clothes in the bloody Taurus. I tossed O'Neill my t-shirt. He balled it up and pressed it tight to his shoulder wound to stop the bleeding.

The plan was to submit to any NYPD car stop or road-block. We'd hand over our fake IDS and try to talk our way out. We would only start shooting if things broke bad. We had to get Quinn back to Southie.

O'Neill took Quinn's death as any soldier did a fallen comrade in the heat of battle. He absorbed the initial shock and stayed in the fight. I did the same. The grief and heart-break would come later. When we were both ready to let it in.

I called Sarah as we sped towards Bryant Park and our Midtown apartment. She was anxious for news. I told her there was a problem and to pack an overnight bag. We would pick her up in five minutes. She asked questions I didn't have time to answer. I told her to hurry, that I'd explain in the car. I smelled her fear over the phone. She knew something was very wrong.

Sarah was waiting for us in front of our apartment building when we pulled up, clutching her overnight bag in front of her with both hands. She got into the Hyundai next to me and behind Philly guy. We sped east towards FDR Drive. Then north to the Bronx. We had to get off this island as fast as we could.

Sarah dropped her bag at her feet. Her wide eyes wandered around the Hyundai's interior, then back to me.

"Did you get her? Where's Quinn?"

The look on my face answered her questions. Sarah started to tremble. Her breathing was rapid and short.

"Where's Quinn?" she shrieked. "Where's Quinn, Frank?"

A wave of nausea washed over me. My stomach lurched. I swallowed the bile down. The desperation in Sarah's eyes stabbed at my heart. I reached out and took her hands in mine.

"He's gone, Sarah."

———

It rained all through Connecticut. The metronome of the wipers against the windshield was the only sound for miles and miles. Philly guy drove the whole way without a word. O'Neill got on his phone when we crossed into the Bronx. He made all the necessary calls to circle the wagons for when we got to South Boston. O'Neill helped me with Sarah for a while. We told her the white lies one does in these situations. That everything would be all right. That the departed loved one was in a better place. Et cetera. I don't think much of what we told her sank in. She was confused. Shell-shocked. We passed through Connecticut in silence.

We crossed into western Massachusetts at around 2:30 a.m. Philly guy stopped for gas outside Sturbridge at an all-night station off I-84 North. He got out and started pumping, head down to avoid the bright lights and cameras.

"I want to see him," Sarah whispered.

"What?" I asked. She hadn't said a word in well over an hour.

"Quinn," she said louder. "You said he was in the trunk. I want to see him."

I blew out a breath. "Sarah... I don't think—"

"I want to see him," she commanded, and reached for the door handle.

I grabbed hold of her. She shook me off.

O'Neill turned around in his seat. "Let her see."

Sarah's expression was set and steadfast. When Philly guy got back into the car, I told him to pull around to the back side of the station, away from the cameras. He started the engine, drove around back by the dumpsters, and parked in the shadows. The pop of the trunk release echoed through the car. We all got out and stood at the rear bumper. I grabbed Sarah's hand. She squeezed hard.

"You sure about this?" I asked.

Sarah nodded. I opened the trunk.

Sarah gasped and staggered backward a half-step.

Quinn was still in the same position. Rigor mortis had begun. Despite the July heat, decomposition had not yet turned him malodorous. Quinn's face was gray and waxy. He looked like a mannequin. His death hit me all over again. I bit my lip. Squinted through the pain. O'Neill bowed his head and walked to the front of the car. Philly guy followed.

Sarah inched towards the trunk. She gingerly reached out and placed her hand on Quinn's body. She yelped. Pulled it back like she'd touched a hot stove. The hand went over her mouth. She shook her head from side to side, repeatedly mouthing the word *no*. I closed the trunk and gently led her away. She buried her head in my shoulder. We all got in the car and drove off. Massachusetts was a quiet state too.

———

We pulled into Gallagher Funeral Home in Boston just shy of four a.m. The rain had slowed to a light mist. The lights of the funeral home were off, the parking lot dark and full of cars. Philly guy parked right in front of the entrance, and we all rolled out of the car, exhausted. Old man Gallagher, in dark suit and tie, was posted just outside the door. He stood completely still, hands clasped in front.

I asked Sarah to go on inside. She said she would come in with us. I acquiesced. We all went to the back of the car. I reached for the trunk, and Philly guy cleared his throat.

"Uhm, I'd better get going," he said. "Best I get rid of this ride."

O'Neill grunted. "Crush it."

Philly guy nodded. He shifted his weight from side to side. He was sweating profusely, eyes wide and blinking. "Hey... About Quinn. I'm really sorry. I didn't mean no disrespect. I would've brought him to the hospital if I thought... you know." He stuck out his hand. It trembled.

Both O'Neill and I accepted his apology. We shook his hand. Philly guy relaxed and exhaled. He would drive out of South Boston this morning alive and well. We said our good-byes and he drove away.

O'Neill carried Quinn's body into the funeral home. The front parlor was full of Irish mobsters. They crowded around to get a look. To see for themselves that their old boss was indeed dead. Anger and muttered curses filled the room. I got a few sharp looks from some of the older guys. I glared back. Gallagher directed O'Neill downstairs. Sarah and I followed him down the old wood staircase. It creaked and groaned under O'Neill's bulk as he descended. I half expected it to collapse. I was happy when I hit the last step.

I surveyed the basement and pulled up with a start. It

reminded me of the bodega basement. And Prisha Baari. I snarled, pressure building in my head. I wiped sweat from my eyes with a balled fist.

O'Neill laid Quinn's body on an elevated metal table. Gallagher patted his arm and said something I didn't hear. O'Neill smiled weakly. Sarah laced her fingers in mine. We all thanked Gallagher and climbed back up the staircase to the parlor.

The mobsters circled O'Neill at the top of the stairs. They treated him with deference. O'Neill ran through the general story of Quinn's death. He didn't mention Prisha or the Saudis. Or the thirty million specifically. I wondered if Quinn had ever told him. It had not been my place to ask. So I never had. O'Neill made a point of telling these angry men that I had killed for the cause last night. That it was me who'd kept the sniper off him and Quinn as we'd retreated. This drew impertinent stares from the men, particularly the gray-hairs. Some asked questions. O'Neill answered truthfully, as best I could tell. Most of these questions focused on the identities of Quinn's killers. Revenge hung in the air like stale cigarette smoke.

An old mobster, one of the handful that had already given me stink-eye, pointed a gnarled finger at me.

"What do you know about this?"

I stepped forward to confront him when another voice rang out from across the room.

"Hey, you're Arthur's boy, ain't ya?" said the voice.

"Yeah—Arthur the rat!" said another voice. "The dead rat."

My mouth dropped open as I studied the face of the man who'd spoken. The room began to spin. I felt dizzy. I started to hyperventilate.

"Maybe he's a rat too!" another mobster said.

White-hot lead burned in my gut. I reeled to face the old fuck. "What did you just say to me?"

A young tough with a bent nose stepped towards me. He asked me what my problem was. I stepped to him. I told him I was his problem.

Sarah screamed. A full-throated scream. The kind that shattered glass and sent cats scurrying under sofas.

"Leave him alone! Stop it!" Sarah held both hands to her face and screamed again.

"You gonna let your little bitch fight your—"

I pulled my arm back when I heard the word *bitch*. My straight right hand landed on his chin, just as the word "battles" escaped his lips. It would be the last thing the young tough would say tonight. He crumpled to the floor. Me on top of him. I wasn't finished just yet. I barely noticed I was getting grabbed and punched from behind. I got one more shot off. A good one. Then two huge arms lifted me off the guy and threw me into a chair across the room.

It was Finn O'Neill. He shouted, and the room quieted. He told everyone to leave. That it had been a long night and not to test him. He stared down the mobsters. No one tested him. There were a few grumbled half-apologies. The guy I'd hit was still on the floor. He groaned as he regained consciousness. O'Neill motioned to one of the men. Told him to get the kid the fuck out of here. That he'd better not see that kid again. The man did as he was told.

O'Neill cleared the room. He clapped a few guys on the back as he escorted them out of the funeral home. I joined Sarah on a sofa in the corner of the room. O'Neill returned and dropped into the upholstered chair opposite us, his legs stretched out in front of him. He rubbed his eyes and exhaled loudly.

I asked O'Neill if it was true. He ran his hand through his hair. Another heavy exhalation.

I leaned forward, pressed him for an answer.

"Look, Frank. I was just a kid then. Like you. I only know what I was told."

"What were you told?"

O'Neill paused. He looked me directly in the eye. "All I know was that your father was an FBI informant. That his testimony would've taken down the whole crew. Quinn included." He cleared his throat. "He had to be whacked, Frank. I'm sorry you had to hear it like this."

I fell back into the sofa. Sarah grabbed my hand. *This can't be.* I slumped to the side, against the sofa armrest.

"Are you sure about this, Finn?" Sarah asked.

O'Neill nodded.

"Quinn knew about this?" I asked.

"He approved it," O'Neill answered. "Had to. That's street life, Frank. You know that." He leaned forward, elbows on knees. "He hated doing it. Hated what it did to you and your ma. He did what he could for you. I know he thought of you as a son."

The word *son* made me wince. I didn't feel like anyone's son right now.

Arthur had not been much of a father to me. Or much of a husband to my mother, Emily. He was never around. He ran the streets and did as he pleased. Quinn had been the only real father figure I'd had growing up.

What was fatherhood anyway? Sperm or succor? I would be one of the unlucky ones that would have to make this choice. But not today. Quinn had died in my arms a mere five hours ago. My father's killer. It would take me more than five hours to unpack all of this.

Sarah leaned in and whispered in my ear, asked me if I was okay. I said I was. But I was pretty far from okay. She said Quinn had loved me very much. I knew he had. Never doubted it. Still didn't. I suppressed the urge to run back down those creaky basement steps. Ask Quinn why he'd never told me. But how do you explain this to an eight-year-old boy? Or a grown man, for that matter? Quinn had chosen to take his secret to the grave. There was nothing left to say.

I thought of my own son, Teddy. Of my own secret, which I had withheld from him. I told myself I had done this for all the right reasons. Quinn no doubt would say the same thing if I could breathe life back into him. Who's to say what's right? There are few absolute truths in this world.

I turned back to O'Neill. I hoped maybe he had something else for me. Something that would somehow fix all this.

"Sorry about tonight, Frank. The guys still hate Arthur. Can't say that I blame them." O'Neill threw up his large hands. "They thought Quinn should've cut ties with you. Sins of the father, you know? But Quinn wouldn't. Some of the old-timers still hold a grudge. Me—I take every man as he comes. On his own two feet. That's why I gave you a chance."

O'Neill stood and stepped to me. He thrust out his hand.

"You're a good man, Frank. Your own man. That's good enough for me." O'Neill's face wore a thin smile.

I stood and took his hand.

A handshake wouldn't fix all this. But it was a good start.

CHAPTER THIRTY

WE LEFT GALLAGHER FUNERAL HOME AT FIRST LIGHT, not long after my handshake with Finn O'Neill. The sun had just started to make an appearance, reminding me the world still spun on its axis. O'Neill had urged us to stay and get some sleep. We'd politely declined his offer. It didn't feel safe, given the way I'd left things with the mobsters. I was concerned they might make a move on me and Sarah. Quinn's old crew now followed O'Neill. My continued presence in Southie would make things awkward for him. It was best we left town now.

O'Neill provided us with a new gunmetal-gray Toyota Highlander. Perfect road camouflage. Another free, clean vehicle. I thought of Duckie and smiled inwardly. These two men. O'Neill and Duckie. Gangsters and car dealers both. It was not the only thing they had in common, of course. They both commanded fear and respect in equal measure in their respective cities. Both were seasoned in the dark arts of the street. Both were cold-blooded killers when it was called for. And now both of them were wrapped up in my shit.

O'Neill said he and his crew would avenge Quinn's murder with or without us, and that he thought it best we join forces. He asked if I knew who was behind all this. I said I did. O'Neill pressed me for names. I held off; said I'd have to think about his offer. It was obvious that Quinn hadn't told O'Neill about Prisha, the Saudis, or even the thirty million. All O'Neill knew was that our would-be abductee was a high-value target and that this was a big-money job. Quinn had shielded him from the rest. For the time being I would as well.

I drove through Southie, head on a swivel. We reached the Mass Pike in one piece. We rode I-90 West in acute silence, each of us wrestling with our own thoughts. Sarah softly sobbed through the pink and orange sunrise as we reached the I-95 Beltway. We pushed towards Worcester and the Connecticut border beyond.

We hit the prelude to Friday morning rush hour when we crossed into Connecticut. The people in the surrounding cars were all applying their game faces for another workday, all anticipating the weekend and their forty-eight hours of freedom. The juxtaposition of what these people were driving to and what I was driving from stretched my mind taut to the point of snapping. Normal people doing their normal commute to their normal jobs. There was nothing about Sarah and me that was normal anymore.

The Connecticut Turnpike was flooded with cars. On-ramps steadily added to the rising tide of traffic. Connecticut is the only state along the East Coast without any highway tolls. That was the thought in my head when Sarah broke the weighted silence between us.

"I can't believe he's really gone."

"Yeah, I know."

"What are we gonna do now?"

"I don't know, Sarah."

Sarah adjusted herself in her seat. She punched the dashboard in front of her. The loud thud made me flinch. I'd never seen Sarah punch anything in all the time I'd known her, going back to high school.

"That woman's gotta pay for this," she said through gritted teeth. "Pay for what she's done." Her eyes were ice cold. Jaw set. She was in this thing to the end. Down for whatever.

Me too. Prisha had to die. No question. But my thoughts were on Quinn right now. How I had burst back into his life. Taken him from his kite flying and into all this. How I'd failed to keep him alive at the theater. That it should have been me who caught that sniper round. I wished I could trade places with him. He'd still be alive if it wasn't for me and my Prisha problem.

But the universe was remorseless. In this life there were no do-overs. I would never get the opportunity to sit down with Quinn. Ask him about my father. Why he'd done it. Ask him did he love me out of remorse? Pity? His sense of obligation? Had anything between us been real? Or just empty words and actions to assuage a guilty conscience? Quinn had taken these answers to his grave. Me, I'd be buried with my questions. Such was the enigma of death.

We hit gridlock outside of Hartford and inched towards

our connection to I-91 South. The futility of the morning commute matched our mood. What were we to do about Prisha Baari?

Sarah had impulsively suggested we point the High-lander west and keep driving all the way to the West Coast. Back to our Oregon life by the Pacific Ocean. It was her head-in-the-sand fantasy. She spoke of it in a wistful tone, swam around the Pacific of her mind. Hiked the seaside cliffs. Dined on organic fare from the co-op. I gave her this indulgence. After a time, she pulled herself out of this alternative reality. It would leave Prisha Baari alive. And that wouldn't do.

I offered that maybe I'd kill Prisha at distance with a sniper's rifle. Poetic justice for Quinn's death. I'd been pretty good with a rifle in my army days. I could take her out at one of her public appearances. After all, Prisha was a U.S. senator now and she couldn't hide forever. She'd have to mingle with the masses at some point. Sarah didn't like this idea. Dismissed it outright as too dangerous and unlikely to succeed. Prisha would now clearly redouble her security efforts. Sarah would not stand for me being back in prison. Or on death row.

We also decided we wouldn't take the chance of turning ourselves in to face our murder charges in the Hewitt case. It was unlikely that Prisha or the new commonwealth's attorney would back down. And Gerry Gonzalez, good as he was, would lose this case in front of a jury. And even if he didn't, our Prisha problem would remain unaddressed.

Equally implausible was anonymously leaking what we knew about Prisha to the FBI or the media. No one would believe us. It would all be packaged as right-wing conspiracy nonsense, a proven CIA trick. And Prisha would live on.

The best option seemed to be to stay the course. Replace Quinn with O'Neill and take another shot at Prisha. Turn her over to the Saudis, collect our thirty million, and disappear for good. O'Neill had already said he was in. It would just be a matter of getting the Saudis on board. I didn't look forward to meeting with Dead Eye to explain what had happened last night at the theater. Given that, I wondered if the Saudis would stay the course with us. If not, they would want their five million dollars back. Should I even return it? We could stretch five million in Montenegro. It would be enough for me and Sarah to start a new life there, free from the long arm of the U.S. government. But Montenegro's sovereignty wouldn't stop Prisha, nor deter the Saudis if we kept their money. Best to give them their money back if we couldn't convince them to give us another try.

The morning commute had ended. Traffic thinned. We were in New York State now, past New Rochelle and approaching the Bronx. The sun was overhead, the temperature already hovering at ninety degrees. A heat mirage rose off the I-95 in the distance. New York was in the grip of a heat wave. The city was a crucible in which to forge our steel.

Twelve hours after Quinn's death, we crossed over the Harlem River on the RFK Bridge and carried on into Manhattan. We immediately hit traffic. Stop-and-go, like my pursuit of Prisha Baari. One step forward, one step back.

Sarah and I made our decision while we were stopped in traffic on FDR Drive in East Harlem. We would stay the course. Make nice with the Saudis and get our second chance. Bring in Finn O'Neill and Duckie. Snatch Prisha. Stick a bow on her head. Hand her over to Dead Eye. Get paid. Get gone. Get justice for Quinn.

I couldn't help myself. I drove down West 45th Street past the Hirschfeld Theatre. It was a full crime scene. Yellow police tape everywhere. The theater was closed and dark. All the excitement of opening night was long gone.

I slowed as I pulled in front of the theater. I relived it all in a flash. Where I'd stood. Where Quinn had fallen. The concrete was still stained with his blood. I looked over to where the sniper had been across the street, saw the branches of the grand oak trees I'd shot through to effect our escape. Saw Quinn's head bobbing as O'Neill raced his dying body down the sidewalk towards our getaway vehicle.

Sarah leaned over me to get a better look. Squeezed my arm in silence.

The blare of a car horn made me jump in my seat. I was unaware I had come to a stop in front of the theater and that a line of cars had formed behind us. Another horn blast. The driver behind me shouted and honked again.

Angry New York guy was right. There was nothing more to see here. Time to move on.

CHAPTER THIRTY-ONE

July 26, 2019
Prisha's safe house; Capitol Hill
Washington, DC

Karlsson sat a solitary vigil in the living room of a small row house in the West Capitol Hill neighborhood. It was a short walk from Prisha's new Senate office in the Capitol building, and only a few miles from where Duckie and Nia lived.

He blinked at the sun streaming through the windows. The same pink and orange sunrise Frank and Sarah were now driving through.

This safe house was Karlsson's idea. He'd purchased it for Prisha a few years ago for just such an eventuality as the fiasco that had occurred in New York last night. It was owned by a succession of companies stacked like Russian nesting dolls, and paid for with money Prisha had siphoned from ODYSSEUS. Good thing too, because the Saudis had shut off the money spigot as soon as they'd learned she had left the CIA. Prisha's only income was her meager Senate salary of $174,000. It didn't deter her. She continued her lavish spending and was never at a loss for money. Karlsson didn't know or care where the cash came from. He had bigger problems to worry about.

Karlsson had argued against the New York trip, but Prisha had insisted on attending the opening Broadway performance of *Moulin Rouge*. In protest, he'd chosen not to make the trip himself and had designated Darius Pierre as his replacement as on-scene commander. Prisha and Pierre were in the midst of a torrid affair, he knew, and Karlsson was happy to let the two of them go to New York without him. Prisha had recently made Pierre the lead on the Luce project. And look what happened. Prisha had deserved what she got.

He had been awakened last night around midnight by a frantic call from Pierre, who had filled him in on what happened. He'd instructed Pierre to drive Prisha straight to the safe house. Karlsson, meanwhile, had made the early morning phone calls. He'd compiled an ad-hoc security team and instructed them all to report immediately to the safe house. He'd placed most of his team on outside perimeter and brought the two best men inside with him. They held their positions and waited.

Pierre had pulled up in the black Suburban sometime after four a.m. Prisha was a mess. Karlsson had put her to bed. Promised her that he'd be right outside her door until she awoke.

Then, he had shut the bedroom door and marched across the living room to Pierre. He'd grabbed him around the throat and demanded an explanation. Pierre had stammered through his report, deflecting responsibility and scapegoating others for his own failures. Truth was, as the driver he had been late for the pickup, and it was this lapse that had gotten two of Karlsson's men killed. Pierre claimed he had tried to extract the sniper but couldn't find him in all the turmoil. No one knew where the sniper was right now. Or if he'd even made it out alive.

Karlsson shoved Pierre towards the door. Told him to get the hell out. Pierre had stood his ground for a moment before he'd turned and left. Karlsson and Pierre would have to address their unfinished business another time.

One of Karlsson's men, a short, stocky ginger with a buzz cut, brought him a mug of black coffee. Karlsson thanked him and raised himself from the dining table chair he had placed against the wall by the hallway that led to Prisha's bedroom. He sipped at the hot coffee and rolled his neck. It had been a long, shitty night. But nothing like the storm that was sure to emerge from that bedroom later this morning.

Karlsson strolled around the empty living room. He had posted his best man, a grizzled white-haired Russian, in the foyer by the front door. The ginger had the back door past the kitchen. The row house was small and quaint. Well appointed, with all the charm and historical lines it had had when it was built in the 1870s. Large, double-hung windows looked out over a treed residential side street. Karlsson fingered open the wood blinds. He spotted two more of his men in separate vehicles, guarding the front perimeter. He bladed the blinds shut, went to the other front window, and did the same.

The walls were original plaster, secured in place by the innumerable coats of paint applied over the past one hundred and fifty years. Prisha had had the place repainted and decorated. The walls now a cream linen color against wide-plank oak floors painted sable black.

Karlsson emptied his coffee mug. He swung by the kitchen for a refill, gave a short wave to the ginger, and returned to his seat.

He blew out a protracted breath. Another sip of coffee. Two of his men had been killed last night. He had been close to one of them. Had been over to the man's house several times. Had played catch with the guy's kids in the backyard. Karlsson blew out another sigh. He had grown weary of it all. Children losing fathers. Prisha manipulating everyone. Nothing really mattered. He stood on his precipice and looked all the way down.

Years ago, Karlsson had stumbled into nihilism and the teachings of Friedrich Nietzsche after his betrayal at the hands of the Swedish army. He agreed with Nietzsche's basic premise that the world is without meaning or purpose, which for him made existence itself senseless and empty. Karlsson found this dire philosophy liberating. If nothing truly mattered, he was free to go his own way. Have his own fun. And that was just what he had done.

Prisha was another breed of cat altogether. A narcissistic paranoid with delusions of grandeur. And a messiah complex. She had an unquenchable thirst for power. What Nietzsche called "will to power." A dynamic he claimed stemmed from feelings of complete helplessness and power-lessness in childhood. Based on her aberrant sexual life, Karlsson figured Prisha must have been sexually abused as a young girl.

Karlsson checked his watch, then looked down the hall at the closed bedroom door.

———

It was mid-morning before Prisha's bedroom door opened. She shuffled down the hall in bare feet, wearing baggy sweat-pants and an oversized pink V-neck t-shirt. She rubbed her eyes with the heels of her palms and let out a big yawn.

Karlsson rose to his feet as she approached. She gave him a long, impassive look without saying a word. She wore no makeup; her long dark hair was haphazardly piled on top of her head. Big-framed eyeglasses sat high on her nose bridge, replacing her usual contacts. Karlsson had never before seen Prisha in this stripped-down state. She looked smaller, more vulnerable. Almost human.

She continued past Karlsson into the kitchen. He heard her pouring herself a cup of coffee. She returned to the living room and sat on the cognac-red leather sofa at the front window. She motioned for Karlsson to sit in the matching high wingback chair. He did as he was told.

Prisha sipped her coffee and waited for the silence to harden. Karlsson held firm. Waited for her to start the show.

Prisha plucked a coffee ground from her tongue and flicked it to the floor. Took another sip of her coffee, then placed it on the low table between them.

"Well, Henrik," she began, "that was a real fuck-up last night. You almost got me killed."

Karlsson wouldn't allow her to pin this on him. He suspected that weasel Pierre had worked on her the whole drive from New York. Explained how this was everyone's fault but his.

"I told you not to go. If you recall," Karlsson said.

"You should've been there last night, Henrik. You weren't."

"You approved my absence, Prisha. And you were the one who reassigned this Luce fiasco to Darius. Not me."

Prisha waved Karlsson off with a flourish of her hand.

"If you had done your job—found and killed those three idiots like I told you to—none of this would have happened."

"This only happened because you had them indicted behind my back. For two years everything was quiet. You fucked this up. Not me."

Karlsson had never spoken to Prisha like this before. Her face flushed crimson, and her dark eyes widened.

"I want them dead! How long have I been telling you that, Henrik?" she screamed. "They tried to kill me last night! And almost succeeded—"

"I'm the one who put that sniper across the street—not your new boy-toy Darius." Karlsson sat bolt upright in his chair, shifted his weight to the balls of his feet. "You'd be dead right now if it weren't for me. You'd best remember that."

Prisha sneered. Sat back into the sofa. "Did you just threaten me, Henrik?"

Karlsson knew he had said too much. Let his emotions show. This was not the time. He had to redirect her before she tasted blood. He changed tack, asked Prisha to tell him what had happened last night. She did, and mostly stuck to the facts. Except for the part about how she had overpowered her captors and zigzagged down the street, dodging bullets, until she'd dived headfirst into a racing Suburban. Karlsson envisioned two bare legs wearing a three-thousand-dollar pair of shoes, toes down, sticking out the side door of a speeding Suburban hurtling down the street. He bit his tongue to keep the smirk off his face.

"You sure it was Luce?" Karlsson asked, covering his smile with his hand.

"Yes," Prisha said. "Of course it was him. And the old mobster. And some other guy. A big guy. The one who grabbed me."

"Any witnesses?"

Prisha shook her head. "We got away before the cops arrived. There were plenty of people out in front of the theater, but most of them were on the ground or running away. I don't think anyone saw me."

"What about cameras?" Karlsson asked. "NYPD's got thousands of cameras all over the city."

"Well, I can't deny I was at the opening. I'll say I was still inside during the shooting. If they catch me on tape, I'll just say it isn't me. A case of mistaken identity. I'll say the cops are trying to frame me. A political witch hunt. Bring ODY in if I need him. We've just got to stick to the denial and we'll be okay."

Karlsson nodded. "You're safe here. You won't be going back to Georgetown until this matter is resolved."

Prisha grumbled that the house was disgusting. It was too small, and the neighborhood was janky. She petitioned to go back to Georgetown. Karlsson struggled to convince her otherwise. They returned to the matter of the shooting.

"What about Doyle? Is he dead?" Karlsson asked.

"Who? The old mobster guy?"

Karlsson nodded.

"Your sniper got him right in the chest. He dropped like a bag of wet laundry." Prisha smiled her full, toothy smile. "He's got to be dead."

Karlsson grunted. "That's not a good thing, Prisha. This

guy Luce is gonna come back even harder against us now. He's not gonna stop." He paused. "If I were him I wouldn't."

"Then what are you going to do about this, Henrik?"

Karlsson weighed his response.

"I want you to grab that bastard's mother," Prisha exploded, startling him. "Mail her fingers to Luce one at a time. See what he thinks of that!"

Karlsson stared at her blankly. "I told you I'm not going to do that, Prisha."

Prisha got off the sofa and began to pace the living room. Karlsson's eyes followed her. She had a hand to her chin, head bowed. Back and forth, back and forth. She finally stopped behind the sofa, then leaned over and gripped the cushions so tight the leather squeaked. She raised her head. Fire danced in her eyes. A faint smile played on her lips.

"You're going to kidnap that girl—the ex-wife," Prisha commanded. "You know, rough her up a bit. And then we hold her for ransom. That'll bring Luce out in the open."

Karlsson stood in protest. "I'm not sure that's going to work."

"Oh," Prisha mocked. "Perhaps I did not make myself clear. That was not a question, Henrik. That was me, your boss, giving you, my employee, direct instruction. You have two possible responses: yes or no." Prisha came around the couch. Stood two feet directly front of Karlsson. "Yes, and we get started planning the kidnapping of Luce's ex. No, and you submit your resignation. Right now." She gave him a mirthless smile. "Which will it be, Henrik?"

Karlsson gazed at this woman, pictured his large hands around her throat. His heart pounded in his ears. He swallowed hard to get the words out.

"As you wish."

CHAPTER THIRTY-TWO

NICOLE PHILLIPS HAD BEEN A SHIT MAGNET EVER SINCE she'd walked off the Florida State campus and into a world that no longer catered to her every whim.

The FBI had found me and Sarah because Nicole hadn't switched out her prepaid cellphones and SIM cards as instructed. Sarah couldn't survive fugitive life with no contact with her baby sister, so new security protocols were in order. Protocols that didn't rely on Nicole doing what she was supposed to do.

In the end, we went old school. Nicole would write a pen-and-paper letter to Sarah, stick it in an envelope, and hand-deliver it to Gerry Gonzalez at his law office. Gonzalez would re-pack the letter in a different envelope and address it to me under my current alias at a little hole-in-the-wall PO box I'd rented for this purpose. Gerry would mix this letter in with his outgoing legal correspondence and give it to his trusted secretary Silvia to mail. Silvia never knew she was a part of our plan. I checked the PO box once a week, on different days at different times, ever watchful that I wasn't being followed or that the Korean proprietors weren't getting suspicious. Sarah would simply reverse this process to get letters to Nicole, who picked them up when she visited with Gonzalez for a few of her own drop-offs. In a digital world, it's sometimes best to go analog.

It was a beautiful late afternoon in the city. It was also Monday. I'd hadn't done a mail run on a Monday in a while. I stepped through Midtown, camouflaged in the herd of other pedestrians going about their city lives. The crisp fall day leeched some of the agitation from the New Yorkers who surrounded me.

I was working on my new look. Both Sarah and I had had to opt into new disguises when we fled Oregon. I'd gone to shaving my head completely bald and growing my beard out long. But not bushy. I hated wearing an unkempt beard and was struggling with this new look as it was. My plan was to grow the beard to my chest, about three inches below my chin. I wasn't there yet, but I didn't look much like Frank Luce these days either. Dark-colored contacts hid my green eyes, and dark sunglasses and a black New York Yankees cap pulled low finished my new fashion statement.

Sarah's new disguise called for more of a sacrifice. She had worn mid-back-length hair since high school and had been blessed with icy blonde hair that women envied and men longed to nuzzle. We both knew what had to be done when we arrived in New York. On the second night, at our kitchen sink, and after an oversized glass of wine, Sarah grabbed the scissors and started cutting. She gave herself a straight bob cut to her neck; she planned to get it styled shorter at a salon the next day. When she was finished, she patted her head and shoulders as if she had suffered an amputation and was feeling for her phantom limb. I told her it didn't look too bad, and she burst into tears. Hugs and more wine followed. We had both loved her velvet plum Oregon hair. Her New York hair would be coal black.

She'd returned from the salon the next day with a spiky new 'do. I'd gasped when I saw her. Man, it was short. But mission accomplished. She didn't look anything like old Sarah. Black retro eyeglass frames with clear glass lenses and dark contacts finished her New York style.

Neither one of us liked our looks. We both equally disliked my long beard and her short hair, but we tried to maintain a sense of humor about the whole thing. We mostly succeeded. Such was the life of most wanted fugitives.

I walked the city often, earbuds dangling from both ears. I never listened to anything, but wanted people to think I was. To think I was distracted and not paying attention to my surroundings. Which of course I was.

I played songs in my head sometimes. My favorite when I was city walking was the theme from *Midnight Cowboy*, a great film that had won the Academy Award for Best Picture in 1969. It was set and filmed on location in New York City and depicted the unlikely friendship between two hustlers: naïve Texas prostitute Joe Buck and dying New York con man "Ratso" Rizzo. The iconic theme song, "Everybody's Talkin'" by Harry Nilsson, inevitably played in my head as I traipsed the city. Like it did now as I headed towards the PO box to check for Nicole's latest letter.

My soundtracks helped me think. About a month had passed since we'd left Quinn's body at Gallagher Funeral Home and returned to Manhattan. I had met with Dead Eye and explained the night at the theater as best I could. He was not happy. I told him we were still operational, that I had replaced Quinn with his right-hand man Finn O'Neill, and added Duckie for more muscle. I'd cajoled him into giving us one more shot and promised we'd deliver Prisha to him soon. Dead Eye had pushed me for a date. I was noncommittal, because truth was, we didn't have any good plan in place. Prisha had been under heavy guard since the first failed abduction and had not returned to New York. We had all worked hard the past thirty days and had made some progress. Duckie had located Prisha at her Capitol Hill safe house. Sarah had made strides to plant a congressional aide close to Prisha. We had established Prisha's new daily patterns with our surveillance: she had cut all the fun from her life. She worked all day in her Senate office at the Capitol building, then went back to her safe house under guard.

We couldn't storm the U.S. Capitol and didn't want to raid her well-guarded safe house. Instead, we were betting on Prisha breaking from her spartan routine. Cutting loose and ditching her security team to have some fun. This hadn't happened yet, and the Saudis were growing impatient waiting. Something or someone had to give.

I arrived at the PO box during my third rendition of "Everybody's Talkin'" and stepped into the cramped lobby. The owner of the place, a short first-generation Korean guy with bad English and worse teeth, eyed me warily. I greeted him with a nod from behind my dark sunglasses. He returned it and disappeared to the back of the store. If the day ever came, he wouldn't talk to the cops.

I found our PO box halfway up the wall, stuck the key in and opened it. One piece of mail. I pulled it out and recognized Gerry Gonzalez's telltale scrawl. I pocketed it, locked the box and, head down, left the lobby. The place did not have any cameras, as far as I could tell, but it was always best to be safe.

I was back at our apartment in fifteen minutes. Sarah sat at our small kitchen table, pecking away on her MacBook. She looked up from the laptop as I came in. My eyes fixed on the black stainless-steel stud in her nose. A matching shade to her new coal-black hair. She'd gotten it the same day she'd had her short hair styled and spiked. Sarah had never admitted it, but her new nose stud was her big F-U to this New York iteration of our fugitive life. She missed Oregon, the ocean, her long velvet plum hair. And missed Quinn most of all. She did her best to act normal, whatever that was these days, but her anger burned just below the surface. I saw it because I had it too. The only road to our salvation ran through Prisha Baari. She was again the unwelcome third party in our relationship.

Sarah had set up a VPN, a virtual private network, that gave us privacy and anonymity on the internet. She also geo-spoofed us, which she explained was a process that hid our geographical location online by changing our IP address to make it look like our MacBook was somewhere other than New York City. She knew her stuff. I, on the other hand, didn't know shit about this but trusted her implicitly.

I handed her Nicole's letter. She closed the MacBook's cover, tore it open and began reading. I went into the kitchen and grabbed another glass and the open bottle of

Tempranillo. Three steps later I was back at the table. I topped off Sarah, poured myself a glass, placed the bottle on the table, and took the only remaining seat.

The wine went down nice. I preferred a full-bodied red but was not finicky when it came to red wine. Sarah held the three-page letter in her hands. Nicole always wrote on the back side of the page, while Sarah never did.

"How's Nicole doing?" I asked.

"Okay," Sarah responded, not lifting her eyes from the letter. "She said Teddy had to have an emergency appendectomy... but that he's doing fine. Not to worry."

"I hope he's all right," I said.

Sarah reached for her wineglass and kept reading. She guffawed. "Oh my god!"

"What?"

"Nicole's got a boyfriend."

"Serious?"

Sarah held a finger up as she read. I waited.

"Holy shit! Nicole says this guy might be the one."

"The one?"

"Yeah. Let's see. His name is Henry Holm. Tall and blond. Nicole says he looks like Dolph Lundgren in *Rocky IV*." Sarah made a swoon face. "Ooh, that guy's hot!"

"He's a Swede, right?" I asked.

"I don't know," Sarah said, licking her lips. "I just know mama like."

"Easy now, Mama," I said mockingly, which drew a chuckle from Sarah.

"Nicole says he's loaded. A lobbyist of some sort." Sarah read on. "Oh shit! She's moved in with him! She says it's only been a month, but she's in love... Teddy likes him."

I didn't like Teddy living with a man Nicole barely

knew. I still hadn't come to terms with another man raising my son. The thought of it turned my stomach.

"What else does she say about this guy?" I asked.

Sarah scanned the pages, turning them over in her hands.

"Not much. Just that she has never been this happy with another man."

"I'm sitting right here, honey."

Sarah laughed. "You and Nicole were always square peg, round hole, Frank. You know that."

A thought flashed through my head. A thought that chilled my blood.

"You said he's from Sweden?"

Sarah looked back through the letter. "Uhm... Yup. She says here he's a Swede. Doesn't say where he was born." She flipped the last page over and yelped. "She gave me a weblink to some Flickr photos of them together! She says the new beau is some kind of secret government lobbyist or something. That he doesn't know she sent the photos, so we can't ever tell him."

I had a bad feeling about all this.

"You want to see him?"

Not waiting for my response, Sarah opened her MacBook and started typing. She was fast. I listened to the ping of the keys as her fingers flew over the keyboard. I watched her from across the table in silence and tried to talk myself out of the growing terror in my gut. It couldn't be. Paranoia was a part of fugitive life. I wrestled with it every day.

Sarah's eyes went wide. A big smile stretched across her face.

"Ooh. He does look like Dolph Lundgren," she cooed.

Sarah spun the MacBook around so I could see the new love of Nicole's life.

It was a gut punch. All the air rushed from my lungs. I slammed against the back of my chair, gasping for breath.

The smiling man staring back at me, the man hugging my ex-wife, was none other than the Viking. Henrik Karlsson.

CHAPTER THIRTY-THREE

SEPTEMBER 2, 2019
FRANK AND SARAH'S APARTMENT; MIDTOWN
NEW YORK, NEW YORK

"WHAT IS IT, FRANK?" SARAH SAID WITH ALARM.

I couldn't speak. I just stared at Karlsson's smiling face. Then Nicole's. She looked radiant. My mind couldn't process what my eyes were taking in. I slammed my finger on the trackpad to scroll through the photo deck. More photos of the happy couple. Some indoors. Some outdoors, in various scenic locales.

My finger froze in mid-air as I took a second gut punch. It was a photo of Karlsson and Teddy together. The Viking on bended knee with his arm wrapped tight around my son's shoulder. Teddy beamed, his posture and expression open. I knew my son to be skittish around most people. He showed no such trepidation in the arms of Karlsson. Teddy looked... happy.

I thought maybe all these photos had been Photoshopped. Maybe staged. I kept scrolling through all the smiling faces, though, and wasn't so sure. The group shots were the most excruciating. The three of them together made the perfect photogenic family. Like models in those stock family photos that come with the picture frames you buy at Michael's or Target.

And yet I couldn't help thinking that I saw something in Karlsson's eyes. Something subtle. Something that said "I've got your family now, Frank. What are you gonna do about it?"

"Frank? Frank!"

I raised my eyes from the MacBook to Sarah. She was wide-eyed. I turned the laptop back around to her.

"What is it?" she implored.

"It's him," I growled.

"Who, Frank?"

I explained to Sarah who the man in the photo was. The man with his arm wrapped around her smiling baby sister. Henrik Karlsson. Prisha's head of security. The man I'd shot in the bodega basement. The man who had killed Charles Hewitt and framed me for his crime. The man who had had a hand in Quinn's death. The man who now hunted us. The man who would kill us on sight. The Viking.

Sarah's face turned ashen. At first, she didn't believe it. Said it just couldn't be, that I must be mistaken. I assured her I was not. You don't forget the face of a man you shot and tried to kill at close range.

We talked it through, and finally accepted the fact that Karlsson had infiltrated himself into Nicole and Teddy's life.

The follow-up question was why, exactly? It didn't take a rocket scientist to see that Karlsson was baiting us. He wanted us to come to him. It was also clear that Nicole and Teddy were now in grave danger. I knew Karlsson and Prisha well enough to know that they would crank this leverage as high and hard as needed to get what they wanted. And they wanted us. Me and Sarah.

That left us with limited options. All of them bad.

I could call Gerry Gonzalez or Duckie, on the assumption that Nicole and Teddy were still in the DC area. But we didn't know where they were. And even if we did, Nicole might not listen to Gonzalez. She certainly wouldn't listen to Duckie, who was a stranger to her.

We could rush a letter back to Nicole. Tell her she and Teddy were in danger, that they needed to get away from her new boyfriend immediately. But Nicole wasn't scheduled to stop by Gonzalez's law office for another week, and that would be too late. Plus, again, Nicole might not believe what she read.

That left the best of the bad options. We both saw no way around this. Nicole and Teddy were in imminent mortal danger. Sarah and I would have to drive down to Washington, DC, try to find them, and rescue them ourselves. I argued for Sarah to stay in New York. She refused and meant it. I relented and suggested I call Finn O'Neill for help. Sarah readily agreed to this. That just left the matter of where the hell Karlsson had them.

Sarah solved this problem. She went back to several of the indoor photos of Karlsson and Nicole; they were selfies. Well-done selfies. Nicole must have taken them. And if she had, she would have used her iPhone. Knowing her sister, Sarah was sure Nicole hadn't disabled the GPS setting on her iPhone. Which meant the GPS coordinates were embedded in the selfie metadata files. Flickr did not strip off this GPS metadata. All Sarah had to do was view the photos' file properties and look for the GPS coordinates. From there, all that was left to do was to plug the coordinates straight into Google Maps and—presto—we would have Karlsson's address. Assuming the selfies had been taken inside his house, which we thought likely.

We agreed this was our best and only chance to save Nicole and Teddy.

Sarah tore into this project and began pulling up photos one after the other. I stood over her shoulder, watching. After a moment, her fingers slowed to a stop. She turned and looked up at me.

"Why don't you go in the other room and try and call Finn," she said. "I'll let you know if I find anything."

"Right. Sorry," I stammered.

Our apartment had only two rooms, so I retreated to our bedroom. I left the door open.

I sat on our double bed, facing the door, and called Finn O'Neill. He picked up on the second ring. I got right to the point. Told him that Karlsson had my ex-wife and son captive, and that we needed his help to get them back. I had to explain who Karlsson was. His connection to Prisha and me. O'Neill asked if Karlsson had been at the theater that night. I told him I didn't know. I never got a good look at the sniper, and said it might have been him. I told O'Neill I was certain that Karlsson was involved in Quinn's death in some way.

That was enough for O'Neill. He told me he was in. Asked me if I needed any more guys. I said no, just him and a good driver/outside man. That O'Neill would come fully armed did not need to be said. O'Neill asked me more questions about Karlsson. I was in the middle of answering them when I heard Sarah's voice.

"Frank! Come here!" she shouted.

I jumped from the bed. Told O'Neill I'd call him later and ended the call. I rushed into the next room and stood next to her at the MacBook.

"Look!" She turned the laptop. "Found it!"

Sarah had Google Maps Street View pulled up. A stately, two-story colonial home was center screen.

"The bastard lives at 15072 Cherry View Drive. North Potomac, Maryland," Sarah said, triumphantly poking her finger at the laptop monitor.

"You sure?"

"Yup. Nicole's selfie had her GPS settings on it, just like I thought. It's gotta be his place." Sarah clicked on another window. "I searched this address and found a few photos. Mostly outside shots. But a few interior ones too." She toggled back and forth between Nicole's selfie and the interior photos of the home. "See? Not an exact match, but close enough. It looks like Nicole's selfie might have been taken in the kitchen, don't you think?"

"Yeah. Could be," I said. My gut told me this was the place. "Show me the exterior again."

Sarah toggled back to Google Maps.

Karlsson's house was immaculate. Made of pale red brick, with four large Palladian windows downstairs. Four more windows, with flower boxes full of bright red and yellow blooms, were stacked above. The lawn was lush green, the trees and shrubs professionally trimmed. A raised cedar deck ran the length of the back of the house. This house had to be four thousand square feet, easy. I guessed four bedrooms.

And I knew North Potomac. It was only seventeen miles north of Silver Spring. Where I'd moved when I was eight and where Sarah and Nicole had both been born and raised. North Potomac was swank. This house topped one million dollars. No doubt.

It was a house just like this that had started everything, I thought ruefully. I wanted to put Teddy in a house like this. It was why I'd tried to get my government benefits restored. This was where my money would go when the cancer took me. Teddy would make new friends and go to high school in a neighborhood just like this. This house was why I'd stepped through Chang Li, the CIA computer tech, and Linda Webb and Charles Hewitt to get to Prisha Baari. It was why Charles Hewitt had had to die. Why I'd gone to jail and committed my first murder.

My son had made it to his house. Just not the house I had envisioned for him.

He now posed for smiling photos in the house of the man who was trying to kill me and Sarah. A house of horrors.

I placed my hand on Sarah's shoulder. She looked up at me.

"We've got to save them," I said.

CHAPTER THIRTY-FOUR

SEPTEMBER 4, 2019
KARLSSON RESIDENCE
NORTH POTOMAC, MARYLAND

I KNEW IT WAS HER FROM TWO HUNDRED FEET AWAY, AS soon as the metallic-red BMW 330i turned onto the street. It was the car Nicole was born to drive. Sarah and I slumped down in our seats as she drove by us. She had her driver's window open a crack; her long blonde hair billowed as she passed.

Nicole pulled her shiny new Beemer into the driveway of the red brick house on the cul-de-sac. We had parked across the street and two houses down. Finn O'Neill and his guy were parked a few houses behind us. Nice residential streets were difficult to sit on for any extended length of time. Cul-de-sacs were the worst. We'd already attracted some attention from the neighbors. Sarah's presence helped.

O'Neill and his driver had already changed spots twice. The light rain was steady enough to keep people off the street and inside their homes.

Nicole stepped out of her car and scanned the street. She looked right past us. The front passenger door opened and my son appeared. Theodore Robert Phillips. I hadn't seen him since our outing at the National Zoo almost three years ago. He'd grown about eight inches and put on twenty-five pounds. Had the same pitch-black hair, which he wore styled and longer now. He was eight years old. The same age I was when my father was murdered and I'd moved seventeen miles south of here. I must have looked a lot like he did now when I'd arrived here from Boston. It gave me a chill.

Nicole and Teddy went to the trunk and removed a few bags of groceries. Nicole said something and they both laughed. They strolled up the walkway, each weighted down with bags in each hand. Nicole set one of her bags on the porch and stuck her key in the front door, and the two of them entered their new home.

It was the same North Potomac house Sarah had found online. No sign of Karlsson yet, but we were definitely in the right place.

O'Neill was here to kill Henrik Karlsson. Kill him for whatever role he'd played in Quinn's death. The details were not important to him. The plan was to wait for Karlsson to come home from work and then make our move. We had to assume it was a standard workday and that he'd probably be home for dinner. This was one of several critical assumptions we had been forced to make to fill in facts we did not have.

It was 4:45 p.m. now. We would wait for Karlsson to arrive and enter the house. Sarah would do the door knock. O'Neill and I would be hiding on either side, flat against the house, guns at the ready. We would rush in no matter who answered the door. We'd gotten lucky here. The front door did not have a storm or screen door, and it opened directly to the outside. We would have direct access inside the house as soon as anyone opened that door. We hoped Karlsson would answer Sarah's knock. I dreaded the thought of it being Teddy. Yet another unknown in our plan. We were counting on the element of surprise to pull this off.

Once inside, O'Neill would control Karlsson at gunpoint. Sarah would have Nicole, and I would have Teddy. We would get them out of the house as quickly as possible, then drive them out of there. O'Neill would then shoot Karlsson in the face. Sarah had insisted that he not kill him in front of Nicole and Teddy. O'Neill and I both agreed to this stipulation.

No battle plan ever survived first contact with the enemy, however. And so it would be for us this night.

———

"We have to go in and get them now!" Sarah said, looking longingly at the front door, which had just shut behind her sister and the boy.

I reached over and placed my hand on her shoulder. "C'mon, Sarah. We talked about this. We wait until Karlsson gets here."

Sarah pursed her lips and turned from me. I pulled my hand back. Sarah fidgeted in her seat, rocked back and forth. Her breathing became more rapid and shallow. She checked her wristwatch incessantly.

"Sarah—"

"How much longer do we have to wait?"

"I—"

"He must still be at work," Sarah said. "We could just slip in right now and get them out before he comes home." Her eyes beseeched me to acquiesce.

"We all agreed our best tactical advantage would be to wait for Karlsson. It'll be safer. For everyone."

Sarah growled and stared forward again. The car fell silent. The only sound was the soft patter of raindrops on the windshield. Time dragged. I dialed up O'Neill and gave him a status update. He insisted we stay the course and stick to the plan. More grunts from Sarah.

Another twenty minutes and still no Karlsson. Sarah had stopped rocking in her seat. She was now quiet and perfectly still. I should have seen it coming.

Sarah grabbed the door handle and leapt out of the car. She marched straight across the street and towards the house. I jumped out and ran across the street to her.

"Sarah! What the hell are you doing?" I said in a low growl.

"I'm going to get my sister and nephew."

I heard O'Neill approach us from behind at a gallop.

"What's going on?" he asked breathlessly.

"New plan," was all I could say. Sarah had us fully committed now, and I would back her play.

O'Neill cursed and fell in on the other side of Sarah. We went up the walkway single file, Sarah leading the way. O'Neill and I drew our weapons, held them against the sides of our legs, then stopped with our backs flat against the house on either side of the door. The solid wood door opened inward, we knew; I took the doorknob side. I would be the first one in. Then O'Neill, tight on my back.

Sarah checked us both with a glance, then stepped up to

the door and pounded on it three times. I focused on my breathing. I was on the balls of my feet now. A coiled spring, desperate for release.

Sarah banged three more times. O'Neill and I exchanged concerned looks.

I saw the doorknob jiggle. Heard the door begin to open. Through tunnel vision I saw long blonde hair. I sprang into the door crack, sweeping the door wide with my left arm, and rushed into the house, securing Nicole in one hand and scanning the foyer with my 9mm. She started to fall, and I jerked her back to her feet. She was crazy-eyed, her mouth a twisted sneer. I clamped my hand over her mouth to mute her screaming.

There was a staircase right in front of me. I quickly cleared it. O'Neill rushed past me and posted up at a set of double doors that opened into the room beyond. Directly to my left was an opening that led to the rest of the downstairs. I released my grip on Nicole and took a quick peek. The living room beyond was empty. O'Neill gave me a quick head nod. He was clear as well.

Sarah entered the house now. She slammed the front door shut, then dead-bolted it, and rushed to Nicole, who was now yelling at us. Sarah grabbed her sister by the shoulders and shook her quiet.

"Is he home?" Sarah hissed.

Nicole just stared at her, dumbfounded.

Sarah shook her again. "Nicole, is Karlsson home?"

"Who?" Nicole's bewilderment instantly turned to anger. "What... what are you doing here?"

"Is he home?" O'Neill shouted at Nicole.

Her eyes darted to him. O'Neill was a large and exceedingly scary man. She shook her head no.

"Nicole!" Sarah still had her by the shoulders. "We don't have a lot of time. You and Teddy are in great danger. We gotta get you both out of here. Now!"

The sisters exchanged a rapid back and forth. Sarah yelling they had to leave, Nicole shouting back incoherently. O'Neill and I went room to room, clearing the house in low ready gun position. Karlsson wasn't downstairs.

O'Neill and I met again back in the foyer, where the two sisters were still arguing. I looked up the staircase and saw Teddy peeking, wide-eyed, through the balusters in the landing at the top of the stairs. I called his name, and the sisters fell silent. Nicole coaxed him downstairs. He ran to her, shaking, his eyes glued to the gun in my hand. I asked him if there was a man upstairs. He shook his head no. Good. I trusted my son not to lie. Plus, O'Neill and I didn't have time to clear the second floor now too.

"How long until he gets home?" O'Neill asked Nicole.

She didn't answer him.

"Nicole—" Sarah started.

"About a half hour," Nicole said.

I checked my watch. 5:10 p.m. Teddy started to cry. He buried his face into his mother. Nicole comforted him.

"It's okay, Teddy. It's just your Aunt Sarah and Frank. You remember Frank, don't you?"

Teddy peered out from his mother's side, still fixated on what was in my right hand. Nicole motioned with her eyes to the gun. I slid it behind my leg.

"Hey, buddy, why don't we all go into the kitchen and I get you a root beer?" Nicole asked Teddy as she rubbed his back.

Teddy agreed, and we followed mother and son into the kitchen.

The kitchen was huge, with dark cherry cabinets and matching granite counters, separated by a backsplash of six-inch cream subway tiles. We circled the cook-top island, which was ringed by eight leather stools. No one sat. Nicole gave Teddy his root beer. He sipped it tentatively and regained his composure. I was proud of him for that. He stole glances at O'Neill, who was fixated on Nicole.

Once Sarah was sure that Teddy was calm, she pulled Nicole aside, away from him. I joined them.

"You and Teddy and in real danger," Sarah whispered in a low, gritty voice. "We need to get you both out of here now."

"What the hell—"

"Nicole, listen. Henry Holm is really Henrik Karlsson—a killer. He doesn't really love you. He's using you to trap me and Frank."

"Shut up, Sarah!" Nicole shouted, startling all of us. Behind her, I saw Teddy turn pale and his eyes widen once more. "You're just trying to ruin my relationship with Henry. You can't stand to see me happy, can you? You're just jealous. Jealous that I've found the perfect man and turned my life around."

The sisters faced off, sparring, reviving decades-old grievances.

O'Neill cut them short, shouting for both of them to stop. Nicole cursed at him. Teddy had started to cry again. I stepped over and tried to comfort him, and Sarah and Nicole kept squabbling. In the middle of this mayhem no one saw the man slip into the kitchen, with a tiger's silence and stealth. One moment, nothing. The next, he was behind Sarah. My gun came up as he put his to the side of Sarah's head. His big arm wrapped tight around her chest. Sarah shrieked. He pulled her tight to him. His human shield. He walked Sarah back two paces from the kitchen island. O'Neill had his gun up and on the man, too.

"Hello, Frank," Henrik Karlsson said. He looked to O'Neill and back to me. "It's been a long time since we've seen one another. It was under similar circumstances, as I recall."

"Let her go!" I shouted.

"So you can shoot me as before?" Karlsson smiled. "No, I think not."

O'Neill started forward. Karlsson froze him with a hard look.

"Henry!" Nicole shouted. She and Teddy wore identical looks of shock and confusion.

"Please... Nicole." Karlsson shook his head at her. He shushed her through pressed lips, then turned his full attention back to me.

"You and your friend here are going to place your guns on the ground—slowly—and kick them towards me. If you do not do this, I will shoot this beautiful woman in the temple."

Sarah struggled against Karlsson. He slid his palm under her chin and raised her head up, exposing her neck. She whimpered.

A freight train ran through my head. "I'm gonna fucking kill you!" I muttered through clenched teeth.

"Perhaps." Karlsson traced the barrel of his gun against Sarah's temple. "But you're not that stupid, Frank. I'll kill her. You know I will."

Nicole shrieked. "Henry!"

"I'm sorry, sweetheart. They're right. My name is Henrik Karlsson."

Nicole started to sob. Teddy sat frozen in place, looking between the two of them, his face a mask of fear.

Karlsson repeated his demand. I had no choice. I placed my gun on the hardwood floor and kicked it to him. I looked to O'Neill. His eyes burned with fury. I told him to do it. He hesitated, cursed, then dropped his weapon and kicked it to Karlsson as well. Karlsson told Nicole to step aside, then lined me and O'Neill up against the wall. In a firm voice he told Teddy to go upstairs. The boy sat unmoving, petrified in place. In a softer voice, Karlsson again asked him to go, said he'd be up to see him later. Teddy looked to Nicole. She nodded and tried to smile. Teddy stood and crept out of the kitchen, turning to get one last look at his mother before he departed. Karlsson stared up at the ceiling until he heard the creaking of floorboards above. Only then did he again level his eyes on me.

"Now, where were we?"

"What the hell is going on, Henry—Henrik?" Nicole shouted. "Is it true? You used me to get to my sister?"

Karlsson confessed. Told Nicole the truth. Told her about his psychotic boss, Prisha Baari, the U.S. senator. That Sarah and I had managed to get on Prisha's bad side, and that she had decided they needed to be dealt with. How it was his job to do that. That he was sorry she had gotten involved in any of this.

"You bastard!"

Nicole stepped towards Karlsson and Sarah. He back-stepped.

"This was all lies? All of it?"

Karlsson's expression softened. He told Nicole not all of it was a lie. It had started out that way, but then things had changed. To his own surprise, he'd fallen in love with her.

Nicole stared to sob. Karlsson's eyes welled with tears. I watched him carefully, but the tears were real. It was true. He did love her. I thought this might be an opening, and I made my move.

"Henrik," I started, "Sarah's got nothing to do with this. Why don't you let her go, and you and I can work this out ourselves."

Karlsson turned to face me. "Yes, Frank. The two of us do have unfinished business." He leaned down and put his mouth to Sarah's ear. "Did you know your boyfriend tried to kill me? Shot me up pretty good. About three years ago, if memory serves. Isn't that right, Frank?"

"Apparently I didn't do a good enough job."

"It's my turn," O'Neill said.

"Excuse me?" Karlsson said, turning to O'Neill.

"You killed my friend Quinn. You're gonna pay for that tonight."

"You must be Doyle's right hand. Finn O'Neill, is it? And I'm betting you're the guy who grabbed Prisha at the theater?" O'Neill grunted. "And what were your plans for our sweet Prisha, huh?"

"Why didn't you fucking people just leave us alone?" I shouted. "You tried to have me killed in jail—twice!"

"Ahh, but you got out and tried to kill Prisha, didn't you? A drive-by shooting, Frank? Really?" Karlsson sniffed.

"We walked away, Karlsson. Two years. And then she re-indicts us for Hewitt's murder. A murder you committed."

"Those two years were hard on you, Frank. Yes? Well, they were hard on me, too. It's hard to walk away. You tried to kill me, Frank. That is something men like us do not abide. We are not so different, you and I."

"Except I don't take orders from a piece of shit like Prisha."

"Yeah, you just fucked her, lost your job, and hit the road for five years," Karlsson snapped.

Nicole gave me an icy look.

"I told Prisha to leave you all alone," Karlsson said. He sounded almost weary. "She's obsessed with getting you out of the way. For her POTUS run. I had nothing to do with the indictments—for the record. I had hoped to never see or hear from you again, Frank."

"What now, then?" I took a short step off the wall towards Karlsson and Sarah.

Karlsson's eyes went cold. He took his gun from Sarah's temple and pointed it at my chest.

"No hard feelings, Frank."

Nicole jumped in front of me. "No! You're not going to shoot anyone, Henry. I know you're a good and decent man." Nicole approached Karlsson gingerly from across the big kitchen, shielding me behind her as she went. "I love you." Another step. "And I know you love me." Another step. "It's not too late for us, Henry. We can all still go to Sweden. Like we talked about. Start over."

Karlsson moved the gun onto O'Neill. Back to me.

"Look at me, sweetheart," Nicole said, steadily advancing. "We can go to the airport right now. The three of us. Me, you, and Teddy. They're not gonna stop us." She looked quickly over at me. "Are you, Frank?"

I said nothing.

Nicole was within five feet of Karlsson now. Inching forward as if on thin ice.

"Give me the gun, sweetheart." Another step closer. "You kill them and you're gonna have to kill me and Teddy too." She smiled at him. "I know you're not going to do that, baby."

She raised her hand to receive it. Karlsson pointed the gun at Nicole's chest. Tears fell from his eyes. His face contorted in a medley of emotions as he teetered on the edge of his abyss.

Nicole took the final step. A step only love could make. The barrel of Karlsson's gun was now inches from her chest. She slowly raised her hand, palm up. Tears rolled down her cheeks.

Karlsson's shoulders slumped. And with a large sigh, he placed his gun gently into Nicole's hand.

The Viking had melted.

CHAPTER THIRTY-FIVE

THE FIVE OF US SAT AT THE MOCHA-BROWN TABLE IN the dining room adjacent to the kitchen. Nicole had enforced our ad-hoc truce by confiscating all our weapons. She and Karlsson sat close together on one side of the oval table, hands clasped. Sarah and I sat opposite them. O'Neill sat to my right, at one head of the table.

The mood had shifted from intense to the awkward giddiness one feels when they cheat death. It was clear from his face that Karlsson was stunned by his turn of fortune. I must have appeared like a ghost to him; he had already written me off for dead.

I was coming to realize how tough Sarah really was. She had just come away from a trained killer pointing a gun in her face. This experience had only seemed to double her resolve to find a way out of this mess. I had heard stories of her ruthlessness in the boardroom and at the negotiation table. I believed them now.

After a few moments, Nicole asked Sarah to go upstairs and check on Teddy. To tell him we were having his favorite pizza tonight. Nicole reached for her cellphone and phoned in the order. O'Neill stepped away from the table to call his driver. He told him to leave the street but stay close. That he'd call him when we were done in here. Sarah came back downstairs and reported that Teddy was shaken but okay. We all returned to our seats.

Karlsson and O'Neill squared off first. With barely contained animosity, O'Neill confronted Karlsson about Quinn's death. Karlsson assured O'Neill that he hadn't killed Quinn, that he hadn't even been in New York that night. He did acknowledge, however, that it had been one of his snipers that had taken Quinn's life. He refused to give O'Neill the man's name. They ended their exchange glaring at one another. The stench of unfinished business lingered in the air.

I shared O'Neill's need for retribution, but not his single-mindedness when it came to Karlsson. Perhaps it was our shared military background. I cut him a little slack. I knew it was Prisha who issued all the orders. Karlsson could have killed me tonight. Killed all of us. And he hadn't. Maybe there was something here to work with.

"What are you doing working for someone like Prisha?" I asked him. "She's a psycho."

Karlsson shrugged. "I don't know." He scratched his chin. "Don't like her much. Never did, really."

"Let's just go, then," Nicole implored. "Get away from her."

"That's not how it works," Karlsson said. "Is it, Frank?"

"You can't keep doing what she tells you to do," Nicole said. "Not after tonight."

"I know." Karlsson sighed deeply. "I've been slow-rolling her on a bunch of shit." He shook his head ruefully, then looked directly at me. "She wanted me to kidnap your mom, Frank. Mail you fingers until you came around."

I snorted, disgusted. Shook my head. Sarah gasped and squeezed my hand.

"Yeah, well, I talked her out of that one," Karlsson stated. "I'm not exactly her favorite now." He leaned back in his chair. "In fact, I'm pretty sure she's gonna try to have me killed at some point." He said it matter-of-factly, like he was commenting on the weather.

"No!" Nicole shouted. She again desperately pitched their immediate exodus to Sweden, and Karlsson rebutted her once more.

O'Neill chuckled and seemed to be enjoying the show now.

Sarah, for her part, remained quiet and studied Karlsson. She was sizing him up, just like I was. Finally, she asked him what he was going to do about Prisha. Karlsson glanced at Nicole. He said he was planning on leaving, but that he didn't have his plan all put together just yet.

I'd been thinking about this since we all sat down together at this table. After Karlsson had spared our lives. I decided to go for it.

"Hey, Henrik." I leaned across the table. "Why don't you join us? Help us get Prisha Baari out of all our lives?"

"What?" O'Neill banged his fist on the table and stared

at me, incredulous. "Fuck that, Frank. This guy just tried to kill us!"

"Yeah, but he didn't," I said.

O'Neill shook his head, a look of revulsion on his face.

"It would solve a lot of our problems," Sarah said. "I for one am prepared to live a Prisha-free life."

We talked the concept through. Nicole asked a lot of questions. It was clear she and Karlsson were a legitimate couple and in love. It was also clear that her master plan was their escape to Sweden. That was her agenda, and it sounded like the best option. Sarah and I took turns neutralizing Karlsson's objections. We went through some what-if hypotheticals, and slowly but surely, Karlsson began to come around. O'Neill was a harder sell. If he'd had access to his weapon, he would have shot Karlsson at the table.

Sarah went in for the closing. "What do you think, Henrik?"

I turned to her. She still bore the red mark on her face from Karlsson's gun. Tough as nails.

The table went silent while Karlsson wrestled with his response. He turned to Nicole, who was nodding her head yes. A thin smile crossed his lips. He caressed her face with the back of his hand. He then turned back to face Sarah and me. He closed his eyes and exhaled hard through his nostrils, like a bull. A deep, quiet breath, and then another exhale. I saw O'Neill about to speak and held up a finger to silence him.

Karlsson slowly opened his eyes. Straightened up in his chair. He opened his mouth to speak and—*Ring! Ring!*

The pizza was here.

———

To say dinner was uncomfortable did not begin to describe the spectacle. It was theater of the bizarre. Nicole had chastised us all to be civil. Teddy was already freaking out and he didn't need any more drama. So we all sat down to dinner. One big happy family. Sarah and I each had a slice. O'Neill had none. Said he wasn't hungry. Teddy started slow but ended up downing half a pie. We told him that what he had seen earlier was a big misunderstanding. That sometimes grown-ups lose their tempers, but that it was all good now. We all smiled for the boy. Even O'Neill. I'm not sure Teddy bought it. Karlsson lightened his mood by saying he'd be up later to play Teddy's favorite video game with him. Inwardly, I shook my head in wonder. The man who had almost killed me would be playing with my son later tonight. Just one more surreal thing about this most surreal of nights.

Pizza time mercifully ended. Nicole sent Teddy back upstairs, saying the adults had to talk. He protested mildly and asked her to come upstairs with him. Nicole said no, and Teddy lingered at the table, not wanting to leave. Karlsson instructed Teddy to go upstairs, said that he'd be up shortly. He said it in that kind but firm dad voice meant to end further debate.

Teddy groaned and got up from the table. He went to leave, and Nicole called him back for a kiss. We all watched him shuffle out of the room and back upstairs.

"He's a good kid," Karlsson said.

I opened my mouth to respond, and Sarah stared me down.

"Okay, where were we?" Nicole grabbed Karlsson's hand.

"Henrik was just about to join us," I said.

"The hell he is!" O'Neill shot back.

"Anyone else need a glass of wine?" Nicole asked, standing hurriedly.

Sarah raised her hand and got to her feet. She and Nicole went to the wine rack in the credenza against the dining room wall. They grabbed a bottle of Sauvignon Blanc, a corkscrew and two glasses, and returned to the table. Sarah took the bottle and pulled the cork. She poured herself and her sister each a full glass.

"What's it gonna be, Henrik?" I asked. "We gonna work together against a common enemy, or go back to trying to kill one another?"

"It's not that simple," he said.

"We have to go to Sweden," Nicole said again. "We could—"

"No!" Karlsson barked. "Please, Nicole. I want to go back to Sweden as much as you do. More. But you don't simply leave someone like Prisha. It's not like I can just submit my resignation. I have too many of her secrets. She'll hunt us down for the rest of our lives. We'll always be looking over our shoulders. What kind of life is that for us? Teddy?" Karlsson paused to look at me and Sarah. "Ask these two what that's been like."

"He's right, Nicole," Sarah said. "It's no life for you or Teddy."

I tried to quell my feelings about my son hiding with Karlsson and Nicole somewhere in Europe. *One battle at a time.*

"I can't go on here, living like this," Nicole said. "You said this lady, your boss, is trying to kill you, right?"

"Maybe so." Karlsson thought. "Probably so." He thought some more. "Maybe I'll kill her first."

"No," Nicole said. "I don't want her people coming after us."

"They won't be able to prove I did it."

"'Prove'?" O'Neill asked mockingly. "This ain't court. They don't need proof. They'll kill you even if they only suspect you whacked her. Or maybe when she's gone, they'll just clean you out—get rid of you for good."

Karlsson shrugged.

"So you see," Sarah said to Karlsson, "killing Prisha won't solve your Prisha problem."

"Then that leaves us back where we started," Karlsson said. "We'll all get our guns back and start up again in the morning."

"Henry—"

"Henrik."

Nicole flinched at the correction. "You're not going to kill my sister and ex-husband." She pointed to O'Neill at the end of the table. "Not even this guy."

"Gordian knot," Karlsson said under his breath.

"Maybe not," I said, as an idea occurred to me. "Maybe we abduct Prisha, not kill her. And cash out while doing it."

"Frank, don't..." O'Neill said.

I told O'Neill it was our only way out. That I'd pay them out of our half of the thirty million. He sneered. I asked him if he had a better idea. He cursed and shook his head. I told him we could make it work. O'Neill took a long look at Karlsson and nodded his approval.

I then shared the Saudi abduction scheme with Karlsson. Nothing specific, just enough for him to understand the concept. I assured him that we would no longer have a Prisha problem after the Saudis got their hands on her. The unsolved disappearance of a U.S. senator would of course be a scandal, but there would be no evidence tying this back to us in any way. I told Karlsson he would not have to meet with the Saudis. That they would not ever know his name or learn of his complicity. Sarah and I would split our half of the fee with him. We would each walk away with $7.5 million U.S., tax-free. More than enough for Karlsson to get back to Sweden with Nicole and Teddy and live a comfortable life.

Sarah, ever closing, followed my pitch.

"It's your only play, Henrik. Prisha is dealt with and we all stay alive. And we all get rich."

Karlsson sat still in his seat, deep in thought. As I awaited his response it occurred to me that he and I were on parallel paths. He loved Nicole as much as I did Sarah. We had both chosen a Phillips sister over Prisha Baari. And we had both gazed deep into our own abyss, and it had not gazed back into us. Neither one of us was a monster.

I decided to trust Henrik Karlsson. I stood from the table and thrust my hand out.

"You sure about this, Frank?" O'Neill asked one last time from the end of the table.

"I am," I said, without ever taking my eyes off Karlsson. I saw the corners of his mouth curl up into the beginning of a grin. "What do you say, Henrik?"

Karlsson held my gaze as he rose from the table. He reached for my hand. Squeezed it with a death grip.

"On one condition," Karlsson said.

"What's that," I said.

"We do this my way."

"How's that?" I asked.

"Trust me," the Viking said with a smile.

PART IV

_____

*It is impossible to suffer without making someone pay for it;
every complaint already contains revenge.*
  —Friedrich Nietzsche

CHAPTER THIRTY-SIX

KARLSSON STOOD AT THE FRONT DOOR OF PRISHA'S Capitol Hill safe house and gathered himself. He had barely gotten a couple hours' sleep the previous night after Frank and Sarah had left. He and Nicole had talked deep into the night about the new plan and their new life together in Sweden. Nicole was fixated on Sweden and her happy ever after. Karlsson knew life didn't work that way.

He shook thoughts of Nicole out of his head and put his game face on. This was to be the make-or-break meeting with Prisha. He had to get it right. He closed his eyes. Took a few deep breaths. He was as ready as he would ever be for this. He turned the doorknob and entered.

He was hit with the smell of breakfast. Prisha had

insisted that one of her security detail have the requisite culinary skills, as she refused to touch a pot or pan. Karlsson followed the bacon and cinnamon scent trail to the kitchen, where he pulled up short in the doorway. His nostrils flared. Darius Pierre was sitting close next to Prisha, tucking into a stack of blueberry pancakes. Their eyes met. Karlsson's hard stare was returned with a sheepish smile dripping with real maple syrup.

"What is he doing here?" Karlsson growled.

Prisha turned to face Karlsson. She was still dressed in her sleepwear, a raspberry-red silk pajama set. Her hair and makeup were game ready. Her plate held a lighter fare than that of her paramour Pierre—a veggie omelet and side sausage. She sipped coffee. Given the time, 8:35 a.m., and Prisha's war paint, Karlsson deduced that this was her third cup of coffee, minimum.

"Good morning to you too, Henrik," Prisha said with her Cheshire cat grin.

Karlsson pointed to Pierre and repeated his question more forcefully.

Prisha winked at Pierre. They shared a private giggle.

"Let's just say that something... came up... and Darius had to spend the night. Does this trouble you, Henrik?"

Prisha was baiting him. He wasn't in the mood for her games this morning.

"I'll come back later," Karlsson said and turned to leave. *Maybe on the next flight to Sweden.*

"Nonsense, Henrik!" Prisha patted the third seat at the round kitchen table. "Sit down and tell me what happened last night."

Karlsson gritted his teeth and took his seat. He slid his chair as far away from the both of them as he could.

"Good morning, Henrik," Pierre said. Karlsson ignored him completely.

"So tell me, Henrik," Prisha intoned. "What went wrong this time? You didn't say much on the phone last night."

Karlsson eyed Pierre. Prisha got the message. She gave a regal wave of her hand.

"Don't worry about Darius," she said. "I've already read him in on your little caper. He can hear anything you have to say."

Karlsson squinted. This was a violation of their trust. Prisha had taken the Luce project from Pierre and given it back to Karlsson after the theater fiasco in New York, with the caveat that Karlsson would work it alone, in strict secrecy. Pierre's renewed involvement would cause additional and potentially serious complications to a plan that didn't need any more reasons to fail.

Karlsson gave a side glance to Pierre. He wore the smug check-mate expression one does when sleeping with the boss. Karlsson would wipe that smile off his face for good soon enough. Prisha appeared satisfied with her handiwork. Pitting her two lions against one another.

She drained the last of her coffee and thrust the empty cup at Pierre. Shook it in front of his face. He silently took it and left the table to get Prisha her refill.

"So, Henrik." Prisha locked eyes with him. "What happened last night?"

Karlsson explained that Nicole had done her job. She had gotten Sarah to show up at his house, but Frank Luce had not been with her. He was supposed to be there, but wasn't.

Prisha's eyes narrowed. "Damn it! More delays? This

thing has already taken over a month. I don't have any more time to wait!"

Karlsson started to respond but was interrupted by manservant Pierre returning to the table with Prisha's coffee. He placed it down on the table in front of her and avoided Karlsson's eyes.

"My plan will work, Prisha. Trust me." Trust was a double-edged sword. Karlsson would wield this sword to his full advantage as well.

"We should have kidnapped her—like I said all along." Prisha took a large gulp of coffee and then slammed her half-empty cup back on the table with enough force to spatter coffee on the cuff of her pajama top. The stain spread, turning the fabric a mahogany red.

"No," Karlsson retorted. "We stick to the plan." He checked Pierre with a glower that pushed him back in his seat, then turned back to Prisha. "It took me longer than I thought to turn Nicole against her sister and ex-husband. But she's fully on board now."

"How can you be sure?" Prisha asked.

"I'm sure."

"Henrik," Prisha countered, "I have no doubts about your prowess in the sheets, but history is full of vainglorious men who have bet on their cocks and lost."

Karlsson snarled, his eyes blazing.

"Oh, so it's love then, is it?" Prisha asked. "You're betting our futures—my future—on love?" Prisha cackled. "Is that what you're telling me, Henrik?"

Karlsson swallowed his anger. Lifted that double-edged sword of trust and ran her through.

"It'll work, don't worry. Trust me."

"So, let me see if I've got this right," Prisha said. "This

Nicole woman has fallen madly in love with you? In less than a month, no less?"

Pierre snorted.

"My, Henrik, aren't you quite the catch?"

Karlsson felt his face burn hot.

"What do you think, Darius?"

Pierre looked at Karlsson, hesitant.

"Look at me, darling." Prisha snapped her fingers. "I'm asking you, as deputy of my security detail, what you would have me do about Frank Luce?"

Pierre mumbled that he agreed with Prisha, that he would have kidnapped and ransomed Nicole as she had wanted.

"You see, Henrik? Even your deputy agrees—"

"Another meeting is already set for next week," Karlsson interrupted. "Nicole will get both Sarah and Frank to the house. She'll use the kid as an excuse. It'll work."

"Does Nicole know what fate will befall her sister and ex-husband?" Prisha asked with a smirk.

Karlsson nodded. "She's fully committed."

"And why will Luce come this time?"

"The boy, Teddy. He's Luce's kid." Karlsson quickly corrected himself. "Nicole told me."

Both Prisha and Pierre found this amusing. Prisha commended Karlsson on his pillow talk, then picked at a piece of cinnamon toast, thinking. Karlsson used the respite to regroup and prepare for Prisha's next salvo. He knew he didn't have her. Not yet.

Prisha drained her cup and placed it gently back on the table. She tugged at the stain on her sleeve and made a face, then raised her head and announced her decision.

"This is what we're going to do. Do your meeting next

week. I have full faith in your skills, Henrik, and have no doubt that if they both show up, you will do what needs to be done."

Karlsson relaxed.

"However," Prisha continued, flashing a smile at Pierre, "if you fail, I'll put Darius back in charge of this. And he'll kidnap the girl, won't you, darling?"

Pierre returned Prisha's smile and nodded.

Karlsson went in for another sword thrust.

"Of course, Prisha," he said. "As you wish." It was his turn to smile. "Why don't you join us next week, Prisha? You've got the stomach for this sort of thing. And as I recall, you enjoyed yourself with Tommy Boone. Given all the trouble Luce has caused you, I think you would enjoy paying your final respects, as it were. It'll be fun. You can play all you want."

Prisha thought about this for a moment, head cocked to one side, tapping her front teeth with a long manicured fingernail. "Yes," she purred at last, her eyes wide. "I would like to see Frank Luce one more time." Prisha touched a hand to her lips. "I do believe I will take you up on your generous offer."

"Very good," Karlsson replied, doing his best to hide his joy at her response.

"I want to make something very clear, though, Henrik." Prisha leaned over the table towards him. "We have little time left. ODY is tested and ready. I intend to make my POTUS announcement next month. And I need this loose end tied up. Do you understand what I am saying?"

Karlsson nodded, and then got wearily to his feet. He had had enough. He had gotten what he came for and wanted to be out of Prisha's presence. "The matter will be resolved next week. Promise." He turned to leave, but made it only a few steps before Prisha called him back to the table. Her expression was cold steel.

"What of the woman—Nicole? What will become of her?"

"That's already been taken care of."

"Good," Prisha said. "No loose ends, Henrik."

CHAPTER THIRTY-SEVEN

SEPTEMBER 5, 2019
KARLSSON RESIDENCE
NORTH POTOMAC, MARYLAND

NICOLE GLANCED UP AT THE KITCHEN CEILING TOWARDS
the cacophony upstairs. Karlsson's booming bass voice.
Teddy's sharp cackle. They were in Teddy's room on his
Xbox playing his favorite video game: *Call of Duty: Modern
Warfare*. Nicole felt Teddy was too young for the game, but
Karlsson had convinced her otherwise. He was only allowed
to play it with Karlsson, and the violence didn't seem to faze
Teddy at all. Just like his father. This might explain how
Teddy had bounced back so quickly from the events of last
night; the boy had been more traumatized by seeing Frank
and his scary friend than he had been by all the guns.

Nicole took a long sip from her wineglass. The last
twenty-four hours had changed everything. So Henry Holm

was not who he said he was. So what? Henrik Karlsson was the same man she had fallen deeply in love with. He was a good man who did bad things. So what? Nicole knew he loved her and Teddy.

Nicole's life had been one long road of broken glass since she'd left college. She'd once thought that Frank Luce might have been the answer, but Karlsson had shown her the kind of love and devotion that women only dreamed of. She now understood why people wrote all those love songs.

More wine. It was all so preposterous. Abducting a U.S. senator. Multi-million-dollar payouts. The mind was so malleable. So fixated on getting its fix, at whatever cost. The impossible became conceivable. The hopeless possible. Achievable. Such was the power of love. Particularly to one first smitten. Nicole was all in with Karlsson. She was down for whatever he had to do.

This whole situation was a shit show, sure, but Nicole would duct tape it together just enough to get them all to Sweden. Her nirvana. His Valhalla.

Nicole finished setting the table. They were having Chinese takeout for dinner. She wondered what the takeout menu scene was in Stockholm, and shuddered at the thought of having to learn to cook. She chugged the last of her wine, placed the un-rinsed glass in the sink, and hollered up at the ceiling for the boys to come down for dinner. She paused. Nothing. She rang the dinner bell a second time. She heard the sound of stomping feet running across the ceiling and down the stairs. Teddy arrived first, out of breath and all proud that he had beaten Karlsson to the table again. Karlsson sauntered in next. He kissed the top of Nicole's head and took his seat next to her.

"How was the game tonight?" Nicole asked.

"I kicked his ass!" Teddy shouted, pointing a taunting finger at Karlsson.

"Language at the table, Teddy," Karlsson admonished.

"Oh, sorry—I meant butt. I kicked your butt!" Teddy glanced at a grinning Nicole. "Sorry, Mom."

Karlsson spooned out the sesame chicken and dumplings, and dinner commenced. Nicole asked Teddy how school was today. He had petitioned for the day off but failed to win his case. Teddy had just begun the third grade, and Nicole wanted him to connect with his new teacher and classmates. Teddy excelled in reading and writing, being an expressive and introspective boy. He hated math, especially all the arithmetic he had to learn this year. Fractions were the worst. He didn't like science much either, except anything having to do with animals.

"I was good at math and science when I was a boy your age in Sweden," Karlsson said. "I will help you."

Teddy beamed. Karlsson's face remained impassive. Teddy's smile quickly faded.

"What's Sweden like?" Teddy asked tentatively.

Nicole jumped in with enthusiasm. She told Teddy he would love it in Sweden. He peppered her with questions: Where is it? (Across the ocean in Northern Europe, near Norway and Finland); Do they speak English there? (No, sweetheart, they speak Swedish.); Is it cold? (Not much colder than here. Now eat your chicken.); Will I make any friends? (You'll have tons of friends—promise.); When are we going? (Soon, Teddy. Real soon.)

Karlsson sat out this entire exchange. He just pushed the food around his plate. Eyes downcast. Nicole saw this and frowned.

"We're all going to love Sweden, isn't that right, honey?"

There was a rising inflection in her voice as she tried to engage him. Karlsson flicked a look at Nicole. She rolled her eyes in Teddy's direction.

Karlsson cleared his throat, adjusted himself in his chair. "Uhm, yeah—sure. Sure. We'll all love it there." He turned to Nicole. "Teddy will be fine in Sweden. I'll make sure of it."

A wintry gale blew through Nicole. "Of course he'll be fine." She gave Karlsson a what-are-you-talking-about look that went unheeded. Karlsson was distracted tonight, growing more and more melancholy since he'd appeared downstairs for dinner. Time to turn this frown upside down.

"How was work today, sweetheart?" Nicole scooped a forkful of fried rice into her mouth. Washed it down with red wine. She gave no fucks for food pairings.

"It was fine," Karlsson responded, stabbing another piece of sesame chicken.

"You meet with your boss today?"

Karlsson nodded.

"Well?" Nicole asked with wide-eyed exasperation. "Is your boss coming over next week—like we talked about?"

"Yeah," Karlsson said. A weak smile appeared on his face. "She said she'll be here."

Nicole brightened. "Just like we planned?"

Karlsson again nodded.

"We're doing the right thing," Nicole said.

"Yeah." Karlsson chewed his chicken. His jaw muscles rippled.

"Okay. I'll call Sarah and Frank. Tell them to come over next Friday night at seven o'clock."

"That'll work," was all Karlsson said.

Next Friday night. Friday the 13th.

CHAPTER THIRTY-EIGHT

September 13, 2019
Karlsson residence; basement
North Potomac, Maryland

We were where Karlsson had placed us, against the back wall of his finished basement. Sarah and I sat two feet apart on brown folding metal chairs that faced the staircase at the front of the room. We had one-quarter-inch polypropylene rope the color of spoiled banana draped around our shins and torsos. We held the loose ends of the ropes in our hands behind the chair backs. I held a loaded 9mm pistol as well. To anyone descending the basement stairs it would look like we were securely tied to our chairs. We had spent the past week practicing wriggling out of our ropes. We both had it down cold.

Teddy was at the babysitter's. Out of harm's way.

We had cleared the furniture out. Pushed it against the wall or put it out in the adjoining garage. The room had an off-white drop panel ceiling and alabaster-gray ceramic tiles on the floor. The walls wcrc also gray, painted several hues darker than the tiles. Fluorescent light shone from the ceiling. The place was as bright and antiseptic as an operating room. Or a morgue.

The plan was pretty simple. Karlsson had done most of the heavy lifting. He would lure Prisha down to the basement. Once he walked her over to us, we would drop our ropes and Karlsson would grab her. He'd tie her up, gag her, and drag her to the garage. We'd stuff Prisha in the trunk of Karlsson's car, and I'd drive her to the meeting spot and hand her over to Dead Eye.

It seemed simple enough.

Sarah insisted on being present for this. Prisha had been in her life for three years now, and I thought it important that she meet her goblin. Have the opportunity to stomp on her foot and spit in her eye. A kind of closure, I guess. And I didn't see any danger in it. Karlsson and I both had guns and were prepared to use them. Prisha would be alone and unarmed. As soon as she entered the basement, she was toast.

Thump. Thump.

They were here. I heard the front door shut, and then footfalls across the ceiling above. Heading to the basement door. It sounded like a herd.

"You ready?" I whispered to Sarah.

"Yeah," she answered in a low voice. She looked ready.

"Remember, follow my lead. Don't stand up until I do."

Sarah nodded.

I took a few deep breaths. This would all be over soon.

The basement door creaked open. I craned my neck to see the first pair of descending legs, clad in 5.11 tactical pants. Then ankle skinny jeans. Then another pair of female legs, followed by jeans and man boots. My heart sank when 5.11 guy hit the bottom of the stairs and turned into the room. It wasn't Karlsson. 5.11 guy was a large African-American man with a shaved head and twitchy hands.

"Who's that?" Sarah hissed.

"Don't know," I replied.

The group broke into two: Karlsson with Nicole, and Prisha with 5.11 guy, whom she called Darius. I got Karlsson's attention. He looked pissed. I rolled my eyes to the stranger in the room, and he shook me off. *Don't worry about it.*

Karlsson acted like he had everything under control. I wasn't so sure, but I had no choice but to follow his lead and see where this went. I milked the grip of my gun. Beads of sweat started to break on my forehead and roll down my face. I did my best to blink them away.

Prisha stared right through me with her dark eyes. A slow grin turned into her triumphant big-toothed smile. She looked between Sarah and me. Sarah let out a low growl.

"*Fraaank,*" Prisha said in greeting. "So nice to see you again." She narrowed her eyes. "We'll talk soon." She turned to her left, stepped past Darius Pierre and stuck her hand out to Nicole. "Thank you so much, Ms. Phillips," she said. "We couldn't have done this without you."

What! Had I just heard what I thought I had? No... no, I thought. It can't be. Nicole wouldn't do this to me. To Sarah. This must be one of Prisha's little games.

Karlsson jumped in between Nicole and Prisha. Nicole

looked at him, dumbfounded. Sarah screamed something, more wail than words. Karlsson whispered something to Nicole, then repositioned her away from Prisha and Pierre and nearer to us. Nicole shook like a sapling in a tempest and was on the verge of tears. Karlsson kept his eyes on Pierre. The tension between these two was palpable.

Prisha whirled on me now. Took three steps in my direction, stopping about six feet in front of me and Sarah. She wore a black wool cardigan over a white t-shirt. She had her hair down and had chosen to wear three-inch heels to this particular event. My face pinched into a scowl at the sight of her this close to Sarah. My gun twitched behind my chair. *Wait.*

"You have no idea what a pain in my ass you've been, Frank Luce," Prisha said. "How I've anticipated this day. I thought I'd feel happier than this, but you know what? I don't feel anything. Just relief. Relief that this is finally over. Relief that you and pretty girl here will finally be gone for good. I'll be announcing my run for POTUS next month. Can you believe that?" She gave me that hundred-watt smile. "You and that hacker of yours thought you could stop me, but ODY 2.0 is up and running. More powerful than the version you spiked at the bodega—what, three years ago now? Come to think of it, you and I have a thing for basements, don't we, Frank?"

"I prefer your office couch," I said, then turned to Karlsson. "What's going on here, Henrik?"

It was Prisha's turn to be confused. Her face scrunched into a question mark. She turned to Karlsson. "Henrik?" She shrieked his name a second time, louder. "*Henrik!* What the hell is going on here? Kill them."

Nicole screamed and started to run towards Karlsson.

"No!" Karlsson shouted in a booming voice that reverberated around the room like a thunderclap. It froze Nicole in her tracks and reset the room.

I was just starting to wiggle free from my rope when Karlsson gave me another knowing look.

Hold.

Shit. I knew from my practice sessions that I could get free from my ropes and on my feet at ready gun in less than five seconds. But that wasn't going to do with these two guys. No guns were out yet, but I figured both Karlsson and Pierre could draw and put rounds through me and Sarah before I could get my first shot off. I knew Pierre was not on my side, but I couldn't figure out what Karlsson was up to. I took the look in his eye to be genuine. This had just become a life-and-death decision.

I went with my intuition.

"Hold," I whispered to Sarah.

Nicole whimpered a few feet from us. She was frozen to the spot, not daring to move.

"Kill them!" Prisha commanded.

Karlsson did not turn to Sarah and me. He turned square to face Pierre. This made Pierre visibly nervous. His hands twitched more.

"Why are you here, Darius?" Karlsson asked him.

"I invited him," Prisha snapped. "It's time for him to see how we do things."

A look of disgust spread over Karlsson's face. "You shouldn't be here." He motioned to the stairs with a flick of his chin. "Time for you to leave."

Darius Pierre didn't move.

Karlsson repeated his command. Told him he wouldn't tell him again.

Prisha started to say something.

"Shut up!" Karlsson boomed at her. His invective blew her back a stutter-step.

The two gunfighters squared off. Pierre's eyes went wide. An amateur tell. He'd lost his tactical advantage and had leveled the action/reaction paradigm. The result of this was that all three of us now knew he was drawing first. Which meant Karlsson's and Pierre's guns came out at the same time. Mine a few seconds later, after I got loose of my rope and jumped to my feet.

Pop. Pop. Pop. Pop. Pop.

The metallic crash of the rapid gunfire reached its crescendo. Pierre dropped to the floor first. Karlsson staggered, looked for Nicole, then collapsed. Loud female screaming. Impossible to tell who.

I checked Sarah in my peripheral view. She was out of her chair and hugging the wall. I ran over to where Pierre lay, grabbed his weapon and tucked it into my waistband. He was bad off but still alive. He mouthed something inaudible. One arm outstretched to me.

I placed the muzzle of my gun an inch from his forehead and pulled the trigger. Twice. Because once is never enough.

Nicole knelt at Karlsson's side, wailing.

Prisha broke for the basement staircase. Sarah sprinted after her, with me in pursuit, and caught her at the top of the stairs. They tussled. Sarah was a hellcat. She dragged Prisha caterwauling back down the stairs by her long raven hair. I helped Sarah tie her tight to one of the folding chairs with our abandoned rope. I mean real tight. She wasn't going anywhere.

I told Sarah to stay with Prisha, and I rushed to Karlsson, who lay dying six feet away.

Nicole was hysterical. I shook her to try to get her to stop screaming. Karlsson had a chest wound that looked bad. He had already lost too much blood. I told him to hang in there. He just shook his head.

Prisha was thrashing in her chair, screaming and cursing at me and Karlsson. I turned just in time to see Sarah wind up and punch her in the face. A good one. It snapped Prisha's head back. Blood flowed from her nose.

"You betrayed me, Henrik!" Prisha screamed. She spat blood on the tile.

Karlsson motioned me to lift his head up off the floor. Nicole cradled his head as well.

"Like you betrayed me..." he hissed at Prisha. He coughed, then choked up blood. He paused to swallow a couple of times. "...with Darius. How long had you been planning to kill me, Prisha?"

"I should have killed you sooner!"

"I know death is one big nothingness. That life is mean-ingless." I raised Karlsson's shoulders higher off the floor. It helped him get the words out. "So I don't fear death." He coughed and spat. "But you! You find great meaning in all this. And it's all about to be taken away from you..." He stopped, unable to say anything more.

Nicole and I gently placed Karlsson's head back on the floor. Nicole planted a kiss on his forehead and held his hand tightly.

"We're gonna get you outta here," I said, squeezing his other hand.

Karlsson shook his head no. "He dead?" Karlsson croaked, shooting his eyes in the direction of Pierre.

"Yeah," I said. "You got him."

Karlsson smiled. "Good."

"Frank, listen," Karlsson whispered in a gravelly voice. "Teddy's a good kid. You're the only father he's ever going to have. Promise you'll be there for him."

Nicole and I exchanged a look. So she'd told him.

I made the promise to Karlsson.

Karlsson turned to Nicole. "Take Teddy to Sweden. My sister will take care of everything. There's money. You'll be fine there." He stopped to catch his failing breath. "You're the best thing that ever happened to me, 'Cole. I love you."

Nicole moaned. Said she loved Karlsson too. She bent down to kiss him one last time. He died in her arms.

A wail erupted from Nicole then, a sound I have never heard before or since. She stroked Karlsson's cheek, then suddenly jumped to her feet and rushed Prisha. She crashed into her with the full weight of her body, tipping Prisha's chair backwards. They both fell to the floor, Prisha screaming and struggling against her ropes. Nicole had a handful of Prisha's hair and was slamming her head against the ceramic tiles. Sarah grabbed Nicole from behind and pulled her off Prisha. Nicole raked her fingernails across Prisha's face as they separated.

Sarah pulled her sister to her feet and held her tight. Prisha was still on the floor, her chair on its side.

"Kill her!" Nicole screamed, trying to break away from Sarah. "Kill her, Frank!"

I slowly walked over to Prisha. Righted her chair and stood it back up. Prisha was out of breath and bleeding from Nicole's tiger scratch on her face. Blood still dripped from her nose and was congealing on her upper lip. Her hair and eyes were wild.

"Don't listen to her," Prisha stammered. "We can work this out."

"It's already worked out, Prisha."

Her eyes widened as realization dawned. "The Saudis?"

I nodded.

"How much are they paying you?" Prisha asked breathlessly. "I'll double it. You're a reasonable man, Frank. We can do business here."

I now saw what this was. Clear as day.

"Is that what this is? Business?" I asked her.

"How much, Frank? Everyone's got a price. I'll pay whatever you want. You and your woman will live in luxury. Boats, cars, whatever you want. Just tell me your price and I'll pay it."

Fucking boats! Cars? I didn't have a price. Never did, really. This was always personal with me. Not business, like it was for Prisha and her Saudi friends.

My obsession with killing Prisha and exacting my revenge had almost cost me what mattered most—Sarah. I had fought my monster for three long years. Had gazed deep into the blackness of my abyss. I had faltered but never surrendered. The monster was not in me, but my vengeance had never left. It stood at my side now. It commanded to be unleashed, to do as it was born to do. To realize its sweet release.

Prisha had had Quinn Doyle killed. And Charles Hewitt. Now Henrik Karlsson. She'd tried to kill me twice— three times, counting tonight. And not just me. Sarah too. My sweet Sarah.

My silence was too much for Prisha Baari to bear.

"I'm a U.S. senator!" she snarled. "I'm gonna be President of the United States! I'm Catherine the Fucking Great!" Spittle spewed from her mouth. She bucked and struggled against her ropes. Her chair tottered and almost tipped over. "Give me your goddamn price so I can get out of this chair!" She shrieked and thrashed some more. "This is over, Frank. Over!"

I looked around. Pierre lay dead in a pool of blood across the basement. Nicole was cradling Karlsson's body once more, a few feet to my right. Sarah stood three feet off Prisha's shoulder to my left.

Sarah and I locked eyes. I looked deep and saw unwavering resolve. No mercy or forbearance. Fire and ice. I know what I saw. Raw justice.

I pulled away from Sarah's soul, all the way out of those blazing blue eyes and back to the basement. I had already seen what she wanted done. I waited for her acquiescence. Sarah dipped her chin ever so slightly. I had what I needed.

I stepped to Prisha. Stood over her, straddling her in the chair. Up close and personal. Prisha went still. Her eyes wide. Her mouth hung open.

"You're right, Prisha," I said. "It's over."

I raised the gun and shot Prisha once in the face. The chair jerked over backwards. I stepped forward. Again straddled the chair between my legs. I stared at the hole I had just put in Prisha's forehead. A different dark abyss. Her eyes were still open wide. I looked into those dead eyes for what felt like a long time. A tornado of rage tore through my chest. The funnel cloud seeking its exit.

I stood over her and shot her again. In the chest. Her body rose and fell with the impact of the bullet. I paused and did it again. Because two is never enough when it comes to monsters.

I stepped back from the dead woman. Stood silently at the foot of the chair, the gun low against my thigh. A torrent of bright red blood splashed my boots as it streamed between my feet.

Three shots. All fatal. All at point blank range. All delivered in righteousness.

Prisha was correct about one thing. This was over.

My rage died with her that day in the basement.

CHAPTER THIRTY-NINE

SEPTEMBER 13, 2019
KARLSSON RESIDENCE
NORTH POTOMAC, MARYLAND

I PICKED PIECES OF PRISHA'S SKULL AND BRAIN MATTER from Sarah's hair and shoulders. They glowed against her black t-shirt under the bright fluorescent lights. She looked down at herself, a look of horror on her face. She patted herself down as if she were on fire, in a frantic effort to rid herself of Prisha's goo. I had it on me too but let it be.

We finished wiping Sarah off, and then she pulled me into a tight embrace. I told her it was over. That we were free. That I loved her. She trembled in my arms. I kissed her and said we had to get out of here. She agreed.

Sarah was holding it together. She had not seen what I had seen in Afghanistan, or done what I'd done to survive in the DC Jail. But here she was. Battle ready and still good to go. She was tough. Good thing, because I'd need her help to get us all out of here alive.

Nicole was draped over Karlsson's body, weeping. We both stepped towards her, passing Prisha, who was still on her back tied to the chair. Her head had slumped to one side, eyes wide, mouth agape. Pink tongue protruding over her teeth. Blood and brain matted in her once beautiful raven hair. She appeared so pathetic in death. Much ado about nothing. Sarah kicked the chair, hard, as we walked by. It slid through Prisha's blood slick and stopped on the tile floor beyond.

Nicole lay across Karlsson's chest, her face buried in his shoulder. Karlsson's eyes were closed, his face serene. As if death was an acquaintance of his, and he had expected this visit all along. Maybe he was right. Maybe nothing really mattered in the end. Dust in the wind and all that. I disagreed to a point. What you do in this life matters. This man had loved my son. Fathered him as Quinn had me. And in the end, he'd kept his bargain. He'd died for it. I supposed Karlsson would always be my favorite guy who ever tried to kill me.

Sarah approached Nicole first, placed a supportive hand on her back. Nicole jumped, looked up at her, then went back to sobbing over Karlsson's body.

"Nicole, honey, we have to go." Sarah laid hands on her again.

No response this time. Sarah repeated herself more forcefully.

Nicole shook her head, still buried against Karlsson's chest.

I gave it a try.

"Nicole, the cops are going to be here any minute. We'll all get caught if we don't go now."

"No... I don't want to leave him here," Nicole mumbled around the sobs.

"We have to," I said.

"We have no choice, Nicole." Sarah rubbed circles on Nicole's back.

Nicole remained silent and motionless.

"You heard what Henrik said," Sarah continued. "He wanted you to leave him here in peace. Take Teddy and run to Sweden. They'll be looking for us soon. You and Teddy will never make it if we don't go right now."

Nicole stopped sobbing. She still wouldn't look at us.

Sarah bent over Nicole. Grabbed her firmly under the arms and pulled her to her feet.

Nicole pushed her sister away, screaming. "This is all your fault!" she shouted, looking between the two of us. "He's dead. Gone... My life is over." She began to whimper.

Sarah reached for her, but Nicole batted her hand away. Sarah did it again, and this time Nicole relented.

"You're Teddy's mother," Sarah said gently. "He needs you to be strong right now." Sarah squeezed her sister's shoulders. "*We* need you to be strong right now."

I looked at my watch. "We need to go get Teddy from the sitter."

"What am I supposed to tell him? About... Henrik?" Nicole choked on his name. She turned and gestured around the blood-spattered basement with her hands. Her eyes took in the totality of the carnage—this macabre subterranean landscape—for the first time, then stopped on the dead bodies of Prisha and Pierre.

"I don't know, Nicole." Sarah tightened her grip on

Nicole's arm. "We'll talk about it in the car. But right now you gotta come with us." She tried to lead Nicole away from Karlsson, but Nicole stood firm as a mule. She brushed Sarah's hand away, then dropped and knelt at Karlsson's head once more to say goodbye. Kissed him one last time. Then, solemnly, she rose to her feet and walked towards the staircase under her own power, head bowed.

We passed Pierre's body as we crossed the basement to the staircase. He had come to rest on his side, his head lying in a halo of blood. I nudged him with the toe of my boot and he flopped onto his back, an arm caught underneath him. I needed to see him one more time. The man who had drawn first and started all of this. But for this man, Prisha would already be in Dead Eye's clutches. We would all be thirty million dollars richer. Karlsson and Nicole off to Sweden, Sarah and I to points unknown.

I understood that it was Prisha who had put us here. That if it hadn't been Pierre who'd drawn his weapon first, it would have been me or Karlsson. It made no difference now. He'd made his choice and I had killed him for it. Like Prisha, Pierre had died with his eyes wide open. Death had snuck up on him and caught him by surprise. I looked down at the gun in my right hand.

We made no effort to clean up the crime scene. There was no point; we could never mitigate all the forensics in here. Hairs, fibers, footprints, blood, fingerprints, DNA. The FBI and the cops would get all of it. The army still had my medical records. The neighbors would give statements about the nice couple and cute boy who lived in the immaculate red brick colonial on the cul-de-sac. That would lead to the local elementary school, where they would find the new student—Theodore Robert Phillips. That would give them the boy's mother, Nicole Phillips. Which would then bring them to me. And Sarah. I figured it would take the FBI less than forty-eight hours to unravel all of this, once the bodies were discovered.

I didn't know if any neighbors had heard the gunshots, or if they had already called the police. We had to get the hell out of here immediately.

We couldn't go anywhere in the bloody clothes we now wore. I rushed us all upstairs to the master bedroom for a quick wardrobe change. We raided the closet, but nothing fit quite right: Nicole's clothes were too tight on Sarah, and Karlsson's were baggy on me. It all fit well enough, though, for a murderer and his accomplices fleeing the scene of a triple homicide.

We raced down the stairs to the front door, me in the lead. I pulled back the curtain of the nearest window a crack and took a quick peek. It was twilight. A full moon shone bright between the breaking clouds. The street was silent. I saw nothing suspicious. That didn't mean shit—only that the neighbors hadn't yet called the cops. Or if they had, they weren't here yet. They would roll thick for a shots-fired call. All lights and sirens. The FBI would not be the first responders, though. They would come in later, with or without the coppers' blessing.

What worried me most was not patrol cars swarming the cul-de-sac, but that Prisha had more goons out on the street. I had no way of knowing if she had brought more than Darius Pierre to this fight. This was the real threat. These guys would offer no surrender nor read us our rights. They would gun us down as soon as we stepped out of the house. I thought of Quinn and the sniper. There were no good answers here. We just had to do it.

I turned to Sarah and Nicole, both stacked right behind me in the foyer. Sarah leaned in for her instruction. Nicole seemed to be in shock.

"Okay," I told them. "Our car is about five houses away. When I open this door, we will all walk—not run—down the street to the car. Stay tight behind me at all times, understand?" Sarah nodded. "Nicole?" I looked at her. She nodded back. "Good. Keep your heads down and walk like everything's normal. If the cops rush us, I want you two to drop to the ground—"

"What about you?" Sarah asked.

"Just drop. Got it?"

I turned and unlocked the front door. Opened it slowly. Nocturnal noise rushed in on the damp night air. Crickets. Wind dancing in the leaves of the white oaks and sugar maples in the front yard. The muffled sound of a distant barking dog. No gunshots. No sirens.

I took a deep breath, exhaled. My hands were down at my sides and I shook them out. My heart was a runaway train. I stepped out of the house and stood on the front porch, hoping to flush out any hidden snipers by offering them an open and easy target. I closed my eyes and awaited the crack of the rifle. I remembered the sound from that night in the theater. I counted to five. Nothing. I opened my eyes and scanned up and down the street. Still quiet.

I motioned for the sisters to come outside. Admonished them to stay tight behind me. Together we walked down the driveway and out to the sidewalk. I craned my neck and saw our gunmetal-gray Toyota up ahead. My heart leapt in my chest. We were going to make it.

I picked up our pace. The full moon lit the silent street.

The night air was heavy and cool. A headwind chilled me as we drew ever closer to our salvation. Almost there.

An old man doddered onto the sidewalk from the house adjacent to our car. He was fifty feet in front of us and headed our way. He was stooped and wore a long wool coat, collar upturned against the cold night air. Stark white hair, the color of the full moon, hung down from his tweed scally cap.

I held our pace. One eye on the approaching old man, one eye on the street beyond. We met him on the sidewalk, a mere fifteen feet from our car. I started to walk around him.

"Evening," the old man said with a tip of his cap. "A fine night for a stroll."

I mumbled some response and gave him a thin smile as we brusquely passed around him.

There it was. Our Toyota gleamed in the moonlight. I reached into my pocket, grabbed the key fob, and pinged the doors open. Sarah jumped into the front passenger seat, and Nicole got in the back. I started around to the driver's side. Anxious to make our escape.

"In the midst of chaos, there is also opportunity."

The old man had come back towards us on the sidewalk. I don't know what he actually said. But I swear that was what I heard. He said it with a knowing smile and a glint in his eyes. I arched an eyebrow at him and then scurried into the driver's seat.

I started up the Toyota, did a hasty three-point turn and headed away from the cul-de-sac. Nicole sobbed in the back seat. I checked the rear-view mirror and thought I saw the old man standing in the middle of the street. He tipped his cap in a jaunty adieu.

I shook myself. Focused on getting us to safety. A

handful of left and right turns and we were out of the neighborhood and onto the main streets. Nicole murmured directions to Teddy's babysitter between choking sobs. Five
minutes later, we pulled up in front of her house. Nicole
gathered herself and went in to get our son. Sarah and I sat in
silence, unable to speak.

I felt vulnerable sitting there. Parked by the curb. Waiting. I looked around and saw nothing but the darkness that
surrounded us.

I checked my rear-view mirror. For an instant, I saw once
more the old man in the shadow of the full moon. In that
instant, in his presence, I felt his warmth. A calm came over
me. I would get us out of this. We would all be okay. Somehow. Someday.

It was then that it hit me.

The old man resembled Quinn Doyle. An older version
of Quinn, had he lived into his eighties. Or maybe not;
maybe I just wanted him to.

Either way, it didn't matter. It was good to see Quinn
again. I needed it.

CHAPTER FORTY

SEPTEMBER 14, 2019
O'HARE INTERNATIONAL AIRPORT
CHICAGO, ILLINOIS

I DROVE ALL NIGHT. ELEVEN HOURS AND SEVEN hundred miles later we approached the labyrinth that was O'Hare International Airport. The patter of rain that had followed us across Ohio and Northern Indiana had given way to mid-morning sun.

The trip was chaos that first couple of hours. Lots of crying, most of it coming from the back seat. Nicole did her best. Teddy got upset when he saw her upset, so she tried to keep it together. Sarah helped from the front seat. Teddy asked a lot of questions: Where are we going? Why are we going? Where is Henry? Among many others. Nicole bounced from one white lie to another. Now was neither the time nor the place to hash out all that had happened, or what yet must be done. Sarah was Nicole's willing accomplice in all this. I mostly stayed out of it. Kept my eyes on the road and the speedometer at a safe sixty miles per hour.

My passengers fell asleep in Pennsylvania, one by one, sometime after midnight. I was grateful for the reprieve. I drove the Interstate in silence. My mind wandered. I had lived a lifetime in the past ten years: ruination; divorce; homelessness; fatherhood; love; death; sacrifice; atonement; salvation.

I stole glances at Sarah as she slept next to me. I loved her even more for all she had done in that basement. I vowed to spend the rest of my life repaying her with my love and gratitude. Prisha Baari was dead. Sarah and I just had to make a clean getaway and we would be free. Free to be our true selves under false names. A bargain I was more than willing to make.

I stopped only for gas. Sometimes someone would stagger into the gas station with me to go to the bathroom. But mostly they all stayed in the car and fell back to sleep after I got back on the Interstate. I filled up on gas station Pop-Tarts and protein bars, and that's what kept me going through those solitary early morning hours.

The car came back to life as the sun rose. A plan slowly came together. Nicole called the airline and booked two one-way tickets to Las Vegas. Leaving O'Hare later this afternoon. She would rent a car at the airport in Vegas, and she and Teddy would drive to Los Angeles, where she would contact Karlsson's sister to make arrangements for their escape to Sweden. Sarah told Nicole we'd wire her some money in LA to get her through. Nicole said Karlsson had already procured her and Teddy false Swedish passports and identification. Karlsson's sister would forward them to her once she got to LA. Teddy had a rough couple of months ahead. My heart ached for him.

Awkward conversations and more awkward silences accompanied us for the remainder of our trip. Teddy had more questions. Nicole answered with more white lies, the kind mothers are forgiven for telling their children. Nicole maintained her false bravado. She told Teddy all about Las Vegas, and how much sun and fun they would have in LA. She assured him they would meet up with Karlsson in Sweden. This was one lie that made both me and Sarah cringe.

We pulled into the domestic terminal drop-off just before eleven a.m. I was anticipating and dreading this goodbye in equal measure: glad to get Nicole and Teddy safely on their westbound flight; sad to be letting go of my son again. I reminded myself it was all for the best.

I parked at the curbside drop-off and rushed out of the car to fetch the bags in back. I stagger-stepped and leaned against the side of the car for balance. I hadn't slept in over twenty-four hours and was running on Pop-Tart power. My brain was wilted oatmeal. The cacophony of the airport immediately put me on edge.

I handed Nicole and Teddy each their bag. We were live parked and the clock was ticking. I was actually grateful this goodbye would be rushed. We pantomimed our way through it. Sarah and Nicole embraced. Nicole said she'd pick up a phone in LA and call her. I thought "Oh shit... Not again," but held my tongue. The sisters each smiled through their tears.

Sarah wrapped Teddy in a big hug. He tolerated it for moment and then squirmed out of it. She kissed him. Told him to be a good boy and mind his mom.

It was my turn.

I turned and said goodbye to Nicole. I wished her luck. I decided not to offer her my hand. It felt like a stupid gesture in light of all we had just been through together. Nicole stared through me with what appeared to be anger. I knew her well enough to see that it was really pain. I stepped forward and gave her a hug. She gave me a reverse-Teddy: squirmed at first then held tight. I whispered "Good luck" in her ear. She told me to take good care of her big sister. I promised I would.

Nicole pushed off and swiped a tear from her eye.

My son stood clutching his bag in front of him with both hands, his clear signal he did not want any part of hugging me goodbye. And why would he? I was a stranger to him, despite my need for this to be otherwise. Karlsson had been more of a father to this boy than I, his biological father, had ever been. Much like Quinn Doyle and my own father, Arthur. I thought about how that had played out. I desperately wanted something better for me and my son.

But better wasn't in the cards today. I futilely offered my son my hand. He shook it weakly, and only after Nicole told him to. I didn't blame him one bit.

The short toot of a car horn behind us interrupted our moment and ended our goodbye. Nicole and Teddy straggled to the door and into the terminal. I watched my son join the gaggle of fellow travelers. Heavy fatigue settled on my shoulders and buckled my knees. The thought that I might never see my son again overwhelmed me. Sarah saw it in my face and steadied me with a firm arm around my shoulder.

Another horn blast, this one less polite. I gestured at the guy behind us as we both jumped back into our Toyota. I eased away from the curb and into traffic.

Airports were about beginnings and endings. I hoped for both.

———

I awoke in an empty hotel bed one block from Grant Park in downtown Chicago. Daylight streamed through the sheer curtains. The alarm clock on the nightstand read 2:41 p.m. Next to the clock was a handwritten note on the hotel notepad. It was in Sarah's elegant hand:

Hey -

Glad you got some sleep! I'm out and about downtown. I made dinner reservations for 6:30. Steakhouse okay? Be back around 4:00.

Love you,
Me

We enjoyed our sixteen-ounce Chicago-cut ribeyes that night. So much so that we decided to stay. Chicago was the third largest city in the U.S., and as good a place as any to hide. We ditched the Toyota for a 2012 metallic-blue Honda CR-V that we purchased for cash on Craigslist. We rented a furnished apartment downtown for three months. We continued with the false identification and disguises we had had in New York, confident they hadn't been compromised. We lay low and stayed to ourselves.

Sarah did speak to Nicole in Los Angeles. It turned out that Karlsson had, in fact, had everything arranged with his sister. Nicole and Teddy landed in Sweden six weeks after

Karlsson was killed. Nicole had hit it off with the sister, and Karlsson's family were welcoming to them. Teddy was struggling with Karlsson's death and his new surroundings. Nicole said he was a resilient kid and that he would be okay.

Prisha's murder was all over the news. As we expected it would be. No suspects had been identified. The powers that be had ensured that the public was being fed a sanitized version of the story. Prisha was being lionized. A selfless public servant cut down in her political prime. Karlsson and Darius Pierre were never mentioned in the press coverage. The FBI and CIA held much more information that hadn't been made public. I wanted it to stay that way.

The FBI weren't the only people looking for us. I knew that the remainder of Prisha's goons might harbor sufficient anger and loyalty to come for us. And then there was the CIA, Prisha's former employer. They had no doubt partnered with the FBI and would take us out at first opportunity. Even the Mexican Mafia, who would have a long memory of the death of their friend Swoll at the hands of Duckie and me.

But I thought our biggest threat came from the Saudis. After a few days in Chicago I contacted Dead Eye from a new phone and explained what had happened. I told him I had had no choice but to kill Prisha, and that I alone was responsible. He told me his people were deeply troubled by what had occurred. Dead Eye wanted to meet, an invitation I said I was unable to accept. I offered to return three million of the five-million-dollar deposit, arguing that Prisha's scalp had to be worth at least two million to the Saudis. He got pissy with me on this point. I reminded him that this contract had also cost us the life of Quinn Doyle, and that his life for Prisha's was no fair trade as I saw it. Sarah made the three million fund transfer back to the Saudis, and we never heard from them again. Which didn't mean all was forgotten. Not by a long shot.

My accounting to Finn O'Neill was more difficult. He was furious we had left him out of Prisha's abduction. I pleaded with him. Explained that Karlsson had insisted on this, that he had held all the cards in getting Prisha to the basement. He had feared that O'Neill would shoot Prisha on sight, which even O'Neill admitted was a likely outcome. I went through in detail the events that had transpired in the basement, emphasizing that we had intended to stick to the script and deliver Prisha alive to Dead Eye, but that Darius Pierre had shown up and everything had gone sideways.

I told O'Neill we were splitting half the holdback from the Saudis, and that Sarah would transfer his million to him. He called me an idiot for returning one penny to the Saudis. And he never came out and said it, but I knew he was glad Prisha was dead. He didn't care about all the money he'd lost.

O'Neill made me explain in excruciating detail how I'd killed Prisha. How she had died. He wanted every detail, every word spoken. It felt pornographic but I indulged him. I think it gave him the release he needed. He said I'd done good, taking her life over the money. He said he would have done the same thing.

We talked for hours. In the end, we got it all cleared up. Finn O'Neill and I were good. He said I was good with his crew too. I could come back to Southie anytime. Anyone gave me or Sarah any shit, we were to tell him and he'd take care of it. Enough said.

Finally, O'Neill wished me luck. Said I was a standup guy as far as he was concerned. I told him the same. He told me to give him a call if I ever needed anything. I thanked him. We would see each other again, he and I. We ended the call as friends.

So Sarah and I had a myriad of scary people looking for us. Most wanted us dead. The rest wanted to put us behind bars forever. The funny thing was, despite all this, Chicago was one of the best times of our lives. Prisha was no longer the evil mistress in our relationship. I no longer carried the weight of all that rage. We both felt lighter. Freer than we'd ever been before.

We had grown accustomed to the protocols of fugitive life in Oregon and were confident in our ability to stay one or two steps ahead of our pursuers. But here's the thing about fugitive life: they can only want you so bad and hunt you down so hard. The first thing you need is money. We had forfeited our big Saudi payday, but we would find enough money to lead the simple life we both craved. And, if we were smart and willing to sever ties with all but a few trusted friends and family members, there wasn't a hell of a lot they could do. Sarah and I could count the people we kept on one hand. Combined.

It's a big country. An even bigger world. I liked our odds.

One day, the temperature dipped into the teens. A stiff wind off Lake Michigan dropped the windchill below zero. Sarah announced she had had enough of Chicago. We both agreed we'd spend Christmas 2019 someplace a little warmer.

We each packed a bag, got in our metallic-blue Honda CR-V, and headed south.

Love is blind; friendship closes its eyes.
    —Friedrich Nietzsche

EPILOGUE

November 4, 2020
Frank and Sarah's apartment
La Jolla, California

I awoke refreshed, having slept through the night again. The dawn was breaking on a new day. Morning sun sliced through the bladed window blinds and cast horizontal shadows across Sarah and me. I crept out of our bed, grabbed her MacBook, and hushed the bedroom door shut.

I shuffled across the bleached hardwood floor, through the living room and into our fancy designer kitchen. I hit the button of the twelve-cup coffee maker and filled the bottom of my oversized mug with an inch of whole milk.

We now lived in La Jolla, California, a dense suburb thirteen miles north of downtown San Diego. We'd only been here a month and were enjoying it quite a bit. La Jolla had lots of upscale bars, restaurants, and coffee shops, and some great city parks. A haven for many retirees. Sarah and I had retired, in a manner of speaking. We felt right at home in our new digs.

We'd gotten lucky with this apartment. It was a one-bedroom corner unit on the fourth floor, furnished, with two open-air decks: a pocket deck off the bedroom and a larger wrap-around, L-shaped deck off the sliding glass doors in the living room. Both decks afforded unobstructed views of the Pacific Ocean only 250 steps away. It was an open floor plan with off-white walls and dark cabinets. Lots of windows made it feel bigger than its 748 square feet. The place set us back four grand a month. It was worth every cent.

After Chicago, we had wintered in Santa Fe. Then drove north to Montana and took the Alcan Highway through Canada into Alaska. We'd spent this past summer in a quirky little ski town forty miles south of Anchorage that looked like the Swiss Alps. The September early morning temperatures dipped enough to put us on the road again. Four thousand miles later, we pulled into La Jolla.

I took my first cup of coffee out on the L-shaped deck off the living room. The last remnants of pink and gold lingered over the ocean, the sun now fully visible over the horizon. It promised to be another warm and sunny day. I took my first long gulp of coffee. Tilted my head back to catch the warmth of the rising sun on my face. It was still quiet, the neighborhood not yet fully awake. My favorite time of day.

I was much lighter now. No longer shouldered my rucksack of rage. No more sleepless nights. No more eye twitches, something I'd picked up in Oregon and never shed. I was free. Free as the kites Quinn used to fly so gracefully. I gave Quinn a silent toast with my next sip of coffee. I missed my old friend.

That was one of the hardest parts of fugitive life. Missing old friends. Sarah and I did manage to hold on to a few, though. Sarah talked to Nicole once or twice a month. Nicole was doing better, but still had her moments of despondency and lingering anger over the death of her beloved Karlsson. She had grown close to Karlsson's sister. They had become the best of friends, and that helped. Both Nicole and Teddy liked Sweden and were picking up the language. Teddy did well in school and had started to make a few friends. He had taken Karlsson's death particularly hard, however, and had suffered a major relapse upon his arrival in Sweden. He was still withdrawn and distrustful of strangers, but was seeing a therapist and making some progress.

We planned on visiting Nicole and Teddy in Sweden for a month next summer. We agreed to discuss telling Teddy I was his biological father. Both Sarah and I had pressed Nicole on this. She was receptive to the idea but remained noncommittal.

I had stayed connected to Finn O'Neill and Duckie, my two amigos. Both were doing well. Running the streets of their respective cities. Making money, keeping people in line. It was good having these two at my back and a phone call away.

Both Sarah and I stayed in touch with our favorite attorney, Gerry Gonzalez. He was our hub in many ways, receiving and transmitting information to and from a variety of people we ourselves could not risk contact with. My mother, Emily, for one. Sarah's childhood friend Becky, for another.

We had a good life, Sarah and me. Ours was a minimalist life, to a degree that would make the Buddha himself proud. Everything we owned could fit in the back of our used

BMW X3, our biggest possession. We rented, leased, borrowed and recycled everything we could. We leased only furnished apartments and did it month-to-month. Our standing rule was to own no winter clothes. If the temperature dipped below the tolerance of our wardrobe, we simply picked up and moved to more hospitable environs.

It was a simple life that suited us right down to the ground. But it was not cheap. Quinn had left us the bulk of his estate, which Finn O'Neill had funneled (I believe the technical term is laundered) to us tax-free. O'Neill, ever honorable, followed Quinn's instructions meticulously, and we got every penny Quinn wanted us to have. Quinn's generosity and Sarah's savings and shrewd investments were what funded our fugitive life.

O'Neill reluctantly accepted the ten percent gratuity (the standard money laundering fee) we insisted upon, and everyone was happy. Except Uncle Sam and the tax man, of course. But what was just one more felony.

Sarah and I still had outstanding arrest warrants in Virginia for the murder of Charles Hewitt. And we were still FBI fugitives, based on our extensive interstate travel to avoid prosecution. But we had hope. Gonzalez said a little birdie in the Commonwealth's Attorney's Office had told him that the state was having major difficulties with their star witness Linda Webb. Still, we kept our go bags packed for Montenegro, just in case. I kept my passable Montenegrin language skills current. We both hoped it didn't come to that. Fingers crossed.

The big news for us came in May of this year, soon after we arrived in Alaska and eight months after Prisha's death. An anonymous source leaked an explosive document claiming that a consortium of Saudi billionaires was responsible for Prisha's death. It alleged that this group had violated U.S. immigration law in bringing a young Prisha Baari into the U.S., then coerced and blackmailed her as she ascended the ranks of the U.S. intelligence community. The document claimed that Prisha had stood up to the Saudis as a U.S. senator and had paid for her patriotism with her life.

The Saudi government and royal family vigorously denied these allegations and dismissed them as fanciful conspiracy theory. The specific facts contained in the dossier were ridiculed or ignored. It became an international scandal for a couple of weeks. Diplomats scurried between the White House and the Royal Palace. Whatever the two countries made of this was decided behind closed doors. The story ran strong for a while and then disappeared behind 24/7 coronavirus coverage. Nothing like a world pandemic to distract a distracted populace.

I noticed with interest that the dossier cast Prisha in an angelic light, as a victim intimidated and terrorized by the Saudis into doing their evil bidding. It conveniently omitted many things, such as ODYSSEUS and Prisha's use of same to gain her Senate seat. And all the murders and attempted murders committed in her name. The press labeled Karlsson Prisha's lover, an allegation that infuriated Nicole. Given this, I suspected one of Prisha's people had leaked the dossier. In the end, the press made a martyr out of Prisha, morphed her into a victim of the Illuminati and shadowy global monied interests.

Gonzalez told us he had been approached by the FBI when this story broke. The agents said they wished to speak with us. They made it clear that we were not suspects but merely "persons of interest" in connection to Prisha's death.

Gonzalez of course told the agents he hadn't spoken with us in over a year and that he had no idea where we were now. They reminded him that it was a felony to harbor federal fugitives. He didn't budge an inch. Gonzalez opined it was unlikely the FBI would charge us with Prisha's murder. The U.S. and Saudi governments were happy to keep the skeletons in the closet.

While this was good news, it didn't mean the U.S. or Saudi Intelligence services wouldn't do a little off-the-books work on Sarah and me. We kept our wits about us and our bags packed.

I stubbed my toes on the bottom rail of the sliding glass door on my way back inside for my second cup. I hobbled into the kitchen, cursing under my breath. I sat down at the table and rubbed my foot. The pain quickly subsided. There was a time in Oregon, in the thick of my chemotherapy, when this little toe stub would have sent me through the roof. Sarah had made certain I stayed current on my check-ups. I was still NED—no evidence of disease. The doctors were careful to explain to us that this didn't mean I was cured, but the cancer was no longer a daily part of our lives. I was grateful for that.

I took my second cup back out to the deck, fired up the MacBook and checked the headlines. I was surprised to see the presidential election results. I had totally forgotten yesterday was election day. I started reading.

The slider rolled open and Sarah emerged onto the deck. She held a coffee mug in both hands and squinted into the morning sun. She walked up behind me, kissed the top of my shaved, bronzed head, then plopped down in the seat next to me at the small glass table facing the ocean.

"How'd you sleep?" I asked.

"Like a rock," Sarah responded through duck lips, and with playful affectation that made me laugh out loud.

She sipped her coffee, eyes forward on the water. Sarah was now a redhead, her hair grown out to shoulder length. She had stopped wearing her contacts and had gone back to her own striking blue eyes. She was back to the bohemian look she had first cultivated in Oregon. It suited her. I still buzzed my head clean but had shaved off my long beard. I now wore only a trimmed goatee that hung two inches from my chin. I chose to keep my green eyes hidden behind dark contacts. We both favored our current selves over our New York looks.

"How's the tat?" I asked.

Sarah leaned back in her seat and pulled down the waistband of her sweatpants with a finger. I leaned over to look. Sarah and I had gotten tattoos together last week. My first, her second. This new one was on her right hip, just below her belt line. It was another black ink vector drawing, this one the setting sun over the Pacific Ocean. The same view as from where we now sat. A compass face was overlaid on top of the sun, its needle at true north.

The skin surrounding the tattoo was pink and swollen. Sarah tentatively poked at it with her finger.

"How's it feel?"

"All right. You?"

I told her mine felt fine. I'd got my tattoo high up on my right thigh, near my hip. I had wanted it at the base of my neck, but needed it to be concealed in public at all times. Yet another concession to my fugitive life. For my tattoo I'd chosen a two-inch black shamrock with the words Truth, Beauty, Freedom, and Love in green Gaelic script on each of the four leaves. These were the four words inscribed on the marquee of the Hirschfeld Theatre. The marquee under which Quinn Doyle had been shot. I was not a big tattoo guy, but I'd had to get this one. Just this one.

"You getting any more?" I asked.

Sarah shook her head. "This one's my happy ever after."

"Huh?"

"Happy ever after," she continued. "The setting sun, true north." She looked around her. "This—right here, right now—is my happy ever after. I won't be needing any more ink." She gave me a big smile and turned back to the ocean and her coffee mug.

I joined her. The morning sun rippled over the Pacific. I nursed my second cup. We sat in blissful silence.

She was right. This was our version of happy ever after. We were soulmates. We led an authentic life under false identity. We were smart and tough. Battle tested. They wouldn't catch us. Whitey Bulger and his girlfriend were the FBI's most wanted fugitives for seventeen years. That was a pretty good run. Seventeen years would take Sarah and me into our sixties. And that was all right with me.

I reached over and squeezed her hand. She squeezed back.

"What are you reading?" Sarah asked, pointing at the open MacBook.

"Oh, Mo Udell got re-elected to a third term," I said. "Got fifty-nine percent of the popular vote."

Udell had successfully spearheaded an effort last year to repeal the Twenty-Second Amendment to the Constitution that prohibited anyone from serving more than two presidential terms. Udell would be the only U.S. president, other than FDR, to serve a third term.

"Really?" Sarah asked.

We both turned back to the ocean. Sarah put down her coffee and rubbed her neck, squinting into the sun. I closed the MacBook. Below us I heard the slam of a car door, the start of an engine. I followed the flight of a seagull over a palm tree to a distant rooftop. Sarah still stroked her neck.

She finally broke the silence and said what we were both thinking.

"This would have been Prisha's year," Sarah said. "For POTUS, I mean." She paused a beat. "What the hell do you think we'd be looking at if she'd won?"

We both laughed. Had some fun trading post-apocalyptic scenarios of a Prisha presidency. Each of us trying to outdo the other.

Sarah raised her mug in toast. "I'm glad that wicked witch is dead." She slugged the remainder of her coffee back.

I thought of Prisha Baari. The Saudi Consortium. President Mo Udell. And ODYSSEUS. A snake uncoiled and slithered up my spine.

"Uhm, I hate to say this..." I hesitated, "but do you think ODYSSEUS could have had anything to do with Udell getting his third term?"

"Don't know. Don't care," Sarah said flatly, never taking her eyes off the Pacific Ocean.

I chuckled. She was right.

DC was three thousand miles away. And we were a million miles from that life. I didn't care what happened in that swamp. I threw my head back, closed my eyes, and soaked up the warm rays of the rising sun.

I would not look into that abyss. I preferred sunlight to darkness.

AFTERWORD

I hope you enjoyed my third novel, Raw Justice, the second book in my Frank Luce thriller series and sequel to Talion Justice.

Let's stay in touch. Click here (newsletter) to sign up for my free monthly newsletter and receive exclusive updates and insights on me and my author adventure.

Visit my Amazon Author Page (author page) to check out my other novels, including First Citizen, my stand-alone fast-paced thriller about an army general seeking absolute power, and the FBI agent who opposes him.

And lastly, if you enjoyed Raw Justice, please consider leaving me a review on my Amazon Raw Justice book page. It would help other readers find the book, and would also really make my day.

Enjoy.

ABOUT THE AUTHOR

Rick Bosworth is an attorney and retired FBI agent who worked and supervised street gang, drug, terrorism, and intelligence cases in six different offices during his 25-year bureau career. He survived the LA Riots, South Central, and the Northridge Earthquake as a street agent, and paper cuts, endless meetings, and ceaseless vexation as a squad supervisor and program manager.

Rick has walked dark alleys and Beltway power corridors, arrested killer gang members and briefed Cabinet members, all the while asking himself the same two questions: Why? What if? His answers became the basis for his first novel, First Citizen, and influenced the books in his Frank Luce thriller series.

Rick writes page-turning novels that make you think and feel. Juicy tenderloin thrillers, sautéed in literary prose and served with a buttery side of history and philosophy.

He lives with his wife on the shore of Lake Superior in Michigan's Upper Peninsula. When he is not writing, Rick enjoys hiking in the woods, sipping good bourbon, and slapping at his acoustic guitar. See what he's up to at his website, rickbosworth.com.

RAW JUSTICE

ISBN Number: 978-1-7341412-4-5 (eBook) ISBN Number: 978-1-7341412-5-2 (Paperback)

Published by UPrising Publishing, LLC 2020 Upper Peninsula, Michigan